SOME AWFUL CUNNING

Other Books by Joe Ricker

(*) Coming Soon

JOE RICKER

SOME AWFUL CUNNING

DOWN & OUT
BOOKS

Down & Out Books
3959 Van Dyke Road, Suite 265
Lutz, FL 33558
DownAndOutBooks.com

The characters and events in this book are fictitious. Any similarity to real persons, living or dead, is coincidental and not intended by the author.

Cover photograph by Joe Ricker
Cover design by Lance Wright

ISBN: 1-64396-086-5
ISBN-13: 978-1-64396-086-9

ONE

She had the perfect amount of fear in her eyes. They darted beyond him to the pointed corners of the room, where she searched for some consolation for what was happening, what had already happened—some kind gesture or comforting embrace from the truth perching on her shoulders. Each breath Melissa took splintered a sharp ache through her ribs, like fingers had bored their way through the thinner gaps of pain that were already there and squeezed, crushing her into another shape to lift her from the world she knew and shake what life was left in her lungs. Mashed fibers of muscle tingled along either side of her spine.

Ryan noted every miniscule adaptation in her eyes while she thought—a cautious awareness of any movement. He sat motionless, watching her acceptance of where she was, a recycled anticipation of the pain that had already drummed the chorus of a song she was trying to forget. Fear. Enough for him to know that she'd do everything he'd told her.

Beyond her fear, a coiling panic flexed her pupils in the pulsing of the light from the lamp in the corner behind her. The silence in the room began to drone a new noise in her head—blaring static.

Her son squatted between her thighs where she sat on the polyester comforter at the edge of the bed. He'd draped his arms over her knees, the frail seams along the calves of her jeans convenient crannies for his roving fingers. Sputtering came from his bottom lip, and Ryan looked down at the boy's purple-bruise raccoon mask—the fragments of white tape still on his skin that had bandaged the split in his nose.

The woman lifted a shoulder slightly, wincing at the struggle to turn just a few degrees to check the clock again—one minute and forty-six seconds since her last check. Her back was rigid, and the panic in her eyes had drifted, replaced by something else that she didn't have the capacity to acknowledge just yet, but it was him, Ryan sitting across from her on the wooden chair he'd pulled from the desk.

Ryan reached down to the cuffs of his dark gray suit, perfectly settled on the contour of his body. The fabric was still flat and neat despite the long hours he'd driven, silent, with the boy in the front seat next to him sleeping most of the way. Melissa hadn't slept, hadn't made an attempt to notice the landscape. She'd just sat in the middle of the back seat watching the road ahead of her until they'd arrived there, in the hotel room. Now, she stared at Ryan's hand. At the edge of his left palm, where his pinky should have been, was a small, mangled bump of flesh. She hadn't noticed until then. He pulled his cuffs down to his wrists, saw her and the child staring at his scar. Ryan stopped his movement, and the boy looked up, digging his middle fingers into the holes he'd made in his mother's jeans.

"What happens now?" she asked.

"Now, you live your life, and I go to Texas to make sure Victoria Williams thinks you're dead."

His voice cooed into her soundtrack of static—a raspy, whiskey-scorched voice wallowing in the shadowy room. She focused on his eyes, a placid, motionless depth. Then she looked away, peered at the overlapped edges of beige wallpaper in the corners of the room where they were almost invisible.

"What did you do to your pinky?" the boy asked.

Melissa squeezed her knees together around the child then winced. "Hey, don't be rude."

Ryan clasped his hands together and leaned forward, toward the boy, a flickering patience at the edges of his lips as he grinned. "Gator took it off."

The boy's eyelids retracted, and the cerulean blue of his irises peered up at Ryan. "An alligator?"

"That's right. Chomped it right off while I was walking down the road."

The boy scrunched his face, one eye closing almost entirely, the thin white line of lingering tape bent away from his skin. "In Albuquerque?"

"Yep."

"But there are no alligators in Albuquerque."

"He was my pet alligator."

The boy stopped poking at the seams of his mother's jeans. "Pet alligator?"

"Yeah." Ryan tapped his left leg. "I kept him right here in my pocket."

"Alligators are too big to be in your pocket."

"He was just little then, and I carried him around with me everywhere I went."

"Even to the bathroom?"

"Even the bathroom."

The boy turned to look at his mother and whispered,

"Can you take an alligator to the bathroom."

Melissa flinched against the child's movement into the sling around her arm. The finger-length bruises over her neck wimpled when she swallowed. "If it's your pet, you can take it anywhere you want."

The boy snapped his head back toward Ryan. "Where is your alligator now?"

"Well, the alligator got too big to fit in my pocket, so I had to let him go."

"You let him go? Where did you let him go?"

"I let him go in a swamp far, far away from here, where he would have enough space to be with the other alligators like him."

"But why did your alligator bite your finger off?"

Ryan weighed his response against what the boy and his mother had already been through. "Sometimes, the things that we have in our lives hurt us. And maybe they don't mean to, but it's what they do. That's how we know when to let things go."

The child worked his bottom lip back and forth into his mouth, staring at the scar on the Ryan's hand.

"Like what my dad did to me and Mom?"

"Something like that."

"Can I touch it?"

Melissa flexed her legs around the boy's ribs again. "Stop being rude. You don't ask people things like that."

The boy looked down at Ryan's feet. "I'm sorry."

"That's alright." Ryan rubbed his palm over the edge of his scarred hand. At times, human touch felt like the annoyance of flies buzzing around his face. Other times, it made him feel like his skin would peel from his body, tear away like thin fabric and all that would be left would be the

4

tightened flex of muscle covering his bones. Once, he'd let a woman take his hands in a cluttered room when he was drunk on absinthe in some dank corner of New Orleans. After just a sweep of her thumbs over his knuckles, the woman flung his hands from hers, the hazy clouds in her blind eyes swirling chaotically and she repeated *bokor, bokor, bokor* until he rushed out of there.

He extended his hand to the boy.

Melissa gave Ryan an apologetic look, an expression slightly more relieved than the look of worry on her face. She nodded and the boy moved forward to his hands and knees and reached one hand out to touch the scar. The pressure of the boy's tiny fingers squeezed at the gnarled flesh.

"It's cold," the boy said. "Does it still hurt?"

Ryan shook his head. Melissa leaned forward and pressed the forearm of her free arm over her thigh. The boy drew his hand back, a flittering smile on his face. He held his hand up and tucked his smallest digit into his palm. Then used his other hand to hold the finger down and observe the four fingers he held out.

"Alright, you," Melissa said. "Time for you to take a bath."

The boy crawled across the dark green carpet on his hands and knees into the bathroom.

"How did you know he liked alligators?"

"I know a lot about you and your son." Ryan pulled a purse and an envelope from the top of the dresser behind him. "Everything you need to know about your new life is in here." He held up the envelope. "Birth certificates, social security cards, resume—all the things you need to move forward." He handed her the envelope and held out the purse. "In here, your license, checkbook, receipts, a little cash.

Day-to-day stuff." He tossed the purse on the bed beside her. "Your back story is written in a narrative so it's easier for you to absorb. You'll want to make that sink into your son's head as much as possible. There are about a dozen pictures for you to keep around. They're Photoshopped, obviously, but they coincide with the narrative. It helps with the transition, especially for him. The mind will build false memories. That's all in the envelope."

She flicked the corners of the envelope with her thumb then placed it on the bed beside the purse, watching her own movement. Her mother had probably found the letter she'd left, which made worry set in about what might happen if someone else found it. "How many times have you done this, *relocation?*"

"Enough to know that everything will be alright as long as you stick to the guidelines I told you about."

"Roy can't find me here?"

Ryan shook his head. "Neither will Victoria."

Melissa rubbed her shoulder. "I never thought I'd live in Oregon."

"The important thing is that you're living."

"What happens tomorrow?"

"Tomorrow you go to your new apartment. A woman named Annabelle will pick you up and help with the rest of your transition. You're safe now."

"Thank you, for all that you've done. I'm not sure why you decided to help me."

"You reminded me of someone I wasn't able to help." He stood to leave the room. "This is where you are, and you can never go home."

* * *

As he left her in the room, he thought about her question. *How many times have you done this?* Never. In seventeen relocations, he'd never betrayed a client, and he wouldn't have, but a week after Victoria Williams' bodyguard Wendell hired him to relocate Roy, they decided to add duties to the job. Victoria wanted assurance that Roy would be in the clear for what he'd done. She wanted Melissa and her son relocated, too. The type of relocation that Ryan didn't hire himself out for.

He made his way to the barren interstate that extended east toward the cities he'd already been to, where he'd completed this process before, undoing the ties that cinched the helpless to their mistakes or other terrors they couldn't escape. Despite the hours he'd spent driving Melissa and her son to Oregon from New Mexico, Ryan could still feel the tension in his hands from his meeting with Roy, the smell of the bar where he'd found him—liquor and sweat on Roy's skin.

Ryan had made arrangements through Wendell to pick Roy up at the bar where he worked as a bouncer. He found Roy outside the door on a chair under the light of the bar picking at the thin scabs from the fingernail wounds Melissa had left on his arms when she'd gasped for breath and tried to fight him off. An hour out of town, Roy made the call to his stepmother to let her know that he was safe, that he'd be in touch in a few weeks. When he hung up, Ryan wrapped a thin steel cable around his throat.

Ryan could still taste the dust in the dry air he'd breathed when Roy was beneath him, his knee between Roy's shoulder blades, the cable taught around his hands. He'd wanted Roy to feel how much damage was being done. Wire would have cut through, would have made it too quick, and Roy wouldn't have had the chance to tap against Ryan's fore-arms. As if that was an appropriate call to mercy. Ryan had seen Melissa's back, the eggplant shade of bruising in giant patches the size of continents that Roy's pounding fists left in their voyage. *I guess you can only get it up for your step-mother*, she'd said to Roy before it started. On the ground, Ryan had pulled the life from Roy, let it seep into the air and drift above him, where the vibrant light of the stars shined down on Roy's ending.

If he had done everything he was told, Melissa and her son would be dead, and Roy Williams would be alive, wait-ing for everything to clear before he could find another woman to damage. If Ryan had done everything he was told, he wouldn't be driving to Dallas to lie to Victoria Williams about what he'd done with her stepson.

In the darkness of the highway, the foggy glow of the next city hovered in the distance. Headlights on the other side of the median crested the hill he was approaching, like glinting eyes rising out of brackish water. He shifted his focus to the white line separating the shoulder lane. The world was nothing more than a swamp full of alligators—motionless predators lurking in murky water that the helpless were try-ing to wade through.

TWO

The splashing in the pool had gone still before Victoria Williams surfaced at the other end. She found her footing on the slick tile at the bottom and stood in waist-deep water. Droplets beaded against the tanning oil on her skin, her stomach flat from two-a-day Pilates sessions. She leaned back and dunked her head below the surface to slick her hair over her head then wiped the water from her eyes, toned arms flexing as she pulled herself out by the railing. The cement around the pool was hot, and she moved quickly on the balls of her feet back to her lounge chair at the edge of the pool, where Wendell picked up a fresh towel and handed it to her.

"What time is it?" she asked him, taking the towel and drying her face.

He looked down at his watch. "Eleven ten."

She worked the towel down her legs. "And when is he going to be here?"

"Two."

"Bring me the documents on our *relocation expert.*"

"I've got them right here." Wendell pointed down to a folder on the small table next to her lounge chair. "The letter Melissa left is in there, too."

"Excellent." She pulled her sunglasses from the cement next to the chair and positioned herself in it before slipping the glasses onto her face. "You're ready for tonight, yes?"

"I am. But, I—"

"He's a loose end, Wendell. You sure you're ready or might this be an issue for you?"

"It won't be an issue, Mrs. Williams."

The flat stretch of highway outside of Dallas was a tight string of stationary vehicles. Various custom-painted SUVs and vintage Cutlasses were tacked to the road among the tinted-window luxury vehicles and dented trucks with broken air conditioners. Heat rose from the tar in lines of crooked wisps, and Ryan imagined the shiny, custom-painted vehicles melting into colorful puddles along the road. The shrubs on the sides of the highway appeared to be dying along the endless span of brown, but they weren't. Not like the people in the car accident ahead might be dying—colors fading to blurry shades of black and white. He thought about those people, where they may have been heading, what their thoughts might have been before they'd crashed.

The motion to his left, a car pulling forward, gave Ryan the sensation of movement and made him flex the brake, afraid the distraction of his thoughts had made him careless in the traffic. More movement ahead, and he let the vehicle roll forward. Soon, the cars were at their normal pace. Eager drivers who'd been behind him, those who'd sat still for the shortest amount of time, swerved from lane to lane in an attempt to gain time and distance. They could only gain distance. That time was gone. In a few miles, Ryan passed the source of the backup, a small sedan, pieces of it scattered on the median and shoulder, like a Lego structure crumbled between angry fingers and left strewn in a doorway.

The estate, where Mr. and Mrs. Williams lived most of the time, was the smallest of their three homes in Texas. They also had condos in Houston and El Paso. But their lake house in Austin and ranch outside of San Antonio were nearly twice as glamorous as the modernized antebellum-style mansion in Dallas. Ryan expected landscapers and the rhythm of various small engines working the property after he'd been buzzed through the gate, but there was no one. Sprinklers rained water over the flower gardens, plots bigger than the area of most middle-class homes—the colors and shapes of the petals forming a syllabus of flora that he didn't know the names of, and the majority of which he'd never seen before, despite his years of traveling the country.

Wendell waited for him at the end of the driveway, standing on the blacktop like he'd grown from it, like one of those pretentious flowers. In Albuquerque, Wendell had delivered Mrs. Williams' demands, hovering over him stiff-necked, trying to show his former employer, Benjamin, who Ryan worked for, how much of a big shot he'd become out in Dallas. *Head of security,* he'd bragged. Ryan might have turned the job down had he done more for Cripple Ben and Filipino Pin than clunking around junk yards for VIN numbers and making collections for Benjamin's storage services. He'd wanted a chance to live his old life, the life he lived before he'd left New Orleans, and Simon. He wanted to feel like he had a purpose again. And then, after he found out more about the Williams, he found more purpose in betraying them.

Wendell moved toward the car, his goddamn mirrored aviator shades punched over the bridge of his nose like he couldn't take them off if he'd wanted to. Ryan turned off the engine and climbed from the seat, discreetly stretching the stiffness from his back. As Wendell approached, Ryan realized how tired he was from driving, and how badly he just wanted to collect his fee and leave.

"Nice car." Wendell smirked.

Dust hid the forest green color of the Subaru. He tossed his keys to Wendell, who caught them against his tie at his stomach.

"It matches my eyes. Keep her handy." Ryan walked past him toward the door of the house. "Nice suit, by the way," he said as he passed. "Matches the driveway."

Wendell followed him, trotting up the steps to Ryan's left. At the door, he thrust his hand toward Ryan, holding the keys out.

"I'm not the fucking chauffeur."

"Obviously. You're the valet."

"Not the goddamn valet, either."

Ryan took the keys. "My mistake. Who are you?"

"I'm the motherfucker in charge."

"Of the gate?"

"Of security. You not remember me?"

"No. Don't take it personally, though. All you people look the same to me. By *you people* I mean the ones who never take off their sunglasses, not that you're black." Ryan pointed at the door in front of him with his thumb. "You mind?"

Wendell snatched his sunglasses from his face, his left ear lobe flopping from the sudden pull.

"Oh, that's better. Now I remember you, Wendell. You're an interesting man. You grew up in Fayetteville, Arkansas. You played the trombone in the high school band, perhaps you even practiced with the rusty version in your free time. You were a Razorback for just over two years until you popped on a piss test and got kicked out of the ROTC program your junior year, so you dropped out of college. You moved to Dallas and worked at a Subway and then as a dishwasher. Then you started working the door at the bar where you peddled ecstasy, which is how you met Roy. Eventually, you started running E from New Mexico to L.A., because you were a go-getter, and that's how you met Benjamin, and how our paths eventually crossed. You got Roy out of a jam, something he's been counting on from his friends and family his whole life. In return, Roy got you a job with his stepmother, and here you are, the mother-fucker in charge."

Ryan let Wendell absorb what he'd summarized about his life.

"Now, Wendell, I can go on about your love of tennis and how you purposely popped on your piss test because of rumors that you jerked off the quarterback onto a cracker that you may or may not have eaten, but I'd like to get this over with. I'd hate to be rude and let myself into someone else's house. From what I can gather, the reason you're out here is to meet me and bring me to Mrs. Williams so I can get paid. So, if you don't mind, be the motherfucker in charge of that door and let me in the house."

Sweat formed on Wendell's neck and seeped into the brown ring around his white shirt collar. He inched the sunglasses back onto his face and reached down to open the door for Ryan. Ryan entered. Wendell moved slowly but composed himself and led Ryan through the massive great room toward the echoing bellow of Mr. Williams in the sunroom near the back patio. Before they crossed through another doorway, Ryan spoke again.

"By the way, Wendell, I love tennis. Your suit is a Dior, which is sharp as fuck. Move your belt to the left three centimeters. You should know what a gig line is. The most important thing, don't take off your sunglasses to intimidate someone. That shit only works in the movies and on people who are afraid of black people. Alternate your grip when you're doing shrugs. It's either that or you jerk off way too much with your left hand. One of your traps is slightly larger than the other. Your suit will fit that much better. And ditch black. Your skin is too dark. Wear tan. Also, stop wearing white shirts The collars stain too easily."

Wendell's mouth hung slightly open.

"In other words, you'd look less like an asshole."

Wendell clenched his jaw before he spoke. "Mr. Williams is in the next room. I'll go get Mrs. Williams." He turned to walk down another corridor.

"You're not going to introduce me, Wendell?"

"I work for Mrs. Williams, not her husband. He knows you're here. Make yourself at home."

THREE

Victoria came out of the darkness of the corridor to the sunroom where Ryan sat across from Williams. She'd wrapped herself in a black silk sari that stuck to the wet bathing suit on her ass and tits, which made her figure clear, the sway of her hips the most prominent movement from the shadowy hallway to the light of the sunroom. The dame. The black widow. The hyper-sexualized female nemesis. He hadn't expected her to be closer to Roy's age than his father's. Who had initiated the flirtations that led to their affair? She threw her hips slightly more as she walked through the room to the bar, ignoring the presence of other people, making them notice her—the trained gait of superiority. And Ryan hated it as much as he hated loud chewing or people who stood in doorways. Behind the sofa that Williams sat in the middle of, she kept her back to them and poured her martini ingredients into a shaker tin. Ryan thought about Roy's wife and son, how they were probably going through their new apartment and testing out the sparse, inexpensive furniture or fumbling through the few contents in the refrigerator, trying to adjust and absorb all that had happened while Victoria checked her martini olives to see if Sylvia, the servant, had stuffed them with the perfect amount of blue cheese.

Williams loosened his tie aggressively at the sound of the shaking tin, which Victoria shook for quite some time. The others in the room, Sylvia in the back corner near an enormous fichus, Wendell in the doorway with his sunglasses on, and Ryan in the hard leather chair that carried a price tag for its brand name and not its comfort, all remained motionless as Victoria shook the tin, switched hands, and continued to shake without rhythm. Williams had removed his tie and coiled it through the fingers of his fist before she finally stopped and drained the slushy liquid into a martini glass.

"Give it a few more shakes, dear. I don't think it's chilled enough," Williams mumbled.

Victoria turned to her left and Ryan could see her profile—as delicate as the sip she took. She took a deep breath through her nose. "That's just perfect. No more shakes required, darling." She strutted to the other leather chair next to Ryan. "You must be the..." She tried to find the words.

"The travel agent," Ryan said.

"Yes." She took another sip of her martini. "Travel agent. How clever."

Her comment stuck with him for a moment, like a stickiness between his fingers that would linger even after he washed his hands.

"So, Mr.—?" Williams said and stopped, looking confused, suddenly, that he didn't remember Ryan's last name, not realizing that he had never learned it.

"Ryan, sir. Just Ryan."

"Alright, then." Williams took his three-finger drink in one swallow and held the glass out. Sylvia sprung from her station by the plant to retrieve his glass for a refill. Williams leaned forward after Sylvia took his glass and extended a palm to Ryan while he looked at his wife. "Ryan was just telling me about the conditions Roy is in. He says Roy's in a small but cozy place and is adjusting well to his solitude. He says he's doing plenty of push-ups to stay fit."

"Where, exactly, is Roy?"

Ryan thought of the dusty earth where Roy was buried four feet in the ground with a six-inch layer of lime over him.

"Specifics aren't something I can extend at this point, Mrs. Williams. It's far too soon, and it's certainly for the best that you know as little as possible. For the sake of any forthcoming investigation, that is. I'm sure that you and Mr. Williams would handle yourselves quite adequately, but investigators can get a little tricky with these matters. Given your wealth, you'll already be suspected of aiding and abetting. I hope you understand my caution. I'll arrange for contact when enough time has passed."

"I'm hardly worried about some chicken-shit bingo investigation."

Ryan gave himself a moment before responding. "It's simply a precaution to take in the best interest of everyone, including myself. Roy is very secluded. There's no phone service, and access is limited by private roads. He'll be safe until I send my acquaintance out there to bring him back into civilization."

Williams rose. "I suppose, then, that you can work out whatever details are left with Victoria. I appreciate your services, mister...Ryan."

"Yes, sir. Follow-ups aren't typical of my profession, but your wife insisted."

Williams chuckled as he puffed his chest. "Profession?" He took a swig of his fresh drink that Sylvia had just delivered. "Oil, son. Oil is the only profession in Texas other than cattle."

"Yes, well, I'm not from Texas, Mr. Williams."

Williams swirled his drink, staring at Ryan as if there were something more he'd expected Ryan to say. "Sylvia," he said, louder than necessary. "I'm going to my office. Bring the bottle."

"Seems that you're one of the first to leave my husband without words," Victoria said, after her husband had left the room. She lifted the glass to drink. "There are a few more things I'd like to discuss. I've arranged a suite for you at this address." Wendell crossed the room then and handed Ryan a business card. "Consider it a bonus. I'll be in the bar for drinks at nine. We can discuss the other matter then. When you get to the desk, ask for Derrick and tell him you're my guest. He'll take care of everything else."

Ryan took the card. "Mrs. Williams, I really appreciate the gesture, but I do need to get back on the road, so I'd like to collect my fee now."

"I understand, Ryan, but part of your services were acquired without my husband's approval, for lack of better words. I won't have your money until I meet you later this evening. How would you like to be paid, Ryan, cash?" She took a longer sip of her drink.

"Checks are a little too personal for me, so cash is sufficient."

She squinted. "Personal. Yes, I expect you don't get very personal despite being a travel agent."

"My business is about being impersonal, Mrs. Williams."

She glared at him. "If you call me *misses* one more time I'll vomit. My name is Victoria. You can call me that. Or would that be too personal, Mr. Carpenter?"

"No, Victoria. I'll look forward to seeing you tonight." Ryan smiled, not a shred of hesitation at her mention of his last name. He followed Wendell back out to his car, and when he drove through the gate and turned down the road, he wondered what else she knew.

FOUR

Ryan didn't check into the hotel. Instead, he crouched in a dark corner of a parking garage a few blocks away and watched his Subaru to see if Victoria had had him tailed. Other vehicles moved in and out of the garage. Tires squealed from drivers taking the sharp turns on the ramps too fast. The steel cables along the back edges of parking spaces shook slightly as drivers inched too far into the spots. People dribbled through the garage. Lethargic shoppers carried their purchases and a brief hesitation of buyer's remorse before they got into their cars. Restaurant employees shambled out to their vehicles stripping ties and undoing buttons. Couples parked for dinner at nearby restaurants. A small group of young professionals cackled before cramming into an elevator.

Ryan focused on the movement of people as a way to stifle his inner dialogue. The hotel arrangement. Victoria patronizing him. Maybe it was more about Mr. Williams. Her tone had changed when he'd left the room. But how she'd thrown in his last name before he'd left bothered him. Benjamin didn't seem likely. Cripple Ben was paranoid about bug zappers and those sneakers kids wore that lit up along the sole as they walked. He didn't even have electricity in his bar, if that's what it should be called. Pin might have said something, but Pin rarely said anything. Still, that would make more sense. The more Ryan tried to focus on the mundane, the shamble of people through the garage, the more the queries nagged at him. Maybe Benjamin had rubbed off on him a little too much.

Trust your gut, Simon had taught him.

Nine thirty-five p.m. No one had taken a second glance at the dusty Subaru. Ryan pushed away from the corner, a hint of cigarette smoke and car exhaust in the garage, and took the stairs to the ground level. Out on the sidewalk, he strolled away from the hotel to make the block and return from the opposite direction. The air was still hot, and he'd thought about changing his clothes, but he didn't. Sweat split the color of his shirt down his spine into a darker shade of gray. At the corner, he stopped at the feet of a grungy panhandler. His eyes were barely open and he sawed his cardboard sign under his chin. The Staffordshire terrier the man had leashed to his waist looked up at Ryan and adjusted against the cement, wagging its tail chaotically and sniffing at Ryan's shoes.

"Got a dollar, man?" the panhandler asked, looking straight ahead at Ryan's knees.

"Your dog looks hungry."

The man nodded. "Yeah, man. We're real hungry. Got a dollar you can spare so we can get some food?"

Ryan thumbed over the folded bills in his pocket. "Maybe. If you're here in an hour, I'll have a hundred."

Ryan walked away and kept moving toward the hotel. Wendell sat in a brown leather chair in the lobby, near the wall to the right of the entrance, watching the door. The blue carpet under his feet shimmered it was so new. Almost everything was marble. Most everything except the iron legs of the marble tables. Shiny stone. Bright colored modern art hung on the walls. The smell of the garage was still on him, like cigarette smoke on a damp towel or maybe the smell of the panhandler on the corner. He needed to change. He'd attract attention in that place without a clean shirt.

Back at the Subaru, he pulled a fresh white button down and jacket from the hanger in the back seat, carried his soiled shirt to the staircase with him and flung it over the railing on his way down to the street. He walked slowly and close to the building edge of the sidewalk, peering into cars as he passed them, looking for anyone who might have been sitting in there for a while. Nothing seemed out of the ordinary, so he walked through the lobby, waving to Wendell on his way to the bar, and stood next to Victoria just as she checked her watch.

She wore a black dress, pearls around her neck. She'd taken her wedding band off, a red indentation on her fingers.

"You're late, Ryan. And Derrick told me you hadn't checked in."

"Should I offer your friend Derrick an apology?"

"That won't be necessary. Besides, I'm sure he's done with his shift by now."

She guided him to the bar seat beside her with her eyes and perched her gaze on the cushioned leather until he sat. "I just ordered another drink. I'm having a Manhattan. Would you like one?"

"No thanks."

"What will you be drinking?"

"What do they have in a can?"

She gave him a disgusted look, which pleased him with the hope that he could conclude their arrangement sooner.

Her fingers waved at the bartender, a bald, middle-aged man done up in his striped shirt and vest and red bow tie. Ryan had only ever seen two men in his life who could wear a bow tie with authority: Simon and a gray-bearded restaurant manager that he'd drank a few Heinekens with at a bar in Oxford, Mississippi, where he'd been once with Simon for an Ole Miss football game. To Ryan, the bartender looked like he'd wrapped a hemorrhoid around his neck. The man delivered Victoria's Manhattan.

"There you are, madam."

She pulled the look of disgust from her face. "Thank you, handsome. My acquaintance here would like a beer."

Handsome turned. "Very good, sir. We have a wonderful new Belgian—"

"I'll take a Lone Star."

Handsome pursed his lips. "Very well," he said and floated off to fetch Ryan's beer.

"I mistook you for a whisky drinker."

"I am," Ryan answered. "When I drink."

"Well, we're here drinking."

"You're drinking. I'm here to get paid."

"So when I pay you, then you'll drink?"

"When you pay me, I'll be leaving."

"Where are you in such a hurry to get to?"

"Somewhere to drink."

She squinted at him. "You're a difficult man to figure out."

"Maybe you're thinking about it too much, like a crossword. It's simple, really. I did a job. Job is done. Now I'd like my money."

"You must be a Libra."

"Astrology now?"

"It's a hobby. So, are you?"

"No. I'm a Cancer."

Handsome returned with Ryan's Lone Star, wiping the dust from the bottle.

"Cancer. I wouldn't have guessed that."

"Water sign. Elusive. Like other things, apparently."

"So you *are* into astrology."

"I read my horoscope from time to time." Ryan took a drink. The beer wasn't very cold. He calmed his impatience. She didn't correct him, so he guessed she didn't know Ryan Carpenter's birthdate.

"Have you ever had your cards done? Or how about your palms? Has anyone ever read your palms?"

"Once. It didn't go so well."

"That sounds like an interesting story. Do tell. No, let me guess. You have no hope of love? Your lifeline is very short? Something that ruined your day?"

"Didn't ruin mine." He took a quick pull from the beer.

"Oh? Someone else's?"

"Yeah."

"Whose?"

"The reader's."

She reached for the Manhattan and took a sip. "I'd be a horrible fortune teller," she said, after putting the glass down. "Sometimes I'm good at guessing signs."

"Like your husband said, oil is the only profession in Texas."

"That's my husband's profession. I don't have a profession. I have hobbies."

"Aside from astrology and palm reading?"

"People. My favorite hobby is people. That's why I'm quite intrigued by you, what you do. Doesn't your work make you curious about people?"

Ryan shrugged. "I used to be curious, but I've met enough people to realize that they don't surprise me anymore."

"You find them boring?"

"In a sense."

"Do you have any hobbies?"

"I like folding laundry and sharpening pencils."

"Fascinating."

"Reading poetry by candlelight and long walks on the beach."

"So romantic."

"It is when I'm alone." Ryan took a drink of his beer. "I also like getting paid."

"Who doesn't like getting laid?"

Ryan focused his stare at the mouth of his bottle. Was she baiting him? He'd thought about it, fucking her, as soon as she'd swooped through the room at the estate. Perhaps not there. After though. He'd thought about it after, wrapping his hand through her hair and jerking her head back, hearing that startled yip in her voice that would settle into a low moan. "I said, paid," he corrected.

"Yes, back to money. Things getting too personal?"

"I'd need to get business out of the way before I got into anything personal. So, if we could handle that, then I'd feel much more comfortable complimenting you on those shoes and how they match your nail polish."

"A man of detail." She offered a twisted smirk. "Alright then. First, I need to know where Roy is."

Ryan reached into his pants pocket to the card she'd given him earlier. She took the card and glanced at the numbers.

"What is this?"

"GPS coordinates. That's where Roy is, within one

hundred meters or so. There's something you should know about how this works. One phone call makes your son. His new identity won't do shit for him if he gets busted. His prints are already in the system." Ryan reached into his back pocket and pulled out a folded envelope. "This isn't typical, and it's on you, now, what happens to Roy." He slid the envelope to her.

She rubbed her thumb over the card and slipped it into her purse. She took a sip of her Manhattan then dug her fingers in the envelope and pulled out photocopies of a birth certificate and a Kansas driver's license with Roy's photo on it. There was also a photo in the envelope. Black and white. Roy's ex-wife Melissa sprawled out on a sheet of plastic, a bullet hole in her right temple. Melissa had done a good job pretending she was dead. And then she'd ridden in the back of the car in silence all the way to Oregon. Victoria licked her lips.

Ryan thought of Roy's phlegm strung lips, his ears turning purple, the cable disappearing into a fold of skin around his neck. The hiss of the wind against the sand. The song in his head that he'd hummed when he killed Roy—*This little light of mine...*

"It was quick," Ryan said. "In case you were curious about that."

The corners of Victoria's lips quivered into a smile and she tucked the items back into the envelope. "Forgive me, Ryan." She lowered her hand from the bar and scraped the nail of her index finger down his ribs and then his leg. He contained his shudder. "For some reason, I find that arousing. I find you arousing. From the moment I saw you, I wondered what it would be like to have you slip into my pool with me some night." She looked up at his eyes. "Your suite has a hot tub."

Ryan followed her hand as it drifted back up to the bar and the stem of the martini glass. She raised her eyebrows, waiting for his reaction.

"I haven't tried to bruise a cervix in a long time. Seems like it would be a tremendous release, right now, but you're not really my type."

She jawed away the rejection as if a fly had hit the back of her throat. Then she gave him a cold stare. "I'm surprised a man like *you* has a type."

Ryan tried not to find enjoyment in the dialogue. She was used to people pining over her. Even Handsome might pour himself a Drano martini if she told him to. "Most men will stick their dick in anything, but they all have a type—the kind that will ruin him."

"And what is the type that will ruin you, Ryan?"

Ryan leaned toward her, felt her quick breaths against his lips. "The kind of lady who likes to get choke-fucked to Norah Jones."

She brushed her cheek against his to whisper in his ear. "You *are* a savage."

"You seem like the type of woman who's comfortable with that."

She finished off her Manhattan and held her palm up to Handsome who was eager to make her another. She reached to the backrest of Ryan's barstool and leaned toward his ear. "Wouldn't that make me your type? Take me upstairs. I haven't had a cock hit my cervix in ten years. Besides, that's the only place it's safe to deal with your money."

FIVE

Nearly everything in life comes down to who someone is fucking or who they're trying to fuck. Nearly every problem that anyone has ever had has been about who they're fucking that they're not supposed to be fucking. There's no straighter avenue toward violence. As Ryan followed Victoria into the elevator, Wendell stepped in and blocked the doors. As they closed, he flashed the handle of the pistol tucked into his belt.

"I knew I should have taken the stairs," Ryan said.

Victoria stepped to the corner of the elevator. Wendell nudged Ryan to the opposite side, near the numbers, and put the barrel of his gun in Ryan's ribs while he patted him down. He took Ryan's cell phone and reached around him to hit the button for the twenty-second floor. Ryan thought about the gun. Plenty of people had pointed guns at him. It had happened enough that it didn't bother him anymore. His mind never stumbled over an existential crisis or made a plethora of promises to God to make it through the situation. And of all the people who had ever pointed a gun at him, only one of them ever pulled the trigger. His mother. Ryan reached forward and ran two fingers over the line of buttons.

At Victoria's command, Wendell punched Ryan in the kidney, and the pain shot through his balls—a sharp merciless pain that made him feel like he was pissing himself.

"If he moves again, Wendell, break his ribs."

Ryan winced as he spoke. "Ribs would have been better than the kidneys."

"Okay then. His throat next time."

Wendell chuckled while Ryan slowly breathed away the pain, He turned his head to Victoria. "I guess maybe you are my type. But I think Wendell's love tap is going to have some effect on my performance."

Wendell flashed a look of curiosity as he put away his gun.

"Wendell, if he says anything else, crush his throat and his balls."

Ryan winked at Wendell. Wendell gave him a big grin.

On the next floor, they exited the elevator to enter another. Wendell put a hand on Ryan's shoulder to keep him away from the buttons. The music was so quiet that Wendell's low, wheezy breaths were more audible.

On the eighth floor, the elevator stopped. Wendell inched closer to Ryan, his breath tickling Ryan's ear. The couple who entered were transfixed with each other. They ignored the three of them already in the elevator. The woman wore a tight silver sequined dress. Her platinum hair filled the space with a faint aroma of lilac. The man's contour, like the blonde's, was a streamlined, athletic frame. He had a perfect chin and nose, the kind that people liked to see on magazine covers. His stubble was an abrasive exfoliant, especially to the woman's lips that Ryan could see were already raw. The man reached up to touch her arm and brushed against the nickel-sized mole on her elbow and his fingers wilted slightly. He moved his hand down to the small of her back.

Ryan thought of the last time he'd put his hands on a woman. Back when he'd first left Simon and New Orleans, when he thought he could pursue something normal—stable. He'd met her at a campground in South Dakota, near the Black Hills—Laura Quinn. She was on her way to Tahoe. In that moment, there in the elevator, he could smell her again—an evergreen scent on the flannel shirt she'd been wearing when he'd met her. A peppermint aroma on her skin just below her jaw. Her short hair, the half sleeve of tattoos on her right arm—clocks in chains. Maybe he'd fallen in love. It had felt like love when he lifted the edge of her beanie to whisper his adoration into her ear between hisses and cracks in the fire. She left the next morning. *I'll think of you fondly, and I'll think of you often, but that's all it can ever be*, she'd said. He remembered how suddenly he'd realized that he'd never been in love, had nothing that it would ever hurt to walk away from. He had no one to fight with over trivial things, to fight for. Falling in love is a hard way to make a friend.

Sometimes, starting a fight is the best way to make a friend. Ryan needed a friend if he wanted to get out of that elevator before the twenty-second floor.

"You see, Wendell. That's how you wear a suit."

The man turned his chin to his shoulder but didn't look back.

"And I really wish I could show you how to wear that blonde all the way down to my balls. I bet her asshole tastes like key lime pie."

The man drew his hand from the woman's back and shifted his feet. The woman looked at him, an obvious hurt on her face, but the kind of comment she was probably used to hearing from men. Wendell shuffled his feet and looked toward Victoria.

"What do you think, Wendell? I bet you a dollar seventy-five that I could knock the sequins from her dress like fucking dandelion seedlings."

The man created some distance from the woman and turned, his right fist clenched. He brought the fist up as he moved and stopped suddenly.

"Victoria?" His fist loosened.

"Hello, Derrick."

"This fucking asshole with you?"

Victoria looked down at her powder blue nail polish. "Yes, unfortunately. But feel free to teach him some manners."

"Shit," Ryan muttered.

Wendell reached down and took Ryan's wrists in his hands.

"Just so you know, Wendell, since we're on the topic of manners, I hate being touched."

"That's too bad," Wendell responded.

"Just a caution."

Without warning, Derrick punched Ryan in the side of the face. It was a solid hit, a smack that flung its sound around the elevator for a moment, and Ryan's ears rang. His teeth cut into the inside of his cheek, but his knees stayed under him.

"Hard jaw," Derrick said.

"Good punch." Ryan licked the corner of his lip to sweep the blood back into his mouth. "I'm sorry."

"I bet."

"Not you, dickhead," Ryan said and nudged his jaw toward the woman. "Her." He pointed to the blonde. "I have Asperger's. It's a condition that affects my thought process. I say impolite things because I usually don't know they're impolite until someone socks me in the jaw."

The blonde gave him a disbelieving look. "Like Tourette's?"

Ryan shrugged. Wendell was still holding his wrists. "Sort of."

"So you're retarded," Derrick said, glancing toward Victoria. "Sorry, I didn't mean like, you know, Down's Syndrome."

"No, it's totally fine. I am, in a sweeping, generalizing way, retarded. But that's why I'm with Victoria. She pays to watch Wendell beat the shit out of me."

"Are you fucking serious?" The blonde asked.

"How much?" Derrick asked, enthusiastically.

The blonde shifted her body to Derrick. "Really?"

Derrick threw his palms out. "What? He's obviously high-functioning."

The blonde threw a hand up, then jutted it past him to the button for the next floor.

"It's okay, really," Ryan said. "Do you want to hit me, too?"

The blonde looked around the elevator at their faces, shock on Wendell and Victoria's. The elevator doors opened and she marched out. Derrick trailed behind her.

"Well, his night's fucked." Ryan looked over his shoulder at Wendell. "Seriously, though, I really hate being touched."

The elevator doors closed. Ryan tensed.

"Wendell," Victoria said.

Wendell let go of Ryan's wrists, put his big hand against the side of Ryan's face and paused.

"You're not really retarded, are you?" Wendell asked.

"For fuck's sake, Wendell," Victoria barked.

Wendell slammed the side of Ryan's head against the side of the elevator. After his head sprang away, Ryan leaned against the wall, his vision blurred. He wished he'd passed out.

Twenty-second floor. Victoria led the way out of the elevator to the suite, carded the door, and entered. Wendell nudged Ryan into the room, and he took in the fragrance of fresh sheets, the sharp corners of the pillowcases. A glow hovered over the display of small liquor and wine bottles lined atop a slab of marble in the back corner, two bottles of champagne angled in the buckets. Victoria walked to the bar and pulled a bottle from the ice. The rattle of falling cubes against the steel like a quick applause. Ryan scanned the room, waiting for the echo of the pop on the bottle. It came, followed by a low hiss of the pour.

"Have a seat," she told Ryan as she turned.

Ryan crossed the room and lowered himself into one of the many chairs around the suite. He chose the one closest to the glass balcony doors and glanced out into the night, lights that pulsed ahead of the dense black behind them. He thought about how much he missed New Orleans on Fat Tuesday, the flush of drunk tourists from the Big Easy streets.

"There are a couple of ways we can do this, Ryan. Wendell, here, is hoping for one way. I, on the other hand, would like to end this. We found Melissa's note."

"Who the fuck is Melissa?"

"Don't play dumb. It's worse than your sarcasm."

"That's a bruise to the ego. I still don't know what you're talking about."

"Wendell."

He stepped toward Ryan and drew his fist back.

"Not the face," Victoria said.

Wendell looked back at her, his fist close to his shoulder.

"I don't want blood on the carpet."

Wendell adjusted and slammed Ryan in the stomach. Ryan heaved forward, mouthing at the air for breath. His eyes watered. Wendell's leather shoes were polished, a small drop of coffee had hit the edge and dried. Ryan's ears started to burn as his body begged for breath. He slumped out of the chair to the floor, focused on calming himself, the involuntary panic shuddering through his body. Relief finally rushed through him and he forced himself to take in slow breaths as he pushed himself back into the chair. Victoria sipped her champagne. She walked across the room toward them and patted Wendell's shoulder.

"The photo was a nice touch, but I'm not stupid. A man as thorough as yourself wouldn't allow a woman to leave a note with his name on it before he killed her. You're no killer, Mr. Carpenter. I paid you for a job, and you didn't finish the job. Where is she?"

Ryan felt a quick flush of rage, but let it slip away. That's how she knew his name. People do stupid things when they're scared. He didn't blame Melissa. Note or no note, he'd be in the same situation.

"Neverland," Ryan answered.

Ryan flexed his abdomen just as Wendell slammed him again. Again, Ryan slipped to the floor, the gag in his throat, the few sips of the Lone Star he'd had foaming in his stomach. It took less time to catch his breath, but Ryan worked through his reseating slower. He thought about the panhandler and the dog, wondering if they were still there on that sidewalk or if they'd moved on to a convenience store for malt liquor and a can of Alpo.

"Put the handcuffs on him so he stays in the chair," Victoria said. "I don't want this to take all night."

Wendell pulled a pair of handcuffs from his back pocket, old police issue, the kind with a chain between the cuffs.

"Shit," Ryan said. "Not the fuzzy kind."

"Stop with the comments."

"You really don't like my sarcasm?"

"It's actually repulsive."

Wendell cuffed Ryan's wrist then pulled his hands away, drawing them close to his chest in surprise.

"Oh shit." Wendell spouted. "You're missing a pinky." He reached down after a moment and cuffed the other wrist, staring down at the hand. "What happened?"

"Pinky swear gone bad. I promised your mother I wouldn't come in her." Ryan shrugged. "I thought her ass was fair game."

Wendell three-pieced him in the chest and the chair tilted back into the wall. Ryan flexed his mouth, hacking, his heart sputtering.

Victoria finished her champagne and walked back to the bottle to pour another. She carried the bottle back toward him and spoke, just as he caught his breath and began to hiccup. "Ryan Carpenter. Age thirty-four. Born on October nineteenth in Richmond, Virginia. *Libra*. You were orphaned at thirteen and moved to New Mexico five years ago. You have a real estate license but file a 1099 for your legitimate travel consulting business. No wife. No kids. No relatives." She finished the pour and handed the bottle to Wendell who turned and put it on a small table near the patio door. "You see, Ryan. I know what I need to know about *you*. The only thing I need to know now, is where Roy's wife is. The sooner you tell me, the less painful your death is going to be."

"You must be really good with those tarot cards." Ryan

sucked a wad of spit and blood to the front of his mouth and spit on the floor. "So much for the carpet. Are you really going to kill me here, in this room? How do you plan on getting my body out of the building? You going to chop me up in the tub? Did you even think this shit through?"

"I've been thinking about this all day, actually." She sipped her champagne and moved past him to open the balcony door. A slight breeze wafted in. "Wendell will spend some time breaking you apart. Then he'll throw you off the balcony."

"Head or feet first?"

"That hardly matters. Though, he'll make sure you're conscious before he tosses you."

"Mind if I have a look? Kinda want to see if it's worth it."

Victoria gave a quick nod. "Keep a tight hold on him. I don't want him to get any ideas."

Wendell grabbed the chain of the cuffs and lifted, the pressure on Ryan's shoulders tight and painful as he moved out to the balcony. Twenty-two floors below, the hotel pool seemed no bigger than a bucket.

"You scared?" Wendell asked.

"Of heights?"

"No, motherfucker. Me?"

"You? Why would I be scared of you? Because you're going to kill me? What does that matter? The real question is: Am I afraid to die? But you're assuming too much of your role in this. We all die, and it's rarely the way we want to. So, no, Wendell, I'm not afraid to die, so by default, I'm not afraid of you. Your problem is that you care too much about what people think of you. Take, for example, the cracker. I know it's not true. Just an ugly rumor. But you sabotaged your life to get away from it anyway."

Wendell peered over the edge. "So you *aren't* scared. Alright, then. What if I let you jump? If you're not scared to die, why not? Maybe you'd make it."

"To the ground?"

"Nah. What if I took the cuffs off? Think you could jump and hit the pool?"

"To escape?"

"Yeah."

"Fuck, Wendell, you're really into shitty action flicks and poorly plotted storylines, aren't you? At this height, I'd hit at eighty miles per hour. Whether I hit the pool or not wouldn't matter. I'd be a goddamn mess. Are you the type of idiot who thinks gas tanks explode when you shoot them or that you can silence a .22 revolver with a lawnmower muffler? Hell, you probably believe someone can get shot in the shoulder with a 12-gauge slug and still engage in a shoot-out."

Ryan turned to Victoria. "How much are you paying this idiot?"

Wendell's fists clenched. "You talk a lot."

"Happens when I'm aroused."

"Have a seat, Ryan," Victoria instructed.

Wendell squeezed Ryan's neck to lead him back inside, his big fingers pinching on Ryan's carotid, making him light-headed. There was no gentleness in his maneuvering Ryan's arms over the back rest of the chair, either. Ryan adjusted, squirming out the kink in his shoulders and attempting to relieve some of the pain in his wrists from the cuffs.

"Where is she, Mr. Carpenter?"

"Victoria Williams. Married Roy Williams the Third ten days after your twenty-fifth birthday. You attended Texas

A&M and graduated summa cum laude. You were a Tri Delta and class secretary. Your uncle Saul used to fuck you, which is why your father went to prison. The hit man he hired rolled, which might explain my current situation. Your mother married your father's business partner two years after your father went in. Your father got out of prison after a six-year stint and got hit by a taxi in New York and died barely three months after his release. The same time your grades dipped, but you managed to keep your GPA at a 3.93."

"Is that all?"

"You're left-handed and a natural blonde, but you've dyed your hair since college because even if blondes have more fun, they get less respect. You wear a size seven shoe and a size one dress. Your tits are real, which is the only detail I've mentioned that your husband knows about. You've only ever had two procedures—an appendectomy when you were nine and an abortion when you were fifteen, which is how your father found out about Uncle Saul. Uncle Saul was a piece of shit, and he deserved to die. I'm betting he has something to do with your aberrant sexual proclivities."

Victoria's shoulders quivered. She lowered her champagne glass a few inches then raised it quickly to take a drink. When she finished the champagne, she walked to the counter and placed it on the marble with the other glass then went back to the center of the room.

"Are you finished?"

Ryan caught the scent of the dry air—sand and gasoline. "Just one more thing, actually. One phone call makes your son's identity. One phone call sends three men to the cabin where Roy is holed up. They won't ask questions. They won't be gentle. These are the kinds of guys who'll take pleasure breaking apart a man who beats women—the kind of piece of shit that Roy is."

"Wendell," she said, moving toward the door. "Don't make a mess, darling."

And she left.

Wendell moved to the door and bolted it. When he turned, he pulled Ryan's cell phone from his pocket. He flipped the phone open and broke it in half, a menacing grin on his face.

"I'm hungry, Wendell. What time do they end room service?"

"One a.m."

"What time is it now?"

"Oh, you don't have to worry about that. It's going to be a long night for you."

"You've come a long way, Wendell. Once again, you're in charge of the cracker."

SIX

Ryan walked down the street with three to-go containers. The three most expensive entrees on the hotel's room service menu—baked stuffed lobster, shrimp and grits, and a filet mignon with a side of smashed red potatoes and sautéed almonds and green beans. The airplane bottles of whiskey he'd taken from the room clacked together in his pockets as he walked back to the corner where he'd first seen the panhandler. Ryan noticed a smudge of blood on the side of the bottom container and wiped it away with his thumb. The panhandler was still there, chin dropped against his chest, shivering in the dropping night temperature even though that drop only brought it down to sixty-five. The dog was curled next to him under a jacket.

Ryan nudged his foot, and the panhandler looked up at him.

"Hey, man. You got a dollar?"

"No," Ryan answered, "but I've got some food. You mind if I sit down?"

"It's a free country."

The dog shuffled from beneath the jacket and waved its nose in the air, looking up at the Styrofoam containers Ryan carried. He set the containers on the ground and stripped his suitcoat from his shoulders. His back was still kinked and aching from Wendell, and his hand throbbed. The scar at his pinky was scraped and raw. When Wendell had locked the hotel room door after Victoria, Ryan had finally pried the handcuff around the nub of his missing pinky. The dog twisted a shake through its body and the jacket covering it slipped off onto the cement. It huffed and sniffed at the containers on the ground. Ryan ruffled its ears as he sat.

"What's your dog's name?"

The panhandler eyed the food containers. "Ex-Wife," he answered, "because she's a bitch."

"Your ex-wife or the dog?"

"I don't have an ex-wife." He grinned and stretched his neck. "I call her X for short. My name's Adam."

"You hungry, Adam?"

"Yeah, man. I'm thirsty, too."

Ryan pulled one of the airplane bottles from his pocket and handed it to him. "You like shrimp or lobster?"

"Oh, man, I like both. Sometimes, the workers at Milo's give me and X food. Usually, it's just potatoes and some rolls. Meat scraps for X. Sometimes there's some shrimp. Once. Maybe twice that happened. They never give me any booze." Adam tilted the small bottle up and took down the whiskey. "That's good, man. Thanks."

Ryan handed him the container with the lobster. "I've got shrimp and grits that I'll trade you for this coat." He reached down and lifted the jacket that had covered X. X sat, staring at the container Ryan had placed in Adam's lap.

Adam opened the to-go box, the inside top of the lid dotted with beads of moisture. He shut the container and handed it back to Ryan. "Nah, man. That's all I got to keep X warm."

"I'll leave you mine. I just need something different.

Jacket and that hat you're wearing for another meal. You keep the lobster either way."

It took a moment before he agreed and exchanged his hat for the plastic utensils Ryan held out for him. Ryan put the other entrée box with the shrimp and grits at Adam's feet. He pushed the plastic fork through the end of the wrapper and began eating. Ryan opened the other container and took out the filet with his fingers. He bit a chunk off and pulled it from his mouth to offer X. X moved her head slowly toward the meat and took it gently between her teeth. When his fingers were free, she chomped it down. Ryan sat there, continuing the process with X while the man swiped away the stuffing in the lobster then used the plastic knife to peel the meat from the shell. When X had finished the filet, Ryan took a mouthful of green beans then slipped his arms through the man's jacket. He put the hat on and pulled his knees to his chest and patted X's head. The jacket stank of cigarettes and body odor and patchouli, which Ryan hated. A heavy pressure rolled into his sinuses.

Ryan reached into his pants pockets, between the bottles that he'd shoved there—the other half of the bottles he left in the pockets of the jacket. X draped her paws over Ryan's thighs and looked up at him, a sort of *thanks-you-got-any-thing-else* expression waving over her thin eyebrows. Ryan peeled off a couple of hundred-dollar bills in the cash roll he'd taken from Wendell's pocket.

He held them over Adam's food. "Just so you know I'm not trying to mug you. You don't carry a wallet, do you?"

"You want to buy my wallet?"

"Yeah. But only if you have a driver's license or a picture ID. I lost mine, and I need an ID to get a bus ticket. It's kind of an emergency."

"Yeah, man. I got a card for Sam's Club, too, but I never use it. It's expired. But I guess you don't really need a Sam's card anyway."

"Not at the moment."

Adam fished his wallet out of the duffel bag he had propped between him and the cement wall where he sat—a tri-fold red cloth Velcro similar to the wallet Ryan had as a kid that he'd carried his library and lunch card in, a folded sheet of a knots diagrams that he'd torn from the pages of a Boy Scout manual. The wallet had burned up in the fire with everything else—the corpses of his family that his mother had left from her rampage with a 12-gauge.

The fabric of the wallet was sticky and damp, and it took him a moment to peel the Velcro flap open and examine the ID. Adam Crane. The ID was worn, bent at the corners, and the photo wasn't a striking resemblance, so Ryan put a crease through the middle of the photo. It would be enough to make it pass for a while. Enough to get him back to Albuquerque to see Benjamin and get his other papers—a name that Victoria wouldn't know and couldn't track. Enough to get him underground until he could figure out how to handle Victoria. He took the wallet and stood, feeling the pang of Wendell's punches still in his lower back and stomach. He pulled the hat low and pulled the jacket collar up to his chin, then slipped Wendell's sunglasses over his face. A slight relief came over him. By tomorrow, Ryan Carpenter would be a ghost—lost in the hot desert air like a puff of cold mist.

Wendell came to, pain resurfacing where Ryan had jammed the joint of the handcuff into his throat. Everything else was vague, clouded by the flash of Ryan ducking beneath his arms as he fell into the chair that Ryan had been in. He was there, and then he was gone. A concussive pressure had exploded inside his head, Ryan's cupped hands against both of his ears. Ryan had stripped his belt and the last thing he remembered was Ryan throwing it around his neck. Then everything had faded out.

More pain emanated from below his wrist and Wendell turned his head to his outstretched arm, his left hand wrapped in a pink towel covered in ice and submerged in one of the champagne buckets. It took him another second to realize that the towel was pink from his blood. There was a crinkle against his chest, and he reached with his right hand to turn it over, afraid of the horror that might be inside that bloody towel. He read the words on the paper.

Manners, Wendell. It's impolite to point.

There was an arrow drawn to the left, and Wendell looked in that direction to the toilet, where there was a cracker, and on top of it, his severed index finger pointing back at him. His left hand shook and rattled inside the bucket at the sight of his own detached finger pointing back at him a few feet away, and his right hand simultaneously patted the breast pocket of his suitcoat for his sunglasses that were gone. His face twisted into an ugly sneer, and then his lip quivered, and he tried to stop himself from whimpering.

When he felt like he had his sobs under control, he pulled his cell phone from his pocket and called Victoria. She answered quickly.

"Yes, Wendell?" She asked, seeming eager to hear what he had to say.

He smudged the back of his hand against his nose, just in time to muffle a sniffle.

The tone in her voice changed. Something harsher,

without concern for him. "Wendell?"

"He's gone."

"Good. Good job," she said.

"No. I mean—he's—I'm. I—I need help."

"What? Help with what?"

"My finger. It's—"

"Are you calling me from the fucking room? Please tell me you're not calling me from the room."

He wanted to scream at her, call her a stupid bitch, blurt it through the phone loud enough for it to echo in whatever fancy room she was in. "Ryan left the building," Wendell finally said. "He didn't use the balcony."

Her breathing became slower through the phone. "Make sure the room is clean. Meet me at the house." She hung up.

When Wendell got back to the estate, she was waiting for him, pacing the corridor. He walked inside, moving slowly toward her. The towel was still wrapped around his hand.

"What happened?" She asked, taking a hard pull from a thin menthol cigarette.

"He cut my finger off."

"He got away?"

Wendell looked down at his hand.

She blew smoke toward him. "How could that happen?"

"I don't know, but he got out of the handcuffs, and when I—"

"Stop."

She began pacing again, shaking her head, muttering things. Then she stopped, turned to him, and took two quick steps. "He knows where Roy is, Wendell. Do you get that? Do you fucking get that? And now he's probably on his way there. Call your cripple in Albuquerque—however or wherever you found Ryan Carpenter. Pay them whatever they want. Find out where Melissa is and have Ryan fucking handled." She jutted the card with Roy's coordinates on it. "Go there. Find Roy before Ryan does. Get him somewhere safe." She walked away. At the corner to the corridor she stopped and looked back to him. "What did you do with your finger?"

"The finger?"

"Yeah, the one he cut off."

Wendell look at her, puzzled.

"Wendell?"

"I—I—"

"You didn't leave it in the room, did you?"

"No."

"Well?"

Wendell dropped his chin. "I flushed it."

"You flushed it?"

"Unh-hunh."

"Down the toilet?"

He nodded. Victoria looked up toward the back corner of the room, pouted her lower lip, and shrugged approvingly. Then she dragged the echo of her footsteps away from him.

SEVEN

Dirt bike engines whined along the motocross trails behind the gravel pit and the building Ryan walked toward. The structure was brown, sun-faded, nearly the same color as the dead grass and sand and the dirt road that led to it. The sun reflected in glimmers from the mounds of sand and stone in the pit. Electrical cords stretched from a rumbling generator at the corner of the building through a space in a small window near the edge of the roof. The glass had been painted from the inside. Ryan took his sunglasses off before he went into the hallway. His legs were tired from the seven-mile walk, and he was already tired before that, unable to sleep on the ride from Dallas. Bus vibrations made his teeth feel like they'd loosened in his jaw during the trip.

Benjamin sat at the table behind the wall that formed the short hallway to the bar. Ryan saw him in the large mirror behind the two liquor bottles on the back counter—Jack Daniel's. And a backup bottle of Jack Daniel's—all that Benjamin would drink. Ryan knew to look for him there in the mirror, tucked away on the opposite side of the wall behind cement-reinforced cinder blocks. Benjamin sat there so he could see who came in, slip his hand into an open space in the blocks, and grip the 12-gauge double-barrel pointed into the hallway from behind a square of sheetrock. Ryan stood in the doorway, lifted his hand to pick at the fresh splinters of wood in the door jamb at waist level, a small dark blemish at the center of the splinters. The sheetrock on the wall to his left had recently been replaced, where the barrel of Benjamin's 12-gauge pointed at his torso. He touched his knuckles against the primer. Still tacky.

Pin stood behind the bar, two wooden shipping crates stacked on top of each other. Filipino Pin was his preferred name. Somehow, the acknowledgment of his ethnicity felt less degrading to him than the nickname he'd earned. He was enormous, a nonsymmetrical blob, unfit to move quickly even if he'd wanted to. It was no surprise that he made a shitty bodyguard. And he'd taken the nickname before he'd come to work for Benjamin, when he was a bodyguard for a Jewish rapper in Colorado who got his windpipe crushed right after giving Pin his moniker. *What the fuck are you looking at fatso? You look like a burnt bowling pin with an asshole.*

The room was freezing. The new air conditioner hummed quietly above Benjamin's head. Pin put down the pair of scissors he'd been using. He cut coupons. It reminded him of his mother, he'd once said, who died over a pile of unused coupons and an ashtray heaped with cigarettes butts. Pin fumbled a smoke from his pack of Newports, his mother's brand, and held it between his marshmallow thick fingers, the knuckles ashy, long yellow fingernails. He tossed the pack on the bar next to a box of Zebra cakes and stared at Ryan as he approached.

"Those things might kill you," Ryan said.

Pin stared, blinking, sweat running over his fat cheeks and neck. His dark T-shirt was drenched and sucked against the folds of his flesh. He lit the cigarette and took a drag. Smoke hovered at his nostrils and inside his partly open mouth.

"Ryan," Benjamin said behind him. "Come here."

He turned to Benjamin, in the shadow of his half bunker, a blanket over his shoulders. His cane leaned against the table. Ryan pulled the chair out and sat.

The table wobbled as Benjamin leaned forward to hover a shaky hand over his half-filled tumbler. He lifted the glass and took the liquid down. Movement in the floor tremored through Ryan's feet as Pin waddled over to them to refill the glass.

"Leave the bottle," Benjamin said.

Pin smelled like something melting. Ryan caught the odor as Pin reached past him and put the bottle on the table. He couldn't tell what it was, but it was something putrid beyond body odor, like ass sweat and trash had been trapped in a thermos. Pin waddled back to the bar. There was crinkling from the wrapper of a Zebra cake.

"So," Benjamin said. "You're leaving us."

"Job is done. And I've been here too long. Time to move on."

"That's too bad. I have some other things coming up, some transports. I know how much you like the road."

"I appreciate the consideration, but I think I'm going to take to the road for a little more solitude."

"This seems a little abrupt. Everything go okay in Dallas?"

Ryan studied him for a moment. Benjamin was an ex-cop until another cop pulled a spray-and-pray and hit him in the pelvis, which blew out a hip and led him to an early retirement and disability. He liked questions, but only asking them, which sometimes gave away how much information he knew. Ryan hadn't told him he was going to Dallas.

"For the most part," Ryan answered.

Benjamin took a drink. "That's good."

"You have my things?"

"I had Pin pick them up this morning." Benjamin looked over at Pin. "Bring Ryan's stuff over here."

Pin grumbled, and Ryan heard it, the faint scrap of the scissors that Pin pulled from the bar before he tussled Ryan's go bag from the floor. Benjamin drew his hand from beneath the blanket, worked his fingers the way he always did when he wanted to make sure his dexterity was good. Ryan lifted his heels, put his weight on the ball of his left foot, reached down, and grasped the right edge of his chair.

Pin waddled closer, and sucked in a sharp breath. He lifted the bag and dropped it onto the table then drew his hand back, the scissors glinting in the reflection on the bottle of Jack.

Benjamin's lips went to a flat line then the corners twitched, and his lips parted slightly as Ryan slipped to his left and brought the chair up. The scissors stabbed into the particle board base of the seat, and Pin's forward thrust, his tremendous body weight, put the tip of the scissors through the board and the cushion of the seat. Ryan pulled Pin's momentum toward him and shucked it off with the chair. Pin kept moving, following the scissors and the chair downward, his knees slamming hard against the floor. Pin's movement was so slow that both Ryan and Benjamin had enough time take in each other's reaction. Benjamin's smug indifference and calm as he lifted his right hand. Ryan's solemn annoyance. And what seemed slow picked up speed at a pace that sucked the noise out of the room. Pin let go of the scissors, pushed the chair from him as he struggled from his knees by the entrance. Benjamin put his hand into the cut-out as Ryan grabbed the cane. He swung it, a wet slap against the fat on the side of Pin's neck and the sharp sound of the wood breaking as Pin slumped against the door jamb. Ryan speared the broken end of the cane into Pin's shoulder, who screamed and swatted at it. Benjamin fumbled the butt end of the shotgun from the hole and Ryan kicked the edge of Benjamin's table, driving the inch-thick wood into his stomach.

The gunshot was muffled, the smack of one board against another, and Pin's sweat-soaked T-shirt rippled. Ryan snatched the bottle of Jack tumbling from the table. He smashed the bottle straight down over Benjamin's skull then grabbed his wrist to keep him from pulling the shotgun from the wall. Ryan dug the jagged neck of the bottle into the soft bend of Benjamin's elbow, and the arm went limp, fingers curling away from his grip on the shotgun.

A long, gastric drone slipped from Pin, his body still jiggling in the threshold of the door. Ryan tucked his mouth and nose against his shoulder, taking in the unpleasant scent of himself over Pin's death gases. He pulled Benjamin's shotgun from the hole.

Benjamin's right arm lay over the table, bubbling blood. He looked up at Ryan, Jack and blood running down over his face. He tapped at the gash on his head with the fingers of his left hand then looked at the side-by-side barrels of the shotgun. "You're no killer. That's why that Dallas bitch put money on you. Besides, you fucking hate guns." He snuffed out a cough that sounded like an attempt to laugh.

"That's true. I also hate public restrooms." He steadied the gun at his waist. "But every once in a while, you have to take an inconvenient shit."

The disbelief on Benjamin's face changed to a scowl. Ryan

pulled the trigger and the cinder blocks behind Benjamin absorbed a single, sudden burst of red just before the back of his skull slammed against the wall. Benjamin fell forward against the table. The air conditioner continued to hum and the ringing in Ryan's ears didn't pick up until he walked over to the bar and put the gun on the wood above the pile of clippings that Pin had been working on when he'd entered.

They weren't coupons. Shards of plastic credit cards, laminated slivers of Ryan's ID, the thicker, official paper of his birth certificate and passport and social security card. Ryan reached over and took a cigarette from Pin's pack. He lit it and blew smoke through his nose. The cool menthol felt crisp in the room. The bodies on the floor made him realize that the fifty-fifty odds he'd given himself that Victoria hadn't been able to buy out Benjamin were shitty odds. But he hadn't expected Benjamin to destroy his only way underground. He wondered how he was going to get to New Orleans, back to Simon, the only option he had left. He wondered how many more decisions he'd have to make that would turn out bad.

EIGHT

Ryan drove through Texas along the Mexican border in a two-door sedan that he'd pulled from one of Benjamin's storage warehouses. The car had no air conditioning or radio—those units taken out, Ryan was sure, to make smuggling runs. He drove through the lonely, possibly abandoned, sand-beaten towns, making his way to New Orleans, back to Simon. More than once, he'd thought about driving into Big Bend and crossing the border, but Mexico wasn't a place he wanted to be, and it certainly wasn't a place he wanted to get papers. White Americans made good mules. Sometimes, in Mexico, that trumped money. While he drove, and as the heat forced sweat to burrow into his eyes, he thought of all the people he'd moved, their lives shattered into fragments they'd hold in their minds, careful so the edges of those truths didn't cut them. He continued through dead Texas towns, settlements along cattle trails where men got shot in the back over card games or drunken words. Maybe less. Early evening, he arrived in New Orleans, where the damp heat coiled itself over his shoulders in layers. He parked the vehicle at the Holiday Inn, wiped down the wheel and the other things he might have touched. The keys rattled in an empty trash bin, where he dropped them on his way toward the Quarter.

The smell hit him, just after the sound of the bars and the tourists wailed down Bourbon Street, like that section of town had been bathed in rainwater that had filtered through week-old garbage. Then he realized the smell was him. He wanted a shower, a drink, a shave. He needed to see Simon. And he needed to sleep. The comfort of a bed didn't matter. All he wanted was an opportunity to close his eyes without the rush of some terror that he dreamed or was reminded of to shake him into consciousness.

The French-door windows of the Hearts of Gold Café were painted yellow. There was no main door on the street, so the only entry was through one of the parted French doors. The café beckoned curious tourists, and only the locals knew that the place was a tranny brothel. Ryan stood on the sidewalk for a few moments before he entered. People often found what they were looking for beyond those doors, whether they knew what they were looking for or not. The café was a place where the rumors were actually truths that nobody wanted to believe.

Ryan slipped beyond the parted door into the low light of the room. The bartender, Discount Drew, a lanky, slow-moving man except for his quick fingers, stood beside the ice well cracking cans of 7Up under the bar. Drew paused when Ryan entered, looked him over, then went back to his cans. Drew could swipe a bill from a stack of cash while he counted it without anyone noticing. Ryan had, though, and since everyone else he knew had a nickname, he gave Drew one. Ryan walked to the bar and sat down.

"We all thought you were dead," Drew said, not taking his eyes from the cans. "Or you'd gotten married."

"Which would be better?"

"Fuck, man, marriage. At least when you're married you can get away from them. When you're dead you just rot together in the ground."

"Weird and interesting logic, Drew. How's your mother?"

"Mom's good. She's in Shreveport for the week."

"Still counting cards?"

"Yeah, she's still got it. She almost got caught at the Horseshoe in Tunica last spring, but her senility act works well. Regardless, she had to take a few months off. Drove her fucking batshit. Drove me fucking batshit. She ran a seventy-hour game of fucking Yahtzee at my house a month or so back. That's all I can fucking hear now when it's quiet, clicking dice."

"Damn."

"Yeah. It's awful. Worse than hiccups. Need a drink?"

"Among other things."

"I hope a shower is one of them. You looking for Simon?"

"I know where to find him."

Drew moved to the cabinet beside the register and pulled out a bottle of whiskey to carry over to Ryan. He stopped, looking over at The Den where a group of the girls were waiting their turns to approach a customer. The Den was the back booth, below the balcony of the second floor that overlooked the bar, and the girls had claimed it as a place where they could sit, where the lighting was a little dimmer, where they could vet the customers when they came in. They'd share details with the other girls, what the client liked, if he or she were a good tipper, which ones were cops they could trust. Amelia, the tallest of them, and the one who'd been there the longest, had stood when Ryan entered. She peered at him as he made his way to the bar. When

Drew saw her looking, he nodded to her. Amelia slunk away from The Den, her eyes squinted, a death stare on Ryan, the side of his face.

Drew poured Ryan's drink in front of him and returned the bottle. Amelia slid her fingers down the bar. Her hand stopped short of his elbow.

"Where I come from, a gentleman would offer to buy a drink for a lady," she said.

"Guess you'd better go back to where you came from. There aren't a lot of gentleman around here. Even fewer ladies." Ryan took a sip of his whiskey, a deep breath to chase it down.

Amelia leaned to the bar and waved two fingers at Drew. Drew brought the bottle back to the bar with two more glasses and made the pours. She pushed one in front of Ryan. "There's at least one here tonight."

Ryan took another sip, dumped what was left into the glass Amelia had just slid in front of him. "How you been Ames?"

"I've been good. Doesn't look like you have, though. You don't look as clean as you used to. I'm betting it's fortunate for me that I don't have a sense of smell."

"Things change." Ryan looked up at her, her dark brown eyes, the lightness of her brown skin, the purple wig. He lifted the glass of whiskey. "I'm getting closer to good every minute."

"I bet I can get you way beyond good."

"Not that much has changed."

"What's it been six, seven years?"

"Four."

"Four is enough to change a man. Hell, Mr. Lover Boy, I can change a man in four minutes."

"And you can change back into one in four seconds," Drew muttered.

Amelia darted her eyes to him and smirked.

One of girls led two frat boys by the ends of their fingers toward the bottom of the staircase. The man closest to the bar tossed a pile of crisp ATM twenties there. Drew counted them, gave the girl a nod, and she finished making her way up the steps with her dates. Drew slid the cash through a slot in the back wall. He went back to work moving cans of 7Up around the ice well.

Ryan turned to Amelia. "Do you have any rooms available upstairs?"

"See? You'll be better than good when I get done with you."

"I just need the room, Ames. A shower. Maybe some sleep."

"And I thought it might be my lucky day. So disappointing. Upstairs is a date though, honey. Doesn't matter what you need."

"Price still two?"

Amelia looked over at Drew, tapped her right cheek with two fingers. Drew nodded.

"Let's go, Mr. Disappointment."

Ryan dug two more of Wendell's bills from his pocket and put them on the bar. He took his drink and followed Amelia. Three of the girls peered out at him from The Den, leaning into each other, whispering over their glasses. Amelia led him up the stairs and across the balcony, to the room at the end of the hall. The Slam Room. It overlooked the street corner, and Ryan moved to the window as soon as he entered the room. Amelia went straight to the bed. The full-size mattress was concave in the middle from a decade or more of steady use. Amelia sank into it and laced her fingers behind her head. Paths cut through the red carpet down to the fibers that held it together. In some places, the padding showed. There was a small round table in the middle of the room, mismatching chairs. The walls were lined with pallets, chunks of foam between the wooden slats to muffle the noise of clients—men and women who chose the room because of the freedom they had to make noise, to release their frustrations and anger, if that were the case. The shower curtain didn't close all the way around the tub. Water in the toilet was still foamy from where someone else had pissed in it. Ryan turned the knob for the hot water in the shower. Ice cold. He put his drink down on the edge of the sink, let the water run, and stepped back into the room to the window. Down on the street, tourists moved from bar to bar.

"Real classy place you got here, Ames."

"Better than the last place I was in." She got off the bed and strolled over to him where he peered through the curtain. "What are you looking at?"

"Home."

"Where have you been the last four years?"

"On the road."

"You do any work out there? Give someone like me a new home?"

"That's what I do."

"You get lonely doing that?"

Ryan moved his gaze from the street to her. "You get lonely doing this?"

"Hell, no. This is a dream come true, baby. Every day is a good day."

"I need you to do something for me."

"Yeah? You want me to touch you?"

He chuckled. "Flattered, Amelia, really, but no. I need a change of clothes."

She rolled her eyes and dropped her shoulders. "Such a tease. You still the same size?"

Ryan dug into his pocket and pulled out more cash. "Just jeans and a solid colored T-shirt. None of that fucking pillowcase, baggy Mardi Gras bullshit that the tourists wear. And socks. White. Please, no argyle."

She took the money from his hand, careful not to touch him. "Moved almost three thousand miles and I'm still fetching shit for a white boy."

"You haven't already forgotten where this white boy fetched you from, have you?"

She marched out of the room. Ryan went to the door and locked it, checked the window again, and turned to the bathroom. Steam began to slip through the open space in the curtain. There was a used bar of soap in the tray. He checked under the sink, found an open box of baking soda. He stripped down, fabric peeling from some parts of his skin, sticky and stiff. The water spray over his shoulders felt better than the shot of whiskey. Once it was as hot as he could handle, he scrubbed the baking soda into his skin. When he finished, he stood under the water to rinse the pasty residue until the water started going cold. Ryan cut the water off and grabbed the whiskey on the edge of the sink to take it down.

There was only one towel in the bathroom. He left it bunched in the corner and turned the light off before he went back to the window to wait for Amelia. The streets below were nearly vacant, except for the random frat packs and gaggles of bachelorette parties. Each of them uniformed in some monochromatic garb as they staggered toward the next venue. Near the alley directly across from him, a hooker in a short skirt lifted three wallets from a pack of drunks. Amelia moved up the street. Heads turned in bewilderment and awe as she moved past them, except for one person. A wiry-thin man stood on the sidewalk across the street looking up at the window where Ryan stood, the brim of his hat casting a shadow over his face. Little by little, Ryan moved the curtain closed and waited for Amelia.

She tossed the bag of clothes into the middle of the floor when he let her in, and she sprawled out on the bed, rubbing the itch from the wig on her bald scalp. Ryan locked the door.

"I like your outfit, lover boy." She waved a foot at him.

He pulled the jeans from the bag and snapped them out before sliding them over his legs. Amelia sat up, the blue eye shadow rippling while she blinked at him. The fresh denim felt crisp, and he realized how damp the other jeans had been. He went back to the slit between the curtains. The man was gone.

"Why do you do what you do?" Amelia asked.

Ryan turned and grabbed the package of socks and T-shirts. "Why do you do what you do?" He tore at the bag of socks on his way to the bed and sat.

"Didn't your mother teach you not to answer a question with a question?"

Ryan held a pair of socks in his hand and paused. "No."

The socks provided a sense of comfort that reminded Ryan of how tired he was. He wanted to wake up from sleep and enter the world like he had new skin, to become a stranger in an unfamiliar place again. The T-shirt fit well and he stood to retrieve his boots.

"You look better naked," she said.

"I guess the man makes the clothes."

"Why are you being so short?"

He yanked on the laces, pausing in his hurry to tie them. "I'm tired, Ames. It's been a long couple of days."

"You want to—never mind. I almost forgot you like talking about the past as much as you like being touched. Remind me again, why that is."

He rolled up his soiled clothes from the bathroom and dumped them into the plastic bag Amelia had brought his new clothes in. The bag wheezed as he tied the carrying straps together. "Ames, I have to go. Maybe another time."

"The last time you said that I didn't see you again, until now."

"What's another few years, right?"

At the corner of the wall near the balcony, Ryan scanned the bar below. Empty, except for Drew gnawing on a beverage stirrer. Ryan took the stairs at the other end of the hallway to the back entrance. The narrow alley led him to the street he'd seen the man on. The warm air around him was the same, sticky air that had draped a layer of grime over his shoulders when he'd first arrived. He ditched the bag of clothes in a trash can at a sidewalk vendor where he grabbed a beer and continued to move. The Quarter barely had a pulse that night compared to what he remembered. And slowly, he recalled the details of the streets, how familiar they were. He crossed them, backtracked, re-walked blocks, backtracked more, but he couldn't see the man or anyone else following him. The thick air was hard to breath as he made his way to the Monteleone Hotel and stopped. He went inside and ordered a drink at the carousel bar. Another whiskey.

The bar rotated, a little at a time, and he had his back to

the entrance when it was time for him to leave. Simon's was two blocks away. Ryan took six to get there and entered the store at ten minutes to nine. Racks of clothing created aisles in the square room. Wooden crates had been stacked on the tables to provide as much inventory shelving as possible—rolled silk ties, mannequins of different ethnicities with starched shirts and double-windsors standing in every corner. A seersucker garment every six feet. The room smelled of oak and cotton, a scent he wanted to pull from the air and wrap around himself while he slept.

Simon's office, the door behind the counter, was slightly open.

"Back here," Simon called, his voice a soothing hum through the store. Ryan took a step toward the counter when the door opened behind him and he turned to the man he'd seen watching him from the street.

NINE

Patrick held the door to close it quietly, locking the deadbolt when it shut. He moved casually to the right wall and pushed the switches to kill the lights outside—for the sign and the one above the door. Another switch darkened the back of the store. And then another to darken the front. The shim of light from Simon's office and the soft glow from the desk lamp near the register were all that was left of illumination. Patrick turned back to the door and stood in the spot that he'd been when he first entered.

"Welcome home, Ryan."

Ryan took in Patrick's presence, the slinking nature of his movement. "You always were a creepy motherfucker, Patrick."

"And you are still as elusive. I had to give up tailing you, but I knew you'd be coming here."

"I hope you didn't scuff your shoes."

"That's an awful thing to say." He held his outstretched palm toward Simon's office. "Simon first. We can catch up later."

Ryan entered the small room and took the seat across from the narrow table Simon used as a desk. There was an empty glass toward the guest end of the table, a bottle of

Rare Breed beside it. The walls were double sheetrock over a layer of steel, soundproof. Patrick closed the oak door. Simon stood at the mannequin in the center of the room, a row of pins in his mouth pressing striations against his bottom lip. Horn-rimmed glasses rested on his nose.

"Good to see you," Simon mumbled over the pins, the beaded ends waving from his speech.

Ryan remembered when he was younger and he'd heard someone refer to Simon as *The Ferry Man*. He'd learned later that it wasn't a reference to his sexual orientation. Simon had nimble fingers, the tips of the first two of his left hand were hard and calloused from pushing needles through fabric most of his life. Match flames pinched between his fingers would leave nothing more than a black smear.

Ryan pulled the cork from the bottle and poured himself a drink, half glass, and leaned back in the chair. The chair was comfortable, embracing. He wanted to sleep right there. Simon folded fabric quickly against the chalk outlines, drawing the pins from his lips and stabbing them along the lines. He brushed the front of his shirt and suspenders as if some remnants of his labor were there and moved away from the mannequin. He approached Ryan, tightening his yellow bow tie with one hand.

He lowered himself into an identical leather chair across from Ryan and reached over the table for the bottle. "And how was the Land of Enchantment?"

"Enchanting," Ryan answered.

Simon took a deep breath, focusing on the bottle as he poured. He lifted the glass and met the rim of Ryan's. "It is interesting how so much human interaction takes place over a drink."

"We're social creatures. Seems fitting, actually."

"Yes. But I was referring to you, Ryan, why it is interesting. You are not a social creature."

Simon reached to the wall and flipped the switch for the overhead lights. The room went dim with the soft light of the lamp beside him, giving just enough for the two of them to see. Simon pulled an ashtray from the edge of the table and fumbled through a pack of cloves. The smell came into the room, rich and full. He grabbed the bottle again and exhaled smoke toward the lamp.

Simon raised his eyebrows. "I spoke to Annabelle."

Ryan finished his drink and took the bottle from Simon. Simon pulled his glasses off and leaned back in his chair, smoothing his white hair along his skull with the edge of his palms.

Ryan finished his pour and set the bottle down. "How is she?"

"Annabelle is concerned. As am I. I was under the impression that you were done with relocations. At least that is the impression you gave when you left us. You do remember, yes?"

"I remember, Simon."

"And now you are here, back in New Orleans, back to this table, back to the same spot you were sitting four years ago with the same whiskey in your glass. I have to venture to guess that things are not alright with you."

"What makes you think that?"

"Your sarcasm, first of all. *Enchanting?* Sarcasm is the veil you use to hide your nervousness, your hesitation, unrest. That, and you gave a travel package to a woman and a child. Children make the guidelines difficult for people. Too much attachment."

Ryan cupped his glass, moved his thumb around the edge

of the rim.

"Didn't really seem like I had much of a choice."

"The booking?"

"Sludge tycoon out of Dallas wanted a vacation for his son. Some domestic troubles that might have tarnished his reputation. He let his wife handle it, the boy's stepmother. She wanted more, insurance to protect the client. Mostly to protect herself. She took her role as matriarch a little too personally."

"Where is the client now?"

"On vacation."

"The duration?"

Ryan bore his squinted stare into Simon's bow tie. "Indefinite."

Simon leaned back in his chair and took a hard drag from his clove. "You betrayed a client."

"Wouldn't have mattered either way. I was a loose end."

"How did you get a travel package for the other two?"

"A friend in Vancouver."

"Are they solid?"

"Yes. And clean. Very clean."

"And did you get a package for the client?"

"Yeah. Different ticket vendor, though."

"Okay. That should keep them in the clear. And what about you? You had to burn your tickets as well, I assume."

"I guess someone paid for its expiration."

"Dallas?"

"Yeah."

"And your employer?"

"Clipped his fucking coupon."

"Interesting choice of words."

"Inside joke. Well, would be an inside joke."

Simon mashed his clove into the ashtray. "So, is it fair to assume that you need a new travel plan, tickets? The whole package?"

"I wouldn't be here if I didn't."

"That hurts my feelings a little."

"Not my intention, but I don't want to push the ticket I have now too far."

"And where did you get this ticket?"

"Panhandler."

"Did you run it?"

"I didn't have a chance. And I'm here, so I don't see the point."

Simon dug his fingers into his pack of cloves. "What kind of package are you looking for?"

"International. I need somewhere else to lay low for a while, so I don't end up running all over the goddamn country. A few years to let this Dallas thing settle before I can deal with it."

"International packages are extremely difficult to obtain. They are also incredibly expensive."

"That might be a problem."

"How so?"

"I used my fee to get a package for the others. The second half is no longer available, and my employer cleaned out my go bag."

Simon tapped the filter end of the clove against his thumbnail. "What size dress do you wear?"

"I've never gotten fitted for one. Is this a new business endeavor? Are you going to start selling women's clothes? What kind of a question is that?"

"All the hookers with hearts of gold work at the café. If this is the way you will be conducting business out on your own, you would be better suited in the Slam Room. Every package you have to burn is a package that could be used to help someone. Acquisition is becoming harder and harder. You let too much of your emotion guide your decisions."

Ryan pulled the bottle closer to him and filled his glass. Simon held his palms out in bewilderment. Ryan corked the bottle and tapped it in with his palm. He lifted his glass, hovering it at his bottom lip. "I don't remember asking you to book me a guilt trip."

Simon put the clove to his lips, pulled a strand of thread from the cuff of his shirt before he lit the clove. "Ryan, you are remarkable on the road, but since—" Simon tapped his clove, ignored Ryan's scowl. "Omaha wasn't your fault. But it has changed you."

"No. It wasn't my fault. I try to tell myself that. I've even spoken that bullshit out loud, my own fucking pity rally, but it doesn't keep me from seeing her face every night. You vetted the wrong fucking client, and I did the fucking work. All we did was give some motherfucker a hall pass, and then we couldn't do anything about it."

"You did do something about it."

"Yeah. I did something. After. It didn't do a goddamn thing for her."

Simon sipped his whiskey. The two of them sat in the room with the hiss of Simon's clove between them. Ryan, weary, the alcohol drawing on his efforts to stay focused. Simon finished the clove before he spoke again. Ryan tried to blink away the burning in his eyes.

"I did not expect our first conversation of your return to reach such an inimical level. This might not be any consolation for you, but there are seventeen people out there who are living, breathing, enjoying a life without the fear that they needed to escape from. You did that for them. What happened in Omaha was one person taking advantage of that same opportunity. That is why it is not your fault. Any amount of vetting would not have prevented that. And there was absolutely nothing you could have done. So, you can carry that with you. You can be reckless in your decisions. But do so in a way that is unselfish. When you use Annabelle to help with a transition, that brings her into the fold, which brings me into the fold. There is more to your decision than ameliorating your conscience by making a noble choice. There are a handful of people close to you and seventeen others who depend on the security of your decisions. If you are going to set out on a conscious crusade, do so without jeopardizing the safety of our clients that you have helped. If that is your aim, go become a Big Brother, volunteer at a hospital, join the Peace Corps, or any number of altruistic endeavors. Rescue a fucking pit bull. But you cannot function in this gritty, wretched world by doing something munificent that might affect the lives of so many others. You are driven by your compassion, which is something I thought I would not see in you after everything you went through, but you need to maintain balance with that compassion, dear nephew."

Simon had not referred to him as a relative since he was a boy. Ryan felt a sweep of unease, and he couldn't tell if it was because Simon had a point or if he was unsure of what Simon would say next. His unease increased with the longer stretch of silence than before.

"You are tagged, Ryan," Simon finally said. "Someone out there is desperate to find you."

"Good thing I'm a ghost."

"That would be a *good* thing if people did not believe that ghosts are real. And you are real to these people in Dallas."

"That's why I need an international package, Simon."

Simon took a deep breath and ran his palm along the edge of the table. "I can help you now, Ryan, but that is all I will ever be able to do. After this, you are, and forever will be, a wisp of breath. I will cover your international package. But I need something from you first, something Annabelle and Patrick aren't quite suited for."

Ryan clenched his jaw. "What?"

"It is quite complicated, and exceptionally sensitive. It also involves someone close to me, someone you know, which is why I need you to limit the possibility of contingencies."

"What do you need Simon?"

"I need you to go home."

"I am home."

"Your other home."

This is where you are, and you can never go home, darted through Ryan's mind. He remembered when Simon told him that for the first time, after he'd brought him to New Orleans, back when his name had been Everett.

His older brother Lucas made faces at him from across the table, crossing his eyes, letting milk spill from his mouth. Everett laughed and their father entered the room, smacked him in the back of the head. He bit his tongue, tasted blood.

"Eat your goddamn cereal, boy."

He nibbled away, hoping the cereal would get soggy quicker, so the cornflakes wouldn't scrape against his tongue while he chewed. Eye crust on the corner of his eyes made a convenient reason for him to wipe at his face, his tears.

Lucas chewed his food slowly to avoid crunching. Everett soaked up his cereal with the blood from his tongue until he could swallow it without chewing. There was a thump on the kitchen window, a bird. *That happened a lot, but it startled his mother in the kitchen and she dropped the casserole that she'd been preparing. His father kicked the chair out, which toppled into the living room, and he stormed into the kitchen.*

Lucas hovered his face a few inches above his bowl to shovel cereal into his mouth, milk dropping from his lips onto the edges of the table and the floor. Everett saw the flashes of his mother's dress, lavender paisley, heard the grunts of his father's mumbled words. He didn't see Lucas stand up.

"Psst."

Everett held his mouth open, hoping air would relieve the sting on the side of his tongue. Lucas waved him toward the hallway, back to their room. He teared up and tip-toed past the kitchen. His father had mounted her, pushing her face back and forth over the casserole, a stream of blood spreading onto the linoleum where a piece of glass cut her face. His father rose and stood there, stared down at Everett.

"Get your ass to school," he said as he picked up his chair and stepped back to the table.

Everett's hands shook and he pressed them against his stomach. His mother reached over the broken glass and green beans, the breadcrumbs that looked like vomit clustered to her face. She whimpered, noticing him there in the doorway. "Help me."

He took a step toward the kitchen. His father slammed his fist on the table and he jumped. "I told you to get your ass to school. Now, get."

Her look went stern then. The tremble in her hands stopped, and she reached for the towel hanging on the hook at the edge of the counter to wipe the mess away from her face.

"Goddamnit, boy, if I have to tell you again..."

He started to move, slowly, and his mother stood, turned her back to him to face the window.

Lucas crammed his things into his backpack. Everett sat on the edge of his bed, almost started sobbing, but Lucas lunged at him and covered his mouth, forcing him to bite his tongue again.

"Shhhhh. Get your stuff. Let's go."

The gunshot pounded through the house, made it shake. Lucas hunched down. Everett forgot his crying and looked to Lucas for an explanation. Lucas moved to the door. Everett followed. They could see their father's arm stretched across the table, fingers twitching. Lucas stepped out into the hallway. The shucking sound of the shotgun chambering another round echoed along the pine-board walls. An empty shell casing fell to the floor, clicked around, and settled. His mother came around the table from behind their father, the barrel pointed down the hallway.

Ryan finished his drink, still trudging his way out of the memory. "What is it you want me to do there?"

Simon told him. Ryan took in the details as his mind slowed like fading embers until the memory was nothing but ashy gray. His aunt's husband Kurt had killed someone, made it look like an accident so he could acquire a lease on a piece of timberland. Now, someone wanted to kill Kurt, and Ryan was going there to make sure that it happened. Ryan was going home to help Malcolm Hale kill his aunt's husband. Malcolm Hale, the man who saved his life.

TEN

The private detective Williams' lawyer had convinced him to hire did not impress Victoria. He didn't drink, which made her distrust him. She'd expected a PI to be someone sloppy, grumpy, a nothing-left-to-lose type who had a couple of ex-wives and a handful of estranged children. Jonathan Johnson, as far as she could tell, was none of those things. He was perpetually smiling, despite the heat and the film it sealed over his skin from sweat. How could he smile in this heat? She checked her own look of resentment and frustration in the panel mirror below Williams' gazelle mounts. He'd brought them with him to San Antonio, where they decided it would be safer for them. Safety waned in their concerns when they discovered that the air conditioning had gone out. Johnson wore khaki cargo shorts and sandals with Velcro straps over the toes, heels, and instep. It all seemed like a lot of work, all that Velcro. And he wore white, cotton, knee-length socks and two watches on the same wrist. Victoria imagined he had a pith helmet out in his jeep and then wondered why he wore two watches.

Johnson had just informed them that the location Ryan gave Victoria was a rest stop on Interstate 70 outside of Topeka, Kansas.

"Now I'm sure this raises some concerns about your son, Roy, but it doesn't necessarily mean a bad thing. In my experience, people who do this sort of thing take their work very seriously. The Ryan fellah might have just given you guys a random location to keep you from finding out where Roy really is."

"And why would he do that?" Victoria snarled.

"Well, there are a number of reasons, actually. One, it's possible that Roy didn't want his location disclosed. I understand he was facing some serious charges. He might have wanted to make sure even his parents couldn't find him. Two, perhaps Roy and his wife reconciled and decided that it might be a good idea to run off with new identities and leave the past behind. I've heard of that before."

"Roy wouldn't run off from this," Williams spoke, holding his arms out to get Johnson to notice the lavishness of the house.

"I didn't say it was likely. It's just a possibility."

"What are the other possibilities?"

"Well, Mrs. Williams, I'm not sure that we should get into that just yet. It's still early, and it's important for you to remain hopeful. With any luck, Roy will get in touch with you at some point."

"We're out of luck, Johnson. What are the other possibilities?"

Johnson's smile faded for a brief second, but returned, less broad than before. "Well, this Ryan fellah might be keeping Roy from you in order to make financial demands down the road. Those Mexicans do that a lot with family members of the people they smuggle over the border."

Williams dug his hand into the ice bucket on his desk, swirled his fingers through the melting cubes, and pulled out a fistful for his glass. Wendell winced at the sound.

"Or he could be dead," Williams muttered.

"That's, unfortunately, another possibility. And if that's the case, most likely, you can expect some sort of ransom anyway."

Victoria stepped toward Johnson, toward Williams' desk. "Mr. Johnson, are we paying you to invent theories about Roy, or are we paying you to find Mr. Carpenter?"

Johnson's smile finally disappeared. "Actually, I haven't been paid for anything, yet. What we're doing here, why I came down here to see *your husband*, was to offer my experience and guidance in resolving this matter the best way possible. As I understand it, you, Mrs. Williams, hired a man to help your son abscond. Now you can't find your son or that man. My *theories* will help prioritize your options. Whatever those options might be, whatever I do, will come from your husband. I answer to one person, and one person only. That person is whoever pays me." Johnson looked toward Williams. "If that's a problem for either one of you, I'd be happy to get to a place that is much more comfortable than this room."

Williams chuckled. "Victoria, if you don't mind, I'd like to allow a professional to handle this situation. The situation that you got us into."

Victoria swiped a line of sweat from her upper lip. Rapid blinking. "Forgive me, Mr. Johnson. I'm a little tense. Please, inform my husband what you think the best course of action will be."

"I think the best option is to find the fellah that you hired. I say the best because, unless your son gets in touch with you, that's really the only option you have. But I'd have to say that it'll be nearly impossible to track this fellah down. I think I can do it, though, but I'll have to reach out for some favors. Favors…I suppose I can't really call them favors with the price tag they carry. I have a per diem rate within the state. Anything out of state goes up twenty percent on top of travel expenses."

"Do you really think you can find him?" Victoria asked.

"Yes, but it'll take some time. How much, I can't say. I can't say that I can find out what happened to your son, either." Johnson reduced his smile and looked toward Victoria. "I know that's discouraging for you."

Victoria turned from him and sat against the desk. She stared out the window again, the sunlight beaming down on the brown earth outside.

"So what happens? What happens when—if—you find him?" Williams asked.

"Then I let you know where he is."

Victoria turned her head. "That's it? You don't bring him to us?"

"That's kidnapping, Mrs. Williams. I'm a licensed private investigator. If your intention is something nefarious or to avoid the use of legal action, I can put you in touch with someone more comfortable in dealing with those sorts of matters."

Williams wiped the sweat from his brow with the back of his hand and took a step to the corner of his desk. He put his hands on his hips and looked over at his gazelle mounts. "When can you start, Mr. Johnson?"

"As soon as you tell me everything you can about this Ryan Carpenter fellah."

"Good. My wife will handle it from here. You work for her, now." He continued around his desk and left the room.

"Where should we begin?" she asked Johnson, moving

around the desk to stand in front of him.

Johnson unfolded his fingers and dug into the pocket of his cargo shorts for a notebook. "Begin with everything you can think of that will help me track down Ryan Carpenter. It's most likely an assumed name, but if we can get a starting point, that would greatly benefit my search. Where is he from? Did he have an apartment or hotel room that you visited? Did he have an ID that you might have seen? A state would help narrow it down."

"What about a license plate?" Wendell said from the corner.

Johnson turned. "Yes, that might get us somewhere. You remember the number? The state? The type of car?"

It had taken Adam only an hour to find the Subaru after he discovered the key Ryan left in the pocket. Getting it out of first gear or reverse took longer. Downshifting, too, was something that he had to get used to, especially to keep X from flailing around the back or slamming into the dash when she decided to ride in the front. He finally had it down, though, and he had enough money to make it to Fort Collins, where his grandmother lived. She'd let him crash there for a while, if he told her he wasn't drinking or using anymore.

Adam had to go to three different stores to buy beer, the first two refusing to sell to him because he had no ID. He also bought an inexpensive sleeping bag and a thirty-pound bag of dogfood for the trip. The rest of the cash he kept for gas money, hoping that he could find some people on the way who might need a lift and could help with expenses. He spread the sleeping bag out in the back of the Subaru for

X to lie on and used a shoebox he'd found for X's food dish.

Boredom pushed into the car around him with the slow movement of traffic in Dallas. He thought he might find someone near the stretch of outlet stores who'd need a lift, someone to keep him occupied while he drove. He didn't, not even anyone panhandling at the entrance to the grocery store, so he reached behind the seat and pulled a beer from the case. X perched her front paws up on the back seat, stirred by the movement while he slowed at a red light.

"Don't worry, little," Adam said. "I'll only have a couple."

That first beer went down quicker than he'd expected, just short of four traffic signals. He pulled the second, making an attempt to be a little quieter so he wouldn't rouse X again. She lifted her head and perked an ear but remained still other than that. That beer went down slower, and he'd made it through five signals before he had to reach back again. One more, he told himself, thinking that once he got on the highway, the steady driving would eliminate his boredom. The can slipped from his fingers, and he patted the carpet behind the seat to reach for it, keeping his focus on the road. His fingers slipped over the end of the can and it rolled a little farther out of reach.

"Dammit."

He clicked the button for the safety belt, allowing himself to arch over the console. The can was gritty from bits of sand that had clung to it. Back in his seat, he wiped the dirt away against his shirt. He cracked the can and took a celebratory sip.

"Gotcha," he said to the can, and looked up at the traffic signal as it turned yellow.

The brakes were something he'd wished he'd spent more time getting used to. Mostly, he'd focused on the clutch. He realized that when he hit the brake, the engine in the pickup behind him grumbled a little louder.

Impact shot glass over the back seat, and it pelted against the windshield. X yelped at the sudden lurch that shoved her into the seats. The beer toppled between his legs and his body slammed forward, snapping his head back. The pain in his neck was sharp and immediate. He reached for his neck, but the movement made him cry out instead. The Subaru stalled and rolled into the intersection.

ELEVEN

Ryan spent three days in a room at the Ironwood Tavern. The room smelled of piss and cigarettes, but the bartender didn't check his ID when he filled out the small slip for the room rental. He watched the corner store across the street for most of that time, letting the vibration of the road settle, looking for faces he might recognize or one that might recognize him. That was unlikely. Simon had run Adam's ID, and it was clean, so it was enough for him to use for travel, and since Ironwood, Maine, was dragging a decade behind, it wouldn't be an issue for him. The bar, including room rentals, was cash only. He'd only be there for a short time, until Simon got his papers. Ryan would be in Ironwood passing through looking for work, fortunate to find some haying fields and cutting wood, which was what Simon suggested as a way to draw as little attention to himself as possible.

A quarter century had gone by since Simon snuck him away with the help of his grandfather and Malcolm Hale, who had been a deputy at the time and found Ryan after his mother's rampage. He remembered that, shivering and cold in a rock pile despite the sun right above him. That thought took hold of him for several hours while he sat in the wooden chair in the room, flicking specks of green paint from the armrests with his thumbnails. He'd propped his feet up on the sill to look at the store through the screen in the open window. Below the window, boot heels struck the wooden steps of the porch and moved down the length of it to the bar door. The heavy, metal door whined as one of the men pulled it open, and huffed as it closed behind them, and the sounds of the bar were gone.

This is where you are. Welcome home.

Ryan got up from the chair and pulled a rolled black T-shirt from his bag where his other clothes were rolled and held tight with rubber bands. He shook the shirt and pulled it over his head, grabbed the baseball cap from the dresser— a mangled piece of thrift store furniture with three drawers that either wouldn't open or wouldn't close all the way. The maroon carpeted hallway led him to a set of stairs. The sign on the wall said, "BAR," but the arrow on it pointed toward the ceiling. He took the stairs one at a time, got to the landing, and saw the restrooms in front of him. Before he entered the bar, he took a breath. *Your wit and sarcasm will not be appreciated there,* Simon had warned.

The wooden floor was furrowed with foot paths. Even the nail heads had been worn away, leaving sharp nibs to catch the rubber of his boot sole. A bull moose mount hung on the wall in the small space before the bar room, the fur grayed with dust and ash from cigarettes when bars still allowed smoking. A round table and pinball machine were pushed into the corners opposite the mount. He moved into the room and the men he'd heard enter the bar were at one of the two pool tables in the back. Another woman sat hunched in her stool, talking to Nicole, the bartender, and she'd only glanced at him when he'd walked in. She scratched her head above her right ear and slapped the bar. She mumbled something, and whatever Nicole had whispered to her wasn't anything she was happy about.

Nicole perked as he made his way to the bar. Her enormous tits were packed into a shirt that was too small, stretching out the lightning-bolt style *KISS* letters on the front of it. She arched her back, stretching the letters a little more. Blond, and her hair pulled back tight and wound with clear plastic pens holding it in a bun. Her nails were painted orange except for the middle fingers, which were black. Fading blue and red from a tattoo on her shoulder leaked below the cuff of her T-shirt. Thick arms, but without the shaky movement of fat. Ryan pulled out a padded stool and eased into it.

"What can I get you?" she asked, tossing a cardboard beer coaster in front of him.

The cardboard wobbled and settled at the fingertips of his right hand. The bar was wooden. Old black-and-white portraits of what the place used to look like were lacquered to the wood. He asked for a beer. Nicole winked at him before moving over to the reach-in beer cooler. The girl to Ryan's left rolled her eyes at the mirror behind the tiers of liquor when Nicole passed again.

She put the can down delicately on the coaster. "That'll be two fifty."

Ryan pushed the five-dollar bill he'd flattened out across the bar and she brushed the back of his fingers as she took it. At the register, Nicole looked at her friend in the reflection and hit a few keys before the register popped open, change vibrating against itself when the drawer stopped. She returned his change and propped her elbows on the bar to lean closer.

"You're not from around here."

Ryan lifted his eyebrows.

"What brings you to the Tavern in good ole' Ironwood?"

"I'm looking for work, actually. I was told to ask for Malcolm Hale."

The girl next to him snapped her head in his direction. "Who told you that?"

Ryan lifted his beer and took a sip. "A mutual friend of ours. Do you know Malcolm?"

"Everybody knows everybody around here."

Nicole chimed in. "What kind of work do you do?"

Ryan turned his head to face her, something familiar about the other girl nagging his memory. "Whatever I can find."

"So you're a handyman?"

"Of sorts."

"Sweetheart, about the only work you're going to get from Malcolm Hale is throwing hay or swinging a chainsaw. Isn't that right, Olivia?"

Olivia climbed from the barstool and walked out of the bar. The sunlight spilled into the room and Ryan turned his eyes away from the brightness. Nicole had leaned away from him as Olivia made her abrupt departure. The two men shooting pool made their way to the bar with empty beer bottles. When the door closed, Nicole looked back down at Ryan.

"Well," she said, bulging her eyes for a second, "I guess she's a little touchy about working for Malcolm."

"Seems that way."

She emphasized a frown. "Her husband, Malcolm's son, died last winter working in the woods. A tree crushed him." She scraped her teeth over her bottom lip. "I'm Nicole, by the way. In case you forgot."

She went to get beers for the two men at the other end of the bar, made small talk with them, asking when the older of the two men would head back out to New York, and how the greenhouse was treating the younger man. When the two men walked away from the bar and Nicole made her way back to him, Ryan ordered a shot of whiskey. It was a bad idea, but he needed something to keep him even, especially there.

When she brought the shot to him and nudged it across the bar beside his beer, she ducked into his vision. Ryan leaned back and pulled money from his pocket.

"You alright? You look like someone killed your dog."

Ryan huffed. "That happen a lot around here, people killing each other's dogs?"

"Just about every shitty thing you can imagine happens around here."

She took care of the money, and when she returned, the predatory look in her eyes had diminished. "So, where were we?" She sat against a trash can and leaned on the bar. "Oh, work. That's right. There really ain't much, honestly. The kid back there," She pointed to the taller of the two men. Thin, almost skinny, and young—a face that would be perpetually twenty-five. "He works at the tomato plant down in Madison."

Ryan picked up the shot of Turkey. He hovered the glass just below his nose, almost felt the bite it would take out of his throat and put it back down.

"You could always come work for me." Nicole touched his elbow. "If you're any good at back rubs. I won't be able to pay you in cash, though." She winked. Again.

Ryan fought hard to keep his expression calm after she

touched his elbow. Her fingers crept across the bar to his hand. What was it about people that made them think touching others was acceptable? Men who'd grab women's arms to admire a tattoo. It seemed a lot like lifting food from somebody's plate and taking a bite, just to see how it tasted. People didn't need to use their hands to see something, unless they were blind. But maybe things would be better if everyone were blind. They'd acknowledge their other senses, senses that were much stronger than their vision. People would be more courteous. Stupid people might not live as long. Ugly people could get fucked with the lights on.

"You look like you have good, strong hands," she said.

Ryan pulled his hand away and lifted the shot glass. He hammered the shot down his throat then pushed the empty glass away with the ends of his fingers. Nicole asked him if he wanted another. He shook his head and lifted the bottom of the beer toward her. When she turned, he finished it.

Nicole brought him the second beer with less enthusiasm. Ryan thought if he should care that his reluctance to jump on her offer spoiled her interest or hope, whatever it might be. The two men in the back room laughed as they put their cues back into the rack and moved out onto the smoking porch.

"You know, I didn't even think for you to talk to Wes' brother," Nicole said, a bit more enthusiastic than she'd been just a minute before. "He picks up odd jobs here and there when he's up for the summer. He might point you in the right direction. You could also go talk to Matty down at the Superette. He knows everyone. If someone's looking for help, he'll know."

"I appreciate that. Nicole, right?" He didn't want to give her the idea that he'd been paying that much attention.

"Yes. And you're Adam. I saw it on the room reservation slip." She confessed. "It's nice to meet you." She moved to extend her hand for a handshake. Ryan saw it coming and had already slipped from his stool.

"Bathroom that way?"

She looked confused, continued to move her hand forward as if she'd anticipated his question, and pointed toward the hallway behind him. "Yeah. That door you came through. Men's is on the right."

When he turned, he saw that the wall on either side of the archway had been decorated with framed newspaper clippings. License plates ran the length of the room across the edge of the ceiling, some of them so faded or covered with dust the numbers were barely visible. Ryan moved closer to the clippings on the left side of the archway. There was less dust on the glass, but the top edges of the black frames were thick with grime. He wiped away a streak of dust with the back of his hand. *Woman Sets Fire to Home; Kills Family and Self.* There was a grainy caption of the plot where the house had stood. Next to that, a picture of his mother when she was much younger than he could remember her. The paper had yellowed, and he moved down to the next clipping.

Nicole said something about Indian Hill, but he ignored her, moving on to the next clipping and the next, wondering why they'd been framed and mounted on the wall. He glanced up at the moose head as he moved to the right side of the archway. More clippings about his family. *Four Dead in Family Slaying. Massacre on Indian Hill. Small Town Slaughter.* He looked over the walls, the floors, at the linen curtains on the windows. The Tavern would go up in flames in minutes.

He passed under the giant moose, where his shoulders twitched from the sudden crowding of space above him. Two other men made their way to the front door. One of them wore overalls over his bare chest, the curve of his stomach heaving beneath the front bib. The man who followed behind him was thinner, wearing an oversized T-shirt. They made it to the door of the bar as Ryan stepped into the bathroom.

There was no soap in the dispenser on the edge of the sink. All that remained of the paper towel roll was the plastic it had been spooled on. There was a space on the paneling of the wall where a dispenser had been mounted at some point, but there was only the difference in paint color and the four dimples in the wood where screws had been torn out. The mirror had been covered in Plexiglas and there were two urinals and one commode, in a line behind the divider that blocked the entrance. Ryan stepped over to piss in the commode and saw the writing above the toilet.

On Indian Hill lived Rebecca and Paul
Until one day in early fall
Rebecca took a shotgun and murdered them all.
Her head came off with a shotgun blast,
While her house and her family burned down to ash.

Ryan whispered his mother's name. At some point, the sound of it had faded, and there was no sound he could think of when he thought of her, only that look in her eyes, like the well at the edge of the field that they couldn't see the bottom of. And there were the gunshots, those echoes that punctuated the graffiti poem in front of him. The depth and severity of his return hadn't occurred to him. His hands shook with an urge to break something. *This simple fucking town*. Maybe he needed to kick the shaky knees out from under it.

In his first few footsteps as he walked back out to the bar, he tried to shake off the words, fill his mind with silence, even the drone of something annoying, but those words bounced around in his skull, a hollow, chaotic knock. He wanted to fill the bar with the people who lived there and walk through it with the shotgun his mother had tried to kill him with. He'd use birdshot, aim low, take their legs out then step over them as he drenched the walls with gasoline to set the place ablaze. And he'd stand in the middle of the flames just to feel the heat and hear their screams.

The two men who'd entered the bar on his way to the bathroom stood on either side of the barstool he'd left. He walked through the room and reached between them to grab his beer. The fat man in the overalls smelled faintly sour, the reddish hair that sprawled over his back and shoulders glistened with sweat. His cheeks were red, one of those slow, happy bastards who took a lot to rile, but impossible to stop or put down if he got pissed—that potato-bred, country-strong motherfucker who would rip the door off a car to get at someone. The skinny one, whose patchy hair around his chin was much thinner than the growth above his lip, watched Ryan take his beer and move to another seat at the bar. He licked his lips and peered at Ryan while his big friend fumbled over a few flirtatious lines for Nicole, who ignored them.

"Hey, man. We in your way?" he called after Ryan.

"Pete, don't start any shit now. For goodness sake it's still happy hour," Nicole said.

"It's a happy question."

His voice slurred down the bar toward Ryan. Pete slid a

couple of stools closer. Ryan could smell the whiskey, sun-baked sweat, and gasoline emitting from his clothes. His eyes were glossed and there was a sway in his movement that he tried to hide by gripping the edge of the bar.

"Hey, Pete, come on, man. We came here to have a good time. Leave the guy alone."

"No, man. Folk around here got manners. Your s'pose to say 'scuse me when you reach between folks conversatin'."

Ryan took a sip of his beer, stared straight ahead of him, locked his gaze at the bottle of Wild Turkey, heart drumming into a heavy, solid beat.

"You deaf or somethin'?" Pete nudged his friend. "Maybe he's retarded." He slid another stool closer and leaned toward Ryan's face. "You retarded or something?"

Ryan imagined the snap and soft give through the man's skull if he grabbed the back of his head and smashed his teeth into the bar. He swallowed. He attracted this, always. It was as though his path through life was one straight shot through a gauntlet of idiots and assholes who'd run to the edge of the road to meet him. And Ryan would pass through, impervious, until one of them reached out to touch him.

TWELVE

Malcolm Hale sat at the window of his cabin with a .308 across his lap. The window was open, and the cool breeze that blew along the tops of the trees in the spur that the window faced floated into the room. He smelled the faint hint of pine needles, the cracked cones that the red squirrels and chipmunks chewed apart. Down the slope of his backyard, through a stretch of stumps where he had cut away a shooting lane, he looked at the small coffee can that he'd filled with sand and placed down there, nailed to a stump seventy yards out. He'd been shooting throughout the afternoon, taking his time, a single shot every twenty or thirty minutes so the old lady across the street wouldn't call the sheriff. That day, like every day since he'd called Simon, he spent hoping that whomever Simon was sending would arrive soon.

The peak of summer was approaching. Each day bore a little more warmth, and he'd have to hay the Stanley Farm fields soon, before the summer rains came. That would carry him through the deepest part of summer, and would dry things out enough to get into the log yard before fall and hunting season and another winter, when the air would smell like wood smoke and cut pine. He'd be back in the woods, hopefully. Arthur Carlton still hadn't decided on the lease for the land, but he'd promised to hold out until September. It didn't matter, though. Kurt wouldn't make it out there even if he did get the lease. Malcolm saw movement between the two large pines to the right of his window. He brought up the rifle and focused the scope on the flash of movement. The porcupine emerged, a fat, piggish creature waddling over the clumps of a rotting log to the right of the shooting lane. As he closed his eyes, he brought the image of Kurt into his imagination. When he opened them, the porcupine was gone. Past the thin black lines of his crosshairs was nothing but the coffee can.

The rifle nudged his shoulder when he shot, and a little more sand spilled from the center of the can. He pulled the bolt back slowly and caught the empty shell casing as it tumbled out into his palm. The brass clinked against other shell casings in the five-gallon bucket beside him where he tossed it. He debated loading the gun again, but his stomach grumbled and he'd given the deer steak on the counter downstairs enough time to thaw.

The rack where he placed his rifle needed dusting. Gray draped over the pale wood, and he left a trail of finger drags through it before he meandered down the steps from the loft into the cellar, where he grabbed the steak and exited onto the covered porch. Stacked firewood made the porch an enclosure, and he kept a table there to sit at when it was too wet to work. The green Coleman camp stove was cuffed with rust at the edges, but it was functional. He lit the burner with a match and pulled a cast-iron pan from a nail in the rafter to set above the blue flame. There was a steel cooler by the door where he scooped a PBR from the ice inside.

The beer foamed against his teeth, and he swished it around his mouth until it nearly bubbled through his lips.

It was a habit he'd gained at some point, something he didn't even think about and couldn't, if it were pointed out to him, remember how or when it started. The first sip was always the same. One of those harnessed and cultivated mannerisms like people who bit the inside of their cheek when they thought. He could smell the pan getting hot, ready for the steak that he'd slap against the iron. Cooking, especially meat, he did outside. Even in winter. That practice he could originate. There was always some flash of thought when that first hint of sizzling flesh drifted into the air, the memory of burn victims huffing into the wind, back when he'd been a deputy. A few days later, he'd handed his badge to the sheriff, his father. He'd decided that cutting wood would no longer be a side job. As he held the meat over the pan, he accepted the memory that he knew was coming. Fighting it had always been a waste of effort.

The small cabin that sat on the edge of the field was in flames. Rebecca Waugh's leg was propped against the doghouse, her foot pointing toward the moon peeking through the blue sky—that impatient peer, like it couldn't wait its turn for the night. Malcolm kept the brim of his hat pulled down over his eyes, thwarting the smoke that shifted in a large black mass as the wind came up through the fields. It billowed out from the edge of the roof, the corrugated tin tacked down over layers of shingle. There was a spot in the middle of the roof above the kitchen where the tin glowed, pulsed with a faint red, barely visible through the smoke. The windows had blown out, and the wind pushed a stream of lighter gray smoke directly into the faces of the spectators that had gathered. He yelled at them to move the hell back, and he smelled it then as he approached Rebecca, through the wood and plaster and shingles, the faintest smell, but the one that clung to him the most. Burning flesh—the smell he'd come home with from Vietnam.

Cars continued to creep up the hill. People had seen the smoke and ventured there to see what it was. The last big fire the town had witnessed was when the original tavern had burned—a generation before that. People there knew what a big fire looked like. The quiet and mundane history of that town was kept alive by the throb of tragedy. It was what gave people something to talk about, something they could use to be neighborly. Malcolm drew his eyes away from the smoke. More people crept up the hill, got out of their cars and leered—a bigger turn out than Fourth of July. He went to the trunk of his cruiser and pulled out a folded blue tarp. Wind snatched at the corners when he unraveled it and whipped the strands of plastic rope tied to them. Rebecca's dress had flown up over her chest. White panties filled with piss and shit. Her face, and that was all that was left, like a rubber mask he'd seen in horror films, lay out over a dried shit their old dog had left by its house. There was no elegance in death with a 12-gauge. That lay off to the side. And then, at that moment, while he stared down at her, he thought of all the times he'd jerked off thinking about her when they were in high school, when he'd dated her sister, Patricia. He threw the tarp down and took two lunging steps away and puked in the grass. There, faintly draped over leaves of clover, was the spattering of blood that wasn't hers. He'd shot enough deer to know the difference between how blood fell to the ground from running and how it sprayed out from a gunshot.

Malcolm downed the rest of his beer and got another before he flipped his steak. In the wooden chair next to the table, he listened to the hiss of meat cooking and stared into the ends of the firewood in the stacks. He rubbed the muscle above his right knee and he thought about wood, already anxious to get out into the forest. The smell of chainsaw exhaust in the cold, the tightening in the skin on his nose and upper lip, the deer creeping into the yard after he felled a tree. These thoughts crawled into his mind to purge out his memory of the tragedy. The forest became vivid as he thought, his eyes closed, land coming to life in his mind while he moved through the trees in the section of land he'd cut that winter, the bark, the clusters of firs, the seven enormous white pines he'd harvest. The rattle of the skidder chains, the smell of diesel and bar oil that would settle into his cuticles, teased the frays of his imagination.

Then he saw the notch in the pine that had crushed his son Mike, the sloppy angle, the tracks that he'd found near the brook and followed back to that pine. He remembered their mumbling, the crew of shivering first responders and state police and sheriff's deputies while he cut the section of trunk from the crooked pine that had crushed Mike's body. The pine was so gnarled and knotted that Mike wouldn't have gotten a dime in board feet. Malcolm wouldn't have wasted his time felling that tree. He breathed deeply, opened his eyes, and stood to turn off the gas on the stove.

A car pulled into his driveway as he walked inside the cabin to get a plate for the meat. When he came back out, Olivia, Mike's widow, had made her way around the corner. He looked at her, tapped the plate gently against his leg.

"Hey, Pop. Got another beer?"

Malcolm motioned toward the cooler flipped the fork between his fingers. The metal grate rattled when he stabbed the prongs into the steak. Olivia stepped through the doorway into the shade beneath the roof of the porch and fished through the cooler for a beer at the bottom. Malcolm slung the meat onto his plate then carelessly dropped the plate on the table and slumped down in the chair. He reached across his stomach and pulled his antler-handled knife from its sheath. A quick swipe across the meat and he pulled away a generous chunk of steak.

"You hungry?" He said before shoving it in his mouth.

He'd cooked the steak too long. It was chewy, and his jaw became tired, almost ached.

"No."

Malcolm worked the utensils in his leathery hands to cut off another piece. Olivia gulped down the rest of her beer and let out a belch. Malcolm smirked as she got up and fetched two beers from the cooler, cracking open his and putting it next to his plate. She sat on the milk crate and leaned back against the stack of wood.

"Pop, I'm sorry that I've said so many horrible things about Mike." She tossed her empty can behind the cooler with the others.

Malcolm moved his chin toward her but kept his focus on the tines of his fork. "I wasn't much of a husband myself. I suppose I didn't have much to teach Mike in the way of being good to a woman. I'm a little sorry, too, that Mike didn't treat you better. He had a good wife, and he should have appreciated that more."

Olivia squinted along the edge of the stacked firewood that she leaned against then up to the porch rafters and wiped the tears from the corner of her eyes. "That was a real nice thing to say."

He bit another piece of meat off his fork, then cut a long sliver and offered it to her.

She leaned toward him and took it. "You're a doll, Malcolm."

With her knees together, she bit the meat in half and held the remaining piece between two fingers, cautious of dropping it onto the dark stains of bar oil on the floor.

"What do you have planned for the rest of the night?" she asked.

"I'll probably dig around that cooler for the rest of the night."

"There's some guy at the bar asking about you. Said he was looking for work."

"What's he look like?" His heartbeat skipped and broke through into his voice. He watched her to see if she noticed. She chugged at her beer.

"Looks like he has all his fucking teeth, so he's probably not local. Tough. He looks tough. Nicole's certainly interested in seeing him with his clothes off."

Malcolm split the last of the steak into two equal bites and handed the one with less fat on it to Olivia. She hated fat.

"Guess I'll have to head down there to see what kind of worker he might be."

"Yeah, maybe. Everyone says they're looking for work, but they aren't really looking *to* work." She bit into the piece of meat. "I dunno, though. Maybe this guy's different than the people from here."

Ryan spider-legged his fingers to keep himself from forming a fist, waving them in the air below the edge of the bar, while Pete tried his best to get punched in the mouth. Then the bar door swung open and Malcolm walked in, Olivia trailing behind him. Malcolm locked his eyes on Pete, and Pete's face went sober when he saw Olivia. He turned from Ryan and straightened his posture before creeping back to a barstool. Ryan took a breath. His hand trembled against his leg, so he moved it up and palmed the bar.

When the door closed, the light around Malcolm faded and Ryan remembered how he'd stepped into the path of the sun where he lay in the rocks all those years ago—the worried look on his face as he'd looked down on him and then back to all the people who'd gathered at the edge of the road to watch the house burn. Malcolm's face had weathered gray like wood in the sun, and it seemed in that moment, Ryan was still hiding in those rocks. Malcolm's lips parted in a way that would allow something to escape, but he clenched his jaw and turned his attention to the big man in overalls.

"How have you been, Smitty?" Malcolm asked.

Smitty put his hand out for a handshake. "Malcolm, been good. Can't complain."

Malcolm shook the man's hand. "That's good. How's your old man?"

"That stubborn motherfucker won't quit smoking. Doctor told him he'd die within a year."

"Sounds like your old man to me."

"Hey, little darlin'," Smitty said to Olivia. "How you holdin' up?"

She settled in a barstool between Smitty and Pete. "I'm good, Smitty. You get that truck out, yet?"

"Shit. That's what Pete's drunk ass and I been doing all day."

"Maybe you should retire that thing from muddin'. All it seems good for is getting stuck."

Smitty chuckled into the mouth of his beer bottle before he took a sip. Nicole dropped two cardboard coasters at the bar in front of Olivia and at the seat to Pete's left, where Malcolm stood then grabbed their beers. Malcolm rotated the can. The bar was silent except for the whisper of the bottom of Malcolm's can turning on the cardboard coaster.

"Heard you might be looking for work?"

Ryan nodded.

"Hey," Pete spoke up. "That ain't right, Malcolm. Plenty of folks around here could use some work."

Malcolm kept his focus on Ryan. "You speak to me again, motherfucker, and I'll hit you so goddamn hard you'll be chewing with your asshole."

Malcolm took a drink. Pete kept his mouth shut. A small smile crept across Olivia's face. The six of them sat there at the bar, each drinking quietly except for Nicole. Smitty finished his beer and pushed it toward the edge of the bar. Malcolm drank his in rhythm with his breathing. Ryan watched the clock, and Malcolm finished the can in almost exactly three minutes.

"Nicole, get Smitty another, please," Malcolm requested.

Smitty held his thick hands in the air over his beer, palms facing Nicole. "I appreciate the offer, Malcolm, but I have to get going."

Malcolm gave a half shrug and focused his attention back to Ryan. He moved down the few stools between them, and Malcolm caught a glimpse of Ryan's left hand, palming the bar, the missing finger and the scar where he'd pressed a fire heated end of a poker to seal the wound twenty-odd years before. He reached out and gripped the bar for balance.

"Jesus Christ," Malcolm whispered.

Ryan tipped the can toward Malcolm. "He is risen."

THIRTEEN

A sudden sense of relief eased Ryan when he walked out of the Tavern. What would he have done to Pete if he hadn't had a purpose for being there? If it were just another town he was passing through? If he hadn't been in a room where the archway celebrated his family's brutal tragedy like a grim garland? For a moment, he was grateful he didn't grow up there, but with most things Ryan felt gratitude for, they reminded him of where he'd come from, and those things were the result of something that shouldn't provide him with any sense of joy. For some people, living was a slow and painful process. Ironwood seemed like a place where that was true. Maybe the people there wanted to be miserable, because that's what they had to be. Maybe that's what they needed to exist, the same way flies live off shit.

Malcolm led the way to his truck, a Dodge with different shades of brown from where he'd had body work done. The layers of blankets that draped the seats in the truck smelled like they'd been pulled from a damp cellar—stale, with the subdued scent of animal and hay and dust and old wood. Ryan wondered if he'd started putting down the blankets as the fabric of the seat wore thin or if the blankets protected the original seat. There was a revolver between them and a box of shells next to it. Ryan toed the quart of oil on the floorboard to the side. Malcolm grunted as he climbed in and started the truck.

"Don't ever get old, son."

"Hard to get old when you're dead."

Malcolm gripped the wheel, his lips slightly parted to say something, his eyes narrowing as if he'd found Ryan's comment offensive.

"You mind if we eat. It's a little hard for me to take this in, you being here. I think I'll be better on a full stomach. There's a place we can go *down rivah.*"

"Fine with me," Ryan answered, rolling the sound of the colloquialism silently inside his mouth. *Down rivah.* The river meaning the Kennebec.

Malcolm drove south down 201, the rolling stretch of road that Ryan had used to drive into town. A few miles before they entered Madison, Ryan noticed a small wooden sign nailed to a telephone pole. *Hell,* and there was an arrow pointed toward the ditch. At the center of Skowhegan, Malcolm parked the truck along the street near the dull brick buildings where the storefronts were a smattering of handwritten, poster-board signs and smeared glass. They got out and Ryan followed Malcolm down an alley toward the sound of the falls of the Kennebec, where Malcolm entered a restaurant on the edge of the short cliff that overlooked the water. They sat in a back corner, away from the only other patrons whose voices echoed through the room. When the server approached them, Malcolm wiped his palm down the front of his shirt.

The tables were thick pine planks and the matching floorboards warped through the room like tiny ripples. The seats wobbled more than the table. The server promised to be back with the waters and the coffees they'd asked for. Ryan glanced over the menu, the word *apetizer* and the various places a typed price had been crossed out and increased with a price that had been penned in. Malcolm thanked the server when she returned with their drinks. She faded back into the dim light and Malcolm chimed his spoon on the rim of his coffee mug.

"You look like you take pretty good care of yourself."

Ryan crossed his arms and stared at Malcolm who put the spoon down on his napkin, a tan dot forming against it.

Malcolm lifted his mug to sip his coffee. "I guess this is what they mean by an elephant in the room."

"It's a little jarring, honestly, to be here. It's certainly not a place I ever expected to return."

"You know, when I found you in that rock pile, I didn't know what to do. None of us did. Your grandfather was the one who wanted you to—"

"Be dead?"

"All of that was pretty hard on John—sorry, your grandfather. I guess he felt that after what happened to Simon, that beating those boys gave him for being, you know, different, it would be better for you to get a fresh start. If you had stayed after that, in Ironwood...You see the walls in the Tavern? Think you would have had any kind of decent life here? Growing up as the kid whose mother—" Malcolm's hand began to tremble and he spilled coffee onto the table. "I remember that day like yesterday. There ain't a day goes by that I don't think about it, see all those things in my head."

Ryan swallowed. He realized his motivation to blame the living, hold someone responsible for what had happened because it allowed him something to focus on. He wanted to say something about forgetting the past.

The server returned. "Guys know what you want?" she asked tersely.

Malcolm ordered a burger. Ryan the same. The server snatched the menus and darted off.

"She's clearly happy to be here," Ryan mumbled.

Malcolm moved his hand toward his mug again. "Only thing that really makes people happy around here is fucking someone over."

"Interesting pastime."

Malcolm snuffed away a chuckle and they sat silently for a while. Ryan made observations about the restaurant: Dust covered the light fixtures on the walls, ceiling fans spinning at different speeds, drops of ketchup gelling on the floor below the table. Ryan stopped looking around and drank his coffee. They sat in the awkwardness of quiet for a while, the occasional burst of laughter from the bar drawing their attention when one of them felt obligated to break the silence. Eventually, the server arrived with their food, set it down, told them they were out of mustard, and walked away.

Ryan mug was empty. "How does a restaurant not have mustard?"

Malcolm shook his head and lifted the bun on his burger. He replaced it and took a bite, shrugged, and reached for the ketchup bottle at the side of the table.

"Is this a place you come to often?"

Malcolm swallowed. "No, but there's never anybody in here, so I thought it might be a good place to talk about—"

"It's not. We can talk later. Not here."

Malcolm swept crumbs to the floor.

"When we get to the cemetery."

Malcolm's chewing slowed. "Why do you want to go there?"

"Something I have to see. Is it far?"

Malcom shook his head. "Just *up the road a piece*."

They continued to eat. Malcolm ate noticeably slower.

Malcolm kept the truck at a steady pace as they drove back. When they crested the largest hill on 201 and crossed the town line into Ironwood, Malcolm pointed out the silver square in the distance, one of the barns on Ryan's grandfather's land.

"Anybody ask any questions about the fire, the number of bodies?" Ryan asked.

"Fire was pretty bad. Took that place down to the foundation. All that poly your old man coated on the pine inside made it burn a little hotter than most fires. They found a pile of teeth and the bone from your finger. Investigators concluded that you'd burned up. We didn't have to do much more than keep our mouths shut."

They passed through the town and Ryan kept his focus on the dashboard. He'd already seen enough of that place and he wanted to deal with Kurt and move on. *And you can never go home.* For a while he thought about why he had to tell that to his clients. There was the obvious reason, but he didn't understand why anyone would want to return to whatever hell he'd taken them from.

Malcolm drove several miles past Ironwood and pulled off the road to the steep incline leading up to the cemetery. The hinges on the truck door whined as he climbed out of the truck, letting out a soft grunt as he stepped down onto the ground. He left it open and moved toward a granite bench. After Ryan followed him, he saw that it was someone's grave marker. The epitaph read: *Sit a while and listen.* A breeze rolled over the hill, nudged the pine branches at the tree line on the other side of the cemetery and shook brown needles to the soft moss below. Malcolm leaned forward, looking toward the other side of the cemetery and rubbed his hands back and forth over his thighs. Ryan took a seat on the bench, remembering how the cemeteries out west sometimes used small stones instead of grass for landscape.

"We didn't talk about what we saw in the war. My old man was in II with your grandfather. They called the first one the Great War. But then they had another one and realized war wasn't so great, I guess. I haven't forgotten all the things I saw in 'Nam. And I know that you saw much worse in that house. Your own mother? God forgive her." Malcolm stopped his rubbing for a moment, lifted his hat, and rubbed the first knuckle of his right hand against his forehead. "But what I want to do to Kurt is worse than anything I've ever seen. I've never felt like this. I didn't think you'd be the one he'd send. Hell, I imagined you off somewhere living a normal life by now."

Cold crept down Ryan's throat. Malcolm made him wonder if any of it was real, if this world was haunting him, preventing him from resting in the darkness of his grave. His tongue snagged against some of the chips in his molars while he worked it over his teeth. He ground his teeth when he had nightmares. Maybe his mind was where it needed to be or had done what it needed to get him there, his final rest. That feeling writhed under his skin and came out hot on his breath. The man next to him had tried to save him from damage, one way or another, but the damage was done. Damaged people can't be saved. They can only be salvaged.

"This town used to be a good place to live, back when everyone worked in the woods. Ironwood Manufacturing was here, the world's biggest producer of popsicle sticks."

Malcolm shook his index finger in the air. "People were nice to each other then, when they had jobs. When the jobs went, the good people went, too. Now all you have is Section 8 and folks with drug problems. Don't know why they came here. Maybe they were already here and just came out when everyone else left. Or maybe the good people changed. I don't know."

Ryan thought for a moment, about his drive through Texas, how many families had been torn apart by something savage and he'd stepped in to make an adjustment, change the way things might have been meant to unfold. He'd had a family, but there was never the nostalgic desire to see them on Christmas or other holidays. The family he'd had was in the ground, and he was supposed to be next to them.

"Where is the plot?"

Malcolm lowered his head. "It was a quiet service. We didn't announce it or anything, afraid the idiots in town would make a spectacle of it. But they made it a spectacle anyway. They had to replace your mother's tombstone a couple times. People stole it. They got one of them back. Probably would have tried to steal the body, too, if they hadn't..." Malcolm pinched the bridge of his nose. He pulled his hand away and pointed to the eastern corner of the cemetery, to the chain-link fencing around the plot like a dog kennel. "They had to fence it in."

Ryan stood and made his way through the granite monuments toward the fencing. Wind rolled up the dirt path and carried specks of dust that settled into the narrow folds in his ear. He walked between the graves and headstones, the granite slabs scabbed with lichen, toward the markers of his dead family—gray notches in the earth. Insignificant except for the cage. At the fencing, Ryan twined his fingers between the holes and stared in at the age-descending order of the dead—beloved husband and father, beloved wife and mother, beloved brother and son, and him. Everett Waugh.

He looked over at his hand, the mangle at the corner of his palm where the scar of that last day came from, before they were beloved, before they became bathroom graffiti, before a mad rage tore through his life to bring him to another. He sunk into the syllables of those words he'd read in the Tavern bathroom, the rows of newspaper clippings on the wall, and his anger came forward again, beveled and polished, like the sharp edge of the corner of his own gravestone.

FOURTEEN

Olivia sat at a back table in The Kodiak, testing the tension of her egg yolks with the tines of her fork, pressing a little more each second. This was her ritual. She didn't want the yokes bleeding out all over her plate. She wanted it to ooze out, barely disturb the pepper she'd sprinkled over the white mounds. Her sister Jennifer sat across from her, held the handle of a coffee mug, a western omelet and home fries in front of her that were going cold. Finally, Olivia poked through to the yoke. Jennifer lifted her mug to sip her coffee.

"Have you decided?" Jennifer asked, putting her mug down.

"On leaving?" Olivia responded.

Jennifer nodded as she picked up her fork and cut a piece of the omelet.

"Yeah. I'm going to wait for fall. There's nowhere to move to right now. Besides, that'll give it enough time to really be over. Things still come up, you know. Just a couple weeks ago I got a letter from some bank in Skowhegan telling me they were going to close his account."

"Was this an account you knew about?"

"No. Some old account that he hadn't touched in years. Anyway, there was less than three dollars in it. They said they'd mail me a check."

"Can't catch a break, can you?"

Olivia pushed half of an egg onto a corner of her toast. "Tell me about it."

Jennifer plowed a home fry though a pool of ketchup. "Why don't you tell me about the new guy Malcolm just hired?"

Olivia tried to keep her face still. "Not much to tell."

"It's not like Malcolm to hire help, especially not a stranger. What's his name?"

"I didn't ask. Who Malcolm hires is none of my business."

"It bothers you, doesn't it?"

"I hardly give a shit."

Olivia's lip twitched, like a string attached to the left corner of her mouth that pulled ever so slightly on the side of her face. "Liar."

Olivia flushed red, like she always did. Her sister enjoyed catching her in a lie. It started when they were younger, Jennifer pushing her for answers. She'd always been like that, studying people, and they often joked that the only reason she became a cop was because of her propensity to corner liars. And even if someone wasn't lying, Jennifer's stare made them feel like they were. Olivia's face drew back its normal complexion and she lifted her own cup of coffee.

Jennifer held her mug at her chin and shook her head slightly. "How's Malcom?"

Olivia dropped the smirk and bit into her toast. "He's the same as he always is. Why do you ask, Jennifer?"

"It's just weird to me that Malcolm hired help, especially someone who isn't local."

"It's weird to me that you think it's your business who Malcolm hires."

"Just doing my job, Liv."

"You're not doing your job. You're being nosy. It's none of your business. Godammit, you're worse than Nicole."

Jennifer put her cup down as the server approached to refill their mugs. She gave them a smile, which both women returned, then spun her heft to move to another table. Jennifer reached for a creamer. "Let's talk about something else."

"Yeah. Let's do that." Olivia forked another chunk of egg onto a piece of toast.

Jennifer went back to her home fries and the two sat silent for several minutes until the bells on the door of the restaurant chimed and Nicole's voice poured into the room.

"Speak of the devil," Olivia whispered.

Jennifer rolled her eyes over the rim of her coffee mug. "And she'll spot us in—"

Nicole was already rushing toward them. She shuffled onto the bench next to Olivia. "I'm not interrupting, am I?"

Olivia shook her. "No, Nic, just a little sister chat."

The server brought a glass of water and a place setting. "Coffee today, Nicole?"

"Yes, please. Just coffee though."

The server meandered to the coffee pots and returned. The three women waited quietly until she'd moved away.

"So what are you guys talking about?" Nicole asked, tearing at sugar packets and snowing the granules on the table around her mug.

"Oh, the usual," Jennifer said. "Which one of us is gaining more weight."

"Ugh. Let's not even talk about that." Nicole turned toward Olivia. "Did you tell your sister about the new face in town?"

"Actually, we just ended that conversation."

"Oh," Nicole leaned back, frowning.

"Olivia doesn't want to talk about it, but I'd like some details."

"Well, ain't you some awful cunning," Nicole whispered as she reached for more sugar packets.

Olivia pressed her fingers against her temples. "What the fuck does that even mean?"

"Clever, I think," Nicole said and shrugged. She crumpled the empty sugar packets into a ball between her fingers and dropped them onto the table. "This guy came into the Tavern a few days ago and rented a room. Yesterday, he started asking about Malcolm and if he had any work."

"So he knows Malcolm?"

Nicole stirred her coffee. "I guess. Maybe he's one of Mike's friends."

Olivia made a fist, put it to her lips and stared coldly across the table at her sister. Jennifer ignored her, staring down at her mug that she'd put back on the table. Olivia placed her silverware across her plate, crumpled the napkin from her leg, and dropped it onto the utensils.

"What does he look like?" Jennifer asked.

Nicole bit her lip and stared down at her coffee. "Lean, stone-faced, like he'd need a really good, hard fuck to even crack a smile longer than half a second."

"Is there anything else you can think of besides how much you want this guy to fuck you?" Olivia asked.

"Like what? Tell me you wouldn't let that guy bend you over."

Olivia sighed and reached over to the window to scratch off a mashed fly.

"You know if he's going to be at the bar later?" Jennifer asked. "To ask some questions, of course. I don't need to get bent over."

Nicole chuckled again. "You might want to when you meet him."

"Why the fuck would you need to ask him questions?"

"Liv, I'm just going to find out what his story is. People don't come to Ironwood to look for work. I just want to make sure he's not someone who'll end up murdering Nicole when he's done fucking her."

Nicole shot out a wide grin. "Oh that would be thrilling. Either of you ever been choked in bed?"

Olivia threw her hands out, palming an invisible bundle in the air in front of her. "For fuck's sake!"

The server grimaced near the table. Nicole and Jennifer leaned back simultaneously. Olivia turned her head slightly to the Chabots who were a couple tables away, their mouths drawn slightly open in mid-chew. Mrs. Chabot stared bug-eyed behind thick, large-rimmed, plastic glasses. Mr. Chabot had turned his head, the loose skin on his neck stretched and twisted like a wet washrag. He gave Olivia a friendly nod.

"Sorry, Mr. and Mrs. Chabot," Olivia said. "Just remembered something I had to do." Olivia turned back to Jennifer. "Can you give me a ride home now?"

"One second, Liv." Jennifer looked at Nicole. "This guy got a name?"

"Adam."

"What's his last name?"

"Yeah, I'm not really sure about that. It wasn't all that legible on the room receipt."

"The receipt? Did you check his ID?"

Nicole put both of her hands around her mug, a look of embarrassment on her face.

"You didn't check his ID? You're supposed to do that to rent rooms."

"Yeah, I know, but…"

Olivia nudged Nicole from the seat to slide out. "Leaving, Jen."

"Yeah, I gotta get going, too. Sorry, Jen. Have a good day."

Nicole rushed out. Jen picked up the ticket and pulled cash from her pocket. She tossed it on the table and met Olivia outside.

In Jennifer's truck, Olivia rode with her arms crossed over her chest. She'd rolled the window down and the wind blowing in streamed her hair across her face. She tucked it behind her ears and crossed her arms again. Jennifer checked the rearview.

"So Mike's replacement has you a little on edge, hunh?"

Olivia maintained her stare through the window, sweeping over the short line of white houses on Main Street.

"Alright, come out with it, Liv. What's your problem?"

"I'm fine, Jennifer."

She shook her head. "Will you stop being childish?"

Olivia snapped her head toward her sister. "Childish?"

"Yes, Liv. Childish. You're pouting. That's a childish thing to do. Just say what's on your mind."

"Why the fuck do you have to stick your nose in? Why do you give a shit about some stranger looking for work?"

"Well, like I've told you before, it's my job."

"Your job?" Olivia clenched her jaw before she spoke again. "Since when is it your job? Is it a crime to look for work? Is it your job to interrogate everyone?"

"I didn't interrogate anyone."

"Then what the fuck was that, back there?" Olivia pointed over her left shoulder, turning to face her sister.

"What are you talking about?"

"*What's he look like? What's his last name? Will he be at the Tavern later?* I told you I didn't want to talk about Malcolm or his helper and you had to bring Nicole into it because you knew she'd give you what you want. That's all you fucking care about."

"Wow. Is that what's really bothering you? That I asked a few questions about some stranger in town? You know, I expect everyone else to try to keep me in the dark. I'm the law, after all, and nobody likes that. Nobody wants to get too chummy with the local cop. But you're my sister, and you treat me like everyone else does, like I'm using you for information. I hate it. But that's why I ask so many questions. Sometimes, I just want to be one of the girls. Is it so hard for you to treat me like your sister and just talk to me?"

"If you really gave a fuck about being my sister or finding answers, why not find out who Mike was fucking instead of parading around town in your tan uniform pretending you're an actual cop instead of some glorified fucking busy-body."

"Fuck you, Liv."

"Fuck you, Jen."

Jennifer passed the Tavern and took an aggressive right-hand turn onto Olivia's road, forcing Olivia to grab for the door to hold herself from sliding across the street.

"Oh, shit. I forgot to buckle my seatbelt. You going to write me a ticket when you drop me off?"

"Stop. Please. I don't want to fight with you."

"You sure you don't want to go a few rounds on the lawn?"

"Would that make you feel better? You want to throw down?"

Jennifer sped up the truck and passed Olivia's house.

"What the frigg? Where are you going?"

"We're going to ride around for a bit, until you decide to tell me what's really bothering you."

Olivia spoke through her gritted teeth. "I already fucking told you. Now. Bring. Me. The. Fuck. Home."

"Ain't gonna happen, little sister. Sooner you start talking, the sooner I turn around and bring your angry little ass home."

Olivia shook her head and relaxed in her seat. She crossed her arms again and propped her feet on the dashboard, grinding the grit on the bottom of her shoes into the vinyl. She glanced over at Jennifer's gas gauge. "Quarter of a tank? This shouldn't take long."

Jennifer loosened her grip, hovering her open hand over the curve of the wheel and looked through at the gauge. "Plenty of gas."

She headed down the Brighton Road, lumped over the end of the pavement onto the gravel, and reached down to roll the windows up to keep the dust out. The truck bobbed along, the gravel crunching under the tires. She took a left onto Mahoney Hill Road and slowed at the sharp curve that would bring them down into the gully where the road crossed over a stream and beneath the power lines that stretched through a swath of cleared landscape. A group of teenagers came off the power lines on their ATVs and sped through the dust Jennifer's truck had stirred up.

"We going loopin'?" Olivia asked. "Did you bring any beer? That might make this suck less."

"Now there's an idea."

She slowed the truck and pulled it to the shoulder, checked her side-view mirror, and turned the truck around. Brown dust from the gravel spilled into the air behind the truck as Jennifer increased her speed. She slowed and turned down a narrow logging road on paper company land, creeping the truck along the rutted path to keep the engine noise low. When she stopped, Olivia jerked around to look out the windows.

"What the fuck are you doing?" she asked.

Jennifer winked. "Stay put. I'll be right back."

"What? What do you mean, stay put? What the hell did you bring me out here for?"

Jennifer climbed out and pinched the edge of the door to gently push it into the latch. She pulled her shirt down over the handgrip of the pistol holstered inside the beltline of her jeans as she stalked over the mound of road in front of the truck. After she ducked into the woods, Olivia let out a deep sighing breath and opened the glove compartment. There was a stack of papers inside, all maintenance invoices on the truck, an envelope with gas and meal receipts crammed together in no particular order. She stuffed the papers back in the glove box. She pulled down the visor and flipped open the mirror cover. Her complexion was pale. Most of her time, when she wasn't at the New Balance factory, she spent in the house, sulking, trying to figure out what she wanted to do. She checked her teeth even though she was sure there was nothing in them, then slapped the visor up and drummed her hands on her knees.

Jennifer moved quietly through the trees to the ATV trail that ran parallel to the road. The murmur of voices came from the cutoff ahead. She crossed the trail and skirted the woods to the edge of the open space, moving slower. The teenage boys were oblivious to her movement even after she'd stepped from the trees. They sat on the seats of their four-wheelers passing around a pack of cigarettes. A torn cardboard beer box rested on the back end of the oldest boy's wheeler. Mud dried in lines where it had whipped up the backs of their T-shirts.

"You boys have some ID?" she called.

Two of the boys tossed their cigarettes to the side at the sound of her voice. The oldest boy continued to fish a lighter from his pocket and lit his cigarette. Jennifer kicked through the decaying bark toward the center of their circle. The boy took a long, hard drag, staring at her, and blew his smoke at her face. The wind caught it and pushed it back toward him.

"I asked you if you had some ID," she repeated.

"Yeah, I got some ID," he answered, taking another pull from the cigarette.

Benson and Hedges menthol light 100s, a score he'd either found in a car somewhere or a pack his mother might have left on the counter. Jennifer moved around the end of his wheeler to stand at his back. He'd torn the sleeves off his shirt, one of the rips gouged into the fabric on the back just below his armpit. The other two boys sat quietly, smirks flashing on their faces then disappearing when they realized what they were doing.

She knew what his response would be before she said anything. "Let's see it then."

"It's wrapped around my dick, bitch. Why don't you get down and have a look?"

The other two boys chuckled, unable to contain their admiration for the older boy's machismo. She bit her lip, smiling along with them, ready to grab her piece.

"That's quite an offer." She trailed the back of her fingers along the handlebars then gripped the shifter and stroked it lightly, catching their attention. "I might just do that."

The other boys lost their entertained expressions to allow an open-mouthed gaze. Jennifer pulled the pistol from her belt, the metal feeling rubbery in her grip, and stepped around the handlebars to jab the barrel into his groin and cocked it.

"Down here? Is that where your ID is? Funny, isn't it? A cocked gun on your cock."

The boy held his arms to his side, the smoke from his cigarette drifting toward her face.

"What? Nothing to say, now?"

"L-l-look lady. I'm sorry. I didn't—"

She pushed the barrel down a little harder until he winced. "Didn't what? Didn't think?" He shook his head and tried to scoot away from the pressure of the gun barrel. She perked her eyebrows. "Don't fucking move," she warned.

The boy swallowed. Jennifer glanced at the other two boys and pulled her gun away. She moved around the wheeler again and stood behind the mouthy one. He moved his head to follow her and she nudged his cheek with the gun. "Don't look at me. Look at your friends."

The boy turned his head and she wrapped her arm around his neck and jerked him back. She dug into his stomach with the barrel of the gun to move his T-shirt up and slipped the barrel into his belt. "You're a tough guy, aren't you?"

"Unh-uh."

"You sure? You seem like one of those tough guys from the movies. You know, the kind who always tuck a gun into their belt." She pushed the barrel down a little more, the soft crunch of the metal against the boy's pubic hair, and the boy's gut sucked in. "Kind of like this. I always wondered how tough one of those guys would be if they accidentally shot off their dick."

The two other boys sat frozen, their thin arms twitching against the weight they pushed on them. Jennifer pulled her gun from the boy's pants, released her hold around his neck and shoved his back. The boy sprawled to the ground and rolled quickly. She pulled her badge from her back pocket and flashed it to the boys. They all took turns looking at one another.

"Today's your lucky day. I catch you out here again and I'll haul all of you in. And if you ever use that kind of language on a woman again, getting hauled in will be the least of your worries. Any of you speak a word of this to anyone, and I'll come pay a visit to all of you individually." She grabbed the cardboard box of beer from the back of the wheeler. "Get the fuck out of here."

She stepped back and let the boys scramble to start their wheelers and maneuver them to the trail. The engines whined, turning the sputter of thrown gravel into a whisper. She holstered the gun and moved back to her truck.

"Come the fuck on, Jen."

Olivia reached for the door handle, impatient. She had the lever half-pulled when she caught movement, just over the edge of the mound. She hoped it was a moose and leaned forward, barely made out what she thought was the curve of its shoulder. It had been more than three years since she'd seen a moose in the woods, and she smiled with anticipation, inching closer to the windshield, but the movement was gone. "What the fuck is she doing," she whispered, disappointed.

Jennifer's voice jumped into her ear and startled her. Olivia grabbed her chest. Jennifer stood at her window, looking in on her. She lifted her hand and held out a beer for Olivia.

"You said you wanted to go loopin'."

Olivia took the beer. "Seriously?"

"Cowboy cool, but it's better than nothing."

Jennifer moved around the truck, a big accomplished smile on her face. Olivia cracked open the can and when Jennifer climbed in the cab, Olivia said, "We could have just gone to the store and bought some. Where did you find this?"

Jennifer bounced in her seat. "Teenagers are always down in the old cutoff on Saturdays." She lifted what was left of a six-pack of tall boys inside the box, two, not including the one Olivia took a sip from, and pulled one of them from the plastic ring. She swung the last beer onto the seat between them. Jennifer cracked hers and took a drink. She vocalized her satisfaction, but Olivia couldn't tell if it were the beer or her cleverness that she'd delighted herself with. "Cheers, little sister," she said, holding the top of her beer at an angle toward Olivia.

Olivia shook her head, tapped the can, and the two of them took a drink.

"I can't remember the last time I had a beer in a truck."

"I can," Jennifer said.

"When?"

"It was with you. Two weeks before I went to the academy. Dad leant us his truck and we bought three twelve-packs of Rolling Rock bottles."

Olivia laughed. "Holy shit! That's right. But we ended up throwing half of them at signs."

"Yeah, and then little Jamie Hachney saw us and flagged us down."

Almost in unison, *"You're supposed to drink the beers*

first, goddammit."

They laughed together and Jennifer took another drink before turning to Olivia.

"So, you ready to spit it out, yet?"

Olivia lifted the can and scratched her eyebrow with the nail of her thumb. "It's nothing, really. I'm sorry for being so bitchy."

"It's not nothing. Something's bothering you. You should be able to talk to me about it."

"It's stupid, really."

"Will you spit it out already?"

Olivia took a deep breath. "Alright. It's Nicole, okay. We've known her forever, and I should be used to it by now, but goddamn if she doesn't get on my last nerve lately, especially when she starts talking about who she wants to bang. And there's always something, something so fucking dramatic."

"Why does it bother you so much now?"

Another deep breath. "I'm pretty sure she was fucking Mike."

Jennifer's eyebrows raised. "Really? Why do you think that?"

"I found an earring in his truck, one that she's been missing. I don't know. I just get this sick feeling every time I'm around her, anytime she starts talking about sex. I'm waiting for her to fuck up, so I know for sure."

"Mike's dead. There's nothing you can do about anything he did. Maybe he would have turned it around, been a better husband, I don't know. Maybe you should have left him sooner. But he's dead. And trying to figure out how he betrayed you is futile. It's not going to make it better."

Olivia gulped the rest of her beer down. The last few

ounces were warm and foamy, and she sucked it away from her teeth and swallowed. She tossed the can into the woods and reached down for the other beer. Jennifer stared at her.

"Don't give me any shit about littering, Jen."

Jennifer reached her hand across the console and grabbed Olivia's wrist. Olivia shifted her look from the beer tab she was flicking with her finger to the knuckles of Jennifer's hand.

"You're going to be fine. Just get out of here. Don't say goodbye to anyone, just go. You don't owe anybody shit."

Olivia cracked the beer open and lifted it. Jennifer's hand dropped away. Olivia looked at the beer as she pulled it from her lips.

"Definitely not as good as the first one. Let's go get some beer and really do some loopin'."

Jennifer shook her head slightly. "I don't know."

"What? You were just bitching about being one of the girls again. Let's go. Two twelve-packs of Rolling Rock."

Jennifer reached toward the ignition. "What the hell."

FIFTEEN

"Wind and sun," Malcolm said. "The two things you need to make good hay."

Malcolm lay on his back, beneath the hay baler, twisting a piece of twine between his fingers at his side. Dust from the earlier harvest drifted through the band of sunlight that left all but a stretch of light in the shadow beneath the machine. He pulled the strand of twine up to his chest and passed it over to Ryan, who lay in the gravel next to him, staring up into the chunks and lengths of metal that crushed piles of grass into rectangles. Malcolm had his right foot propped against the tension bar on the back of the baler and he flapped his leg slowly, tapping the inside of his knee against a dangling chain. Ryan drummed the fingers of his left hand against the edge of the baling chute while Malcolm showed him where to feed the twine that would tie off the bales.

Malcolm hobbled slightly as he moved to the garage. Ryan paused, looked up the field into the corner where the edge of the hayfield met the square boundary of the small plot of land he'd once known. Home was nothing but a mound in the field where grass and small shrubs grew through the ashy remnants of his family's home. The gray line of the top of the stone wall ran down the field. Pursed-lip scars marked the trees from a century-old run of barbed wire, now rusted and gone except for the lengths that the bark of the trees had swallowed. Malcolm took a step toward Ryan but stopped and stood at his shoulder, slightly taller than him. Ryan's jaw flexed and he rubbed his right index finger along the edge of his belt. In the swaying grass, the past waved for his attention.

He stood at the door, looking down the hallway at his mother and the shotgun.

"Mom?" Lucas' voice skipped down the hall, shrill and high pitched, almost a squeal.

Another gunshot and Lucas flailed back, hit the wall and fell facedown at Everett's feet. His eye twitched, looking up at him until the glisten faded.

"Come here, Everett," her voice cooing as she chambered another round.

Smoke crawled along the ceiling from the kitchen. She moved the barrel toward him, and he ducked back into the room as another gunshot rang in the house and buckshot splintered the pine trim at the door.

For a moment he froze then wanted to climb under the bed. All those red squirrels and chipmunks he and his brother had cornered in the shed and killed with their BB guns—their eyes wide and black, petrified, and they'd shot them anyway. His heart pounded and his mother's soft footsteps down the hall rattled his guts. Lucas' .22 was in the corner, resting against the wall beside the dresser. Baseball mitts and animal skulls displayed on the surface of the pine furniture. He went to the window and rattled the screen loose. It fell, twanging against the spigot outside. As he flung his leg through the opening, he knocked over the jar of baby teeth that he'd been saving and it thumped to the floor, where it rolled down the slant toward his bed post and nudged against it. The end of the shotgun barrel poked into the room as he lowered himself from the window, gripping the sill, tapping his toe against the side of the house for the spigot. She came into the doorway and scanned with the end of the shotgun, remnants of casserole in her hair, and he dropped to the ground.

Another gunshot blasted out the glass and metal frame of the storm window.

The fall to his back jerked the air from his lungs. Pain in his hand, and the finger was missing—a tiny bloody stump of flesh, the hand already drenched in blood. The barrel came through the window and he rolled to his stomach and crawled, pulling himself forward with one hand down the edge of the house. He scrambled around the corner to the back of the house and breath rushed into his lungs. Clamoring, he got to his feet, puking, trying to cover his mouth. East, into the sun, he ran past the doghouse, away from another gunshot as the echo followed him all the way through the field toward the rock pile.

Pain began to crawl away from his trembling, bloody hand and up his arm. His mother sat on the roof of the doghouse and kicked her shoe off, the way she did when she sat on the swing and watched him and Lucas when they were younger try to catch lightning bugs in the antique mason jars they'd find in the dump. She worked her foot against the trigger guard of the shotgun and fed the barrel into her mouth with both hands. He didn't hear that shot at first, not before her head jerked up, hair flinging through the air like swinging arms and she toppled backwards onto the lawn. Then, the sound of the gunshot rolled through the field while black smoke rushed from the opening in the kitchen window.

* * *

Malcolm cleared his throat before he spoke. "I know I said this before, but when I called Simon, I didn't expect him to send you. Still wondering why, honestly."

Ryan wiped sweat from his right eyebrow with the back of his hand. The tips of his fingers tingled, almost buzzed with panic, then vibrated into a rage. He slowed his breath. The anger dissipated as he sifted through the memories and the path that led him back home. But this place wasn't home. His connection to it was nothing more than bathroom graffiti and wisps of smoke from that day that led him out of there. A memory of his grandfather's hand on his shoulder, the large mitt enveloping the bony structure of his child form, fingers tapping against the thin muscle on his chest as they put him in the back of a car during the night, and that car carried him away. His grandfather's tears, his apologetic whisper, sang to him lucidly. And then Ryan focused, followed the swallows to where they perched on the dead, bark-less tree across the yard next to the space where the other barn had once stood.

The last time Ryan had stood in that yard, the driveway hadn't been paved. He and Lucas had ridden their bikes down the dirt tire lanes and kicked their brakes near the house to turn their bicycles sideways in their stunt-like maneuvering. Bright yellow dandelion patches had lined the strip of grass between the lanes, but those only grew along the sides of the stable now. The young maple he remembered had grown to a thick, shade-casting beast. A raised garden bed sat at the edge of the lawn, just before the steep slope of grass into the small orchard that was no more than a dozen dying trees. The granite slab and the cement platform that had led to the milking room were all that was left of the second barn. The dead tree scrawling through the setting of the wood line, where the swallows had perched, was once a leafy cover for his grandfather's afternoon beer. And he saw him, under that tree, the shade so dark, where his grandfather would sip his Schlitz and throw feed to the two peacocks that paraded up and down the edge of the driveway whenever a car pulled in. They'd been the most majestic things he'd ever seen, the animals his grandfather had loved the most.

All that was left of the farm was the dead grass Malcolm would harvest for three dollars a bale. Ryan's memories shifted from color to black and white, still and lifeless and faded. The tines of the tedder chimed like a soft jingle of coins in a pocket when Malcom shook them. Ryan drew his gaze from the places that prompted his flashes of memory. He no longer had the urge to work. The dead tree near where the barn once stood beckoned him to sink into the suppressed memories of his youth—give him a sense of what a regular life would have been.

Malcolm worked a grease gun over the nozzles on the tedder. When he finished, he walked down to the post barn. Metal clanged inside the barn and Ryan glanced over at the noise. There was a sputtering from inside then the guttural rumble of a tractor starting. Malcolm pulled the small Kubota from the bay and wheeled it around to back it up to the tedder hitch. The engine was exposed. The metal hood for the tractor leaned against the edge of the garage, dented, and an abandoned hornets' nest dangled from the grille. Malcolm shifted the tractor into neutral and latched the brake, then climbed down to connect the tedder.

Malcolm spoke louder, close to Ryan's ear. "Just drive

over what's been mowed. Make sure you do two loops, though." He waved Ryan closer to the Kubota and pointed down at the gears. "Keep it in High—2. That should be fast enough."

Ryan climbed onto the machine. The whole thing vibrated into his thighs and lower back, through his spine and into his jaw.

"You good?"

Ryan nodded.

"Hold onto your ass and watch out for woodchuck holes."

Malcolm waved him off and Ryan pushed the tractor into gear. He let out the clutch and pressed down on the small round gas pedal. The Kubota jerked forward, faster than Ryan expected and he cut the wheel to guide it between the garage and post barn. The tedder rattled behind him. He breathed in the smell of cut hay on the wind, looked up at the edge of the field that ran along the road, where the power lines seemed as if they sagged only a couple feet from the ground and cut black lines through the rounded summits of the mountains in the distance.

He tried not to look toward the spot of his old home again while he passed over the hay with the tedder. It spun the cut hay from its flat rest against the ground to clumps of chaos. There was an occasional clang when the tines struck the edges of exposed granite. The sharp, roasted smell of broken stone rose through the smell of hay. The Kubota jerked over the divots and sinks in the field. Patches of sand indicated where woodchucks had tunneled into the ground. One had been hidden by the hay and the Kubota had nearly bucked him off. He finished the first pass and went into the large portion of field for the second, driving the tractor perpendicular over the path he'd taken before.

Malcolm came from underneath the barn where some of the older tractors Ryan thought he could remember were parked between the new posts that had been erected under the stable. Was that all it would have taken to save the other barn, some new posts? Malcolm carried a wrench and used it to point back toward the garage as Ryan returned on the tractor. He guided the teetering tractor along the steep, haggard tire rivets on the side of the slope and pulled onto the driveway. The tines of the tedder screeched against the pavement. The sun was directly overhead and thin clouds passed through to offer a mild reprieve before the sun slapped against the sting and itch on the back of his neck, where hay burrowed into his pores. He put the tractor in neutral and locked the brake. Malcolm was at the back detaching the tedder before Ryan had a chance to climb off.

"How's your ass?" Malcolm asked over the sputtering engine.

"Still there," Ryan answered and rotated his torso to crack his back.

Malcolm pulled the pin from the hitch on the tedder and kicked it free of the tractor. He waved him over to another machine similar to the tedder, parallel bars and more tines like a crooked smile. Ryan backed the Kubota to the machine, and Malcolm explained the rake, how to push the hay into windrows for the baler. The clunky, metal song of the rake chorused behind him as he pulled back out onto the fields. The rolling grunt of the Kubota churned the thoughts in his mind until he lost himself in the thoughts that he refused to talk about.

* * *

His hands vibrated even after he'd climbed off the Kubota. The depleted windrows, from where Ryan stood at the garage, were faded mars in the browned landscape. The backs of his ears burned and he was thirsty. His wrists ached from gripping the wheel of the tractor and his lower back twitched against the tightness settling there. Malcolm came from the garage working the grease off his fingers against a polyester rag.

"Store down the road makes a decent sandwich. You hungry?"

Ryan thought about crawfish po'boys and muffulettas in New Orleans or the gas station burritos in New Mexico as he followed Malcolm to the truck.

Malcolm backed the truck into a parking spot at the store, complaining that he'd almost been hit several times trying to back out into the road. They got out and moved to the shade in front of the store. Ryan glanced across the street at the window of the room he had at the Tavern. Malcom held the door and Ryan waited for Malcolm to guide him to the deli on the left where a portly, flour-dusted woman swiped her hands across her apron and watched Malcolm open the warmer on the counter. The menu was a syllabus of disappointment. No po'boys. No muffulettas. Just *eye-talian* subs. Malcolm pulled out two burgers wrapped in foil and shambled by the woman's ogling to the cooler. He flung one of the doors open and caught its return with his knee then pulled out an orange can of Moxie.

"Something to drink?"

Moxie, his grandfather's staple drink, something that Ryan hadn't experienced since childhood, but the bitter taste still crept over his tongue. He took the can.

Kurt Myers glared at Malcolm and Ryan from the opposite counter at the register. Ryan had studied the pictures Simon had showed him. The glare was almost laughably humorous, like a child making a full attempt to be intimidating. Kurt was lanky, but he had a fat, doughy face. Kurt shifted his glare when he made eye contact with Ryan. Malcolm intentionally kept his line of sight on the counter. He paid, and Ryan followed him back outside.

"Either this town is full of people looking to get punched in the mouth or that was Kurt," Ryan said at the truck.

"*Yessah.*"

Ryan parted his lips and took the burger Malcolm held out for him. He unwrapped the foil and took a bite. It wasn't very good, but he was hungry and the satisfaction of putting something in his stomach outweighed the taste. At least it was better than the last one he'd had. He wondered if Malcolm ate anything but burgers.

Malcolm chomped away, his head moving from side to side. "Fucking cocksucking Norwegian piece of shit."

"Norwegian?"

"Yeah. Real name's *Kjetil, Kajestal* or some shit. Fucking cunt-balls. He goes by Kurt. Posts his land and spends a lot of time on everyone else's. He's wanted the Carlton piece for a decade. That's where Mike died. Where that son of a bitch killed him." Malcolm forced the mouthful of food down with a swallow. "And I've got to see that plump-faced fucking asshole almost every day. Fucking cocksucker."

Ryan lowered his burger. "I'm sorry about Mike."

Malcolm took another bite. Ryan cracked the can of Moxie. He held it at his mouth, thinking back to his grandfather's plastic coffee cup that he drank his from. The smell hit his nose, bitterroot, sarsaparilla, dirt. He took a sip and his teeth went sticky.

"Must still be a Maine boy if you drink that," Malcolm said.

"What exactly is it that you want to do about Kurt?"

Malcolm tongued away the remnants of the burger on his teeth. "I want him to suffer. I want his whole life to fall apart. And that won't take too long. His wife's been fucking some professor from Colby down in Waterville. Guess that's what you get when you let your wife suffer through cancer alone. I used to—shit, I'm sorry. I guess I forgot for a moment that Patricia's your aunt. Shit. I really didn't mean to be rude."

"I think things will be easier on both of us if you just think of me as your help, and not someone who is connected to anyone here. Now, Kurt. You were saying?"

"I want to dump his body in the bog to rot in the mud. I'm ready. I'll do it tonight if we can."

"It's going to be a little while longer."

"Longer?"

"Yes. I'm waiting for something. But that will give me time to find out what I need to about Kurt, and the best way to get rid of him."

Ryan should have drank water. He sat behind the groaning of a bigger tractor that pulled the baler and crushed loose hay into bales. The baler rocked and the mechanism was loud and rumbled over the sound of the tractor's engine. Kurt's truck slowed at the edge of the road and stopped. The passenger window lowered. Exhaust from the tractor fed out just above the engine and the breeze blew it back into Ryan's face. It made him start to feel sick. He'd been out there for over an hour, putting up and down the windrows on the tractor at a mile per hour. He wondered if he'd ever get the sound of that baler out of his head. Kurt was still parked on the road as he moved down the last windrow, and Malcolm drove into the field with his truck, hauling a trailer.

Ryan finished the row and moved the tractor out of the way. He climbed down and walked to Malcolm's truck. Malcolm handed him a mason jar of water. Ryan unscrewed the cap and drank, peeling the dry hay and fumes from his mouth and throat. The insides of his nostril were dry with the dust that had collected there, and he used the bottom of his shirt to wipe it away.

"Seems like we have a fan. That cunt-balls?"

"Yeah. You need a break? Picking these up is the hardest work."

Ryan moved his concentration from Kurt's truck to the field where the bales rested in formation. Some of them had perched on their ends as they pushed through the baler and they reminded Ryan of some Biblical story about a dreamer. The bales were all he had left of his grandfather, a smear of nostalgia wiping away the purpose for him being there. It made more sense to him then, why they'd ushered him away. Every town has its freak, and he'd have been it. What ripped through him, coming the way it always had despite the closure he was gaining on, was guilt splitting lines down the heat in his stomach—how he did nothing to help his mother.

"No. I don't need a break."

Ryan followed the trailer that Malcolm drove between the rows of bales. As he grabbed that first bale and lifted, he imagined how that morning of his childhood would have been different if he'd walked into the kitchen and helped his mother off the floor. The sun spread its heat over him, drying his sweat like blood.

SIXTEEN

Olivia and Jennifer sat on the tailgate of the truck watching Ryan hurl bales of hay onto the trailer. He moved quickly, and Malcolm was more often the one who had to increase his speed to catch up. The last two bales that Ryan picked up, he carried in each hand and hefted into the bed of the truck. Olivia opened the cooler and fished out a beer, setting it between her thighs to pull the empty from her neoprene coozie and toss it over her shoulder. Eight cans lay strewn in the bed of her truck.

"I hope you plan on cleaning those out."

"Just drive around with your tailgate open and let the wind clean it. That's the beauty of having a truck."

Jennifer extended her index finger away from her beer and pointed up into the field. "We should cook them dinner."

"You just want to grill Malcolm's help."

"Maybe you should grill the help."

Oliva stroked her tongue over her teeth and spit into the grass. "I want nothing to do with that man. You and Nicole can fight over him."

Malcolm's truck puttered through the slain field, lolling over the uneven ground. Olivia waved as he swung past them. A clucking metal grind at the hitch twisted through the air as Malcolm maneuvered the trailer into the barn and cut the engine. Ryan got out and slipped into the darkness of the barn to unload the bales. Malcolm flexed his fingers as he walked toward Jennifer and Olivia. Olivia reached into the cooler again and pulled out a beer for Malcolm. He took it and cracked it open.

"I've been looking forward to that all day," he said, after he'd swallowed the beer he'd swished through his teeth.

"Where's your help? We got plenty if he wants one," Jennifer said, with a stream of beer sliding over her lip.

Malcolm turned toward the barn then back to the sisters. He pointed over his shoulder with his free hand. "Working his ass off unloading the bales."

Ryan continued the work, the twine digging into the tendered flesh in the bends at his knuckles. The fading sunlight cast channels through the second floor, which was empty, except for a pile of old televisions and broken chairs in the southwest corner. Rusted metal shelving and old canning jars, a tinge of violet in the glass, littered the opposite corner. Perpendicular lain boards constructed the second floor. They hadn't been nailed down, and hay sprouted from small gaps above. Specks of dust, a hundred years of fragments, floated through the air, through those beams of light, and kept rising. Ryan wondered if they'd ever settle, how many of those little specks he was breathing in to become part of him. His father's work and his grandfather's and *his* father's floated through the air in that place, the work Ryan was doing. Barn swallows swooped close to his head, swerved around the beams inside the barn, and found their nests near the peak of the roof. The rapid flap of their wings swirled the dust in the air. He hefted the last bale from the trailer and nudged it into the corner to start a new row, then went for the two he'd thrown in the bed of the truck. The bales stood in a wall stacked as high as he could lift them.

Ryan walked out of the barn. Kurt's truck was gone. The moving air cooled the sweat behind Ryan's ears and jaw, the soft flesh just above his collar bone. He walked slowly toward Malcolm who leaned against the bed of the truck. Jennifer reached into the cooler and pulled out two more beers. She extended her arm over Olivia's back and handed one to Ryan, who joined Malcolm. Ryan gave her a nod of appreciation and took the beer. The cold can chilled his hand, and he wanted to roll it over his body where bits of hay had nuzzled into his pores in the inside of his elbows and along the skin at his waistline, against the contour of his hip. His T-shirt clung to his chest, almost as tightly as Jennifer's stare.

"He's got a name, Jen. Since you were so interested in it, maybe you should be cordial."

Jennifer's face flushed.

"Name's Adam," Ryan said and gave Jennifer a brief smile. He remembered her.

She extended her arm, and Ryan gripped her fingers. "Jennifer," she said.

Heat pulsed at his temples. Jennifer and Olivia, the sisters he and Lucas had spent time with during the summers. Jennifer, the oldest of them by a few years had been his sitter, even though her title had only earned her money during the school year. He hadn't recognized Olivia, but he should have been reminded by the mousy features—her ears, the elegant little hands. And there was the small scar just above her eyebrow from the fall she took on his bike after the first day of school in fourth grade. Jennifer, though, he knew her before Olivia had said her name. Her settled peer, always evaluating something, the freckles over her nose that had grown darker with the years.

"Nice to meet you," he said, and slipped his fingers from hers.

"Likewise."

"So, what are you boys up to this evening?" Olivia asked. "Jen, here, wants us to make you dinner."

Malcolm tilted his head and lifted his shoulders too long for it to be a shrug. "Dinner sounds good to me."

"How about you, Adam? You got any big plans tonight?" Olivia worked her empty can from her coozie.

"A shower." He wanted to plunge into a cold lake, let the water numb everything in his mind, drift into the current and slip away from that place—that town.

"Jen's got a great shower. You could use hers. It would certainly be better than the shared hallway bathroom at the Tavern."

"Oh, Liv. You're so accommodating." Jennifer flicked her empty beer can into the bed. "Unfortunately, as much as I'd love to have people over, my house is a disaster. Besides, Liv's house is closer, and she has a better kitchen. I don't even have any clean towels." She jerked her hand through the cooler for another beer. "So, Liv, dinner at your place? We've made the mistake of extending an invitation before we figured out the hosting arrangement."

Olivia scooted from the end of the truck. "Come on, guys." She pushed the cooler from the tailgate into the bed.

Malcolm cleared something from his throat then poked his tongue against the inside of his bottom lip. "Maybe—"

"Dinner at my place," Olivia spurted. "Jen's going to

make her specialty. Don't be surprised if it's Eggo waffles."

Jennifer hopped to the ground, keeping her eyes on Ryan.

Ryan tried to find a place in his mind for his childhood nostalgia. For the first time, he remembered the sound of his own childhood laugh, theirs, their squealing voices rising above the crickets in the summer evenings when he and Lucas chased them through the fields with squirt guns or snakes they'd found in the garden. He wanted something other than the echoes of gun blasts that drummed the tempo of his nightmares. More than anything, Ryan wanted some aspect of peace in his mind, the promise that Simon told him he'd never have. Just for a moment, he wanted to savor that. After, he'd wander into the darkness of the night, stalk through the former landscape of his childhood to find something to present to Malcolm. Before that, though, he wanted to see if satisfying the inkling of nostalgia in him, no matter how brief or disguised, would cease his curiosity.

SEVENTEEN

Kurt slammed through his door, sending it hard against the wall. It thudded then shimmied back. A wooden vibration crept through the house. The camera strapped around his neck thumped into his sternum. Something was strange to him, and it surfaced through his anger, making him feel peculiar, as if he'd stormed into the wrong house. Patricia's car was gone, and she was never gone that late in the evening. He wondered where she'd gone off to, started counting the other strange behaviors she'd been exhibiting lately. The door nudged his foot where he stood, and he moved past it into the kitchen to the cabinet above the refrigerator. The cabinet was empty except for a bottle of Dewar's tucked into the back corner. Kurt felt some relief just pulling the bottle down, like he'd caught the ghost that had been haunting him. He grabbed the camera from around his neck then took a tumbler from the dishrack and poured himself a finger of Scotch. Photography had replaced his drinking. Six years since his last drink. It made him mean, Patricia had told him. And in fear for his reputation in a small town, he'd stopped drinking. But Patricia was gone, and Arthur Carlton had held his check long enough for Malcolm to find help. He'd never get the lease on the Carlton lot. All that he'd done, what he'd done to Mike Hale, was meaningless and he was going to lose out on the best acreage of timber in the county.

"These fucking people," he whispered. *These fucking worn out, solemn people.* He left the bottle on the counter and carried the glass with him outside, sat in the rocker on his porch and put the glass on the table next to him.

The sun had already peaked in the sky and began to pull the temperature down with it as it sank toward the mountains. He grabbed the glass, rubbed his thumb against the rim, but left it there on the table. The smoother contour of handles on the wooden rocker he sat in was as warm as the glass. He needed to say something to someone, and his curiosity about the man working with Malcolm had fueled an anger toward Patricia because she wasn't there to listen. Where was she? The setting sun banded the horizon with lavender. The clouds gathered there and curled as if they were glass melting against the sky.

When that first churn of hunger rumbled in his gut, he lifted the glass and sipped the Scotch. It brought back the last taste of it he'd had all those years before, the sour of vomit on his teeth the morning after. His stomach grumbled and a flash of heartburn crept up to the back of his tongue. The tightness of his thoughts loosened as if air had found a way to spread the ideas into separate spaces. He held the tumbler a few inches above the table, deciding if he'd take another sip or put it down. On the horizon, the lavender had faded and the sky was soaked in darkening blue. The last bit of Scotch in his glass went down as if he'd never spent any time away from it. Then he stood and went to the bottle on the counter and poured another.

"Fucking Hale's. Poachers. Backwoods fucking swine."

He couldn't think of them without thinking about their crude and simple way of life, how they patched up their broken things and carried on like they'd found some sort of success, so content with their eked-out existence. And that was the problem with them, their satisfaction with the mundane, their willingness to coast, their failure to exploit or even pursue their possibilities. But for once, Malcolm Hale had bled some ambition into the world and found a way to dismantle all that had fallen into place for Kurt.

Kurt took his camera into the basement, set it down with the bottle and the glass. He flicked a switch over the bench, leaving the room in a red glow, and removed the film from his camera. The Scotch kept the chemical smells down while he held the glass to his lips. Malcolm's helper's face drifted onto the photo paper a little at a time. Everyone has something to hide. He'd hang the photos, come back to them in the morning, and bring one to Sheriff Middler. Maybe he'd learn who Malcolm's new helper was, if he had something to hide like everybody else.

EIGHTEEN

Ryan fanned his fingers out and let the wind push over his knuckles. Malcolm took an occasional glance at him as they drove the road toward Olivia's. Ryan could feel it, Malcolm's apprehension, something he wasn't telling him about Olivia or Jennifer. He could feel it when he walked back into the field to get the tractor and the baler after the sisters had left. Anticipation for the more domestic interaction made his ribs feel rubbery, like they did when he was young. As a child, his father made him stand in the corner as punishment—nose against the wall, the heat of the woodstove hovering a hair's width from his back. He could still feel the edges of the knots in the pine that he'd relieved nose itches against. And that's how he felt as Malcolm drove toward Olivia's, how being in Ironwood was just waiting for someone to let him out of the corner. Malcolm pulled his truck into Olivia's driveway, and Ryan waited for him to lead the way.

Steam hit their faces as soon as they walked through Olivia's front door. Jennifer stood at the stove behind a pot of boiling water. The vapor wafted through the opening in the wall into the living room, where Olivia sat on the couch flipping through an old photo album. She squinted for a moment when Ryan crossed her line of vision. Jennifer threw a towel over her shoulder with one hand and tapped it with a wooden spoon that she held in the other. She lifted a beer from the counter and took a sip.

"I'll show Adam to the shower," she said.

Jennifer stripped the towel from her shoulder and dropped it onto the counter. Olivia told Malcolm to grab himself a beer as Jennifer led Ryan down the hallway. The air thinned and Jennifer turned to face him when she pushed the bathroom door open. "After you."

Ryan stepped into the room, and dropped his duffel bag. Jennifer slipped in behind him. She closed the door, keeping her hand on the knob. A towel had already been laid out, a packaged bar of soap on top of it.

"I think I can get it from here," he said.

"Yeah? I was curious, Adam. What's your last name?"

"Wouldn't you rather have this conversation at dinner? I'm sure I'd be a little more presentable. Besides, the bathroom seems like an awkward place to ask that question. People shit in this room."

"Yeah, you just seem familiar. I can't place it, and my curiosity is getting the better of me."

"Maybe I just look like a guy who needs a shower. I'm sure you've seen that before around here."

She dropped her hand from the knob and lifted her arms to cross them over her chest. "Is your last name something you're having a hard time remembering?"

"No. Not at all," He stripped his T-shirt and undid his belt. Jennifer dropped her hands to her side. He reached beyond the curtain and turned the knob, pulled the plunger down on the tub faucet and the shower head sputtered water. He thought of New Orleans, how even fifteen hundred miles away he was still being harassed with questions before a shower. Ryan pushed his pants to the floor and stepped out of them. Naked, he fingered his socks over his heels and stepped past the shower curtain under the stream of water.

A moment later, he heard the bathroom door close then Olivia's laugh, and the clattering of plates. The hot water drummed against the raw skin on his palms. He flexed his hands and worked his fingers. The baling twine and rough hay had rubbed the edges of his hands raw, more on his missing pinky.

Why was she so interested in his last name?

The warmth of the water seemed like it would never end, and he wanted to remain under that spray, but he rinsed off quickly then stepped out of the shower. As he toweled himself off at the mirror, he noticed all the men's products on the counter: a men's razor, Old Spice after shave, Speed Stick, Barbasol. Even there, hanging in the holder over the sink, Olivia's dead husband's toothbrush.

The three of them were rearranging the chairs at the table as Ryan entered the living room. It was so strange to him—the family dinner—so wholesome, and despite the size of the table, there didn't seem to be enough room. Ryan put his duffel bag near the door. He kept his left hand in his pocket, the scar hidden. People always stared at it, always wanted to touch it or ask how it had happened.

"Feeling refreshed?" Jennifer asked.

"Incredibly."

The plates were set around the table, coils of spaghetti in each and a small cape of steam rising and flapping toward the light fixture hanging over the table. Olivia moved around the table to ladle red sauce onto the pasta, circled around him as if he were a banister or support column that she'd learned to avoid. She put the pot of sauce back on the stove and reached for the small of Ryan's back.

"Have a seat," she told him, making her way to hers.

Ryan pulled the paper towel from beneath his fork and draped it over his knee.

He stood from the table when he finished, taking his plate with him, and rinsed it in the sink despite Olivia telling him that she'd take care of it. He looked out into the living room from the sink, thought about the quiet in the room.

He spoke as he turned, "Thank you for dinner. I'm really tired, so I think I'm going to head back down to the Tavern and get some sleep."

Malcolm shifted in his seat, perhaps to stand, but stopped when Jennifer spoke.

"I'll give you a ride," she said, taking one last bite of her meal. She wiped her mouth as she stood and tossed the napkin on the table.

"I appreciate that, but the Tavern's not far. I'd much rather walk and enjoy the air."

"I insist."

Malcolm's eyes darted from Ryan to Jennifer. "I'm sure Adam can manage to get to the Tavern on his own."

"Yeah, Jen. The man's been working all day. Maybe he just wants some time to himself."

Jennifer clenched her jaw. "I guess you're right. Enjoy your walk, Adam."

"I'll see you in the morning, Malcolm," Ryan said, and grabbed his soiled clothes on his way out.

* * *

Olivia rocked her empty beer can on the table while Ryan moved down the driveway to the road. Jennifer flicked her thumb over the end of her fork. Her eyes had lost focus, but the strain in her cheeks pulsed as her jaw clenched. Malcolm slipped out of his seat, carrying his plate and silverware with him to the sink.

Jennifer spoke. "So, Malcolm, where'd you find this guy?"

A tinny, low thud vibrated when he pulled his fingers from the edge of the plate.

In a rock pile twenty-five years ago.

"We have a mutual acquaintance." He turned to face Jennifer. "A guy I knew a long time ago. He said he knew someone looking for work. I knew I was going to need some help with the wood this season, and if I didn't get any, I was afraid your father wouldn't extend the lease Mike had. I've got a few more seasons in me, I think. The both of you know how hard it is to find good help around here."

"So you don't really know him? Anything about his background? His last name? You just know a guy who knows a guy."

"I know he's a worker."

Olivia looked over at Jennifer who'd drawn her gaze from Malcolm's chest. "Satisfied?" She asked.

"Glad you found some help. I'd better be going, too. I have to get in early tomorrow."

Malcolm stepped forward to take Jennifer's plate. She handed it up to him and left.

Ryan crossed the gravel lot to the steps at the side of the Tavern that led to the rooms on the second floor. The stagnant air in the hallway pressed more dryness through his hay-chapped nostrils. He walked softly and waited at his door for a moment, dismissing the idea that Victoria could have found him there. For safe measure, more out of habit, he nudged the door with his knuckles, and it remained motionless. Then he rapped on the thin pane in the middle of it. No movement inside. The key was jammed in the pocket of his soiled jeans and he tugged at it until it came loose. The pile of clothes unraveled on the floor where he dropped them to lock the door behind him. As he turned to sit on the bed, there was movement in the hallway, the weak boards of the floor sending tiny tremors through his feet. The knock was steady, three quick taps. He opened the door six inches and stopped it with the edge of his boot.

Jennifer lifted the base of her shirt and revealed the badge. "I'm still curious about that last name."

Ryan curled his right hand into a fist with his annoyance that Malcolm hadn't mentioned Jennifer was a cop. "This official county business, deputy?"

"I'm hoping it won't have to be."

"What can I help you with?"

"How about you let me inside. Better to keep this little chat between us."

Ryan backed from the door and Jennifer nudged it into him as she passed. She kicked past his duffel bag on her way to the window. The neon lottery and beer lights at the store went out. "Great view," she muttered.

"It's interesting from time to time."

"Malcolm tells me you two have a mutual friend."

"I guess I'm not the only one you've been asking questions to."

"No. He offered that information after you left. I just want to know how I know you." She turned from the window to face him. "Because I know you. I just don't know how. And I don't like the way that type of thing will keep me up at night."

"Not much goes on around here, does it?"

"More than you might think."

"Well, there's no need to lose any sleep over me."

"I know you."

"You don't know me. But if it's that important to you, maybe you should buy me a drink. That's typically a better approach than flashing your badge for *unofficial* business."

"Sorry, stud. That's not it. You got any ID? See, you're legally required to present ID to rent a room, and it's come to my attention that that didn't happen when you rented this one."

"Don't you mean that this establishment is legally required to acquire a copy of a government-issued ID for any person renting a room? I'm not legally required to present anything they don't ask for."

"All the same, I'd like to see that ID."

"It's out in my truck."

"That's convenient."

Ryan turned and moved to the bed and sat. He unlaced his boots and toed them onto the floor. "I'm a little tired, deputy. Shut the door on your way out."

She shook her head and sighed out a small chuckle. "You smug motherfucker. I'm trying to be nice about this. I don't think you want me to have to put hands on you."

He leaned back on the thin pillows. "You seem like a woman who has a hard time keeping her hands to herself."

"Then maybe you should be thinking of me as a deputy, not someone you can dismiss so easily."

"Goodnight, Deputy." He pushed a corner of the pillow

beneath his ear and rolled to his side, facing her. "Don't forget the door."

She took a step closer to Ryan. "I'm not going to ask you again."

Ryan spun from her as her fingers brushed against his shoulder. He gripped her wrist, swung it behind her back, and pushed her face down on the mattress. In the same movement, just before her face hit the sheets, he snatched the pistol from her belt and tossed it next to her head. "That wasn't exactly protocol, was it?" His voice came out low. "I don't really like being touched."

She tried to push against him, but she was down, firmly against the mattress. He pressed his cheek against hers.

"Maybe we should make a call to your supervisor now to discuss one of his deputies assaulting someone in their room."

Her throat flexed as she swallowed. Her eye movement became more rapid.

"I hate being an ungracious host, but your choice of fore-play doesn't really put me in the mood."

She turned her head, her nose brushing against his lip and she snapped her teeth at it, catching a piece just big enough to bite into. Ryan loosened his grip for a moment then squeezed tighter and dug his thumb into the opposite corner of her mouth. He fish-hooked her face toward the mattress and tore his lip from her teeth.

He growled into her ear, "Sweetheart, the world is a cruel place. It's time for you to go, unless you want to learn more about the world than you probably want to know."

He released his grip and stepped back, grabbing her gun. She flung her hands over the mattress, clenching at the sheets. Then she turned to face him, leaning back against her elbows on the bed. Ryan held the barrel of the pistol in his hand, tapped the grip against his belt buckle and stared down at her. A trickle of blood seeped over his lip. How badly he'd fucked up began to swarm thick in his thoughts.

She sucked in a deep breath, chest heaving. A tear struck her eye and she blinked it away. She stood slowly. That single tear bothered him. Her shoulders quivered. For a moment, he thought she might cry. He thought of the peculiarity of that act, balling, dumping all those rapid huffing emotional breaths. It must help, to cry as an adult. Babies do it because of pain or want, and it seemed that adults had to get used to pain. That was a part of life that they were seasoned by, so pain hurt less. There had to be a lot of pain to make an adult cry. That's what he'd believed when he was a kid, the last time he'd thought with care about an adult weeping. Any other time, when he saw an adult break down, it was fear. And those were a different kind of tears. It occurred to him then, that she wanted control. He was the stranger in her town. That's what he needed to give her, one way or another. Control. He reached up and thumbed the blood from his lip and looked down at it then back at her.

"You're all kinds of fucked up, aren't you?"

"A little more than most, I'd have to say. But you're not so different. I can see that in your eyes."

"Yeah? Maybe we would have hit it off in another life, been something of a whirlwind."

"Maybe. You think you would be man enough to handle that?"

He pressed the handle of her pistol against her hip and she took it. He kept his hands at his side.

"Probably not."

She tossed the gun onto the mattress. There was a brief quiet in the room, a subtle pause, like the sound of rain stopping for a moment when driving below an overpass. Touch is about nothing more than possession, about gaining something. It was about control, about taking. Touch is about violence, and sometimes it's disguised as affection. *The kind that will ruin you.*

Then there was the light slapping sound of her hands grabbing at his face, moving to the back of his head and pulling him in, against her mouth.

She pushed his face away, glared into his eyes. "You're going to regret this," she whispered, and turned him around to push him onto the mattress.

He let himself fall, closed his eyes, waited for the shiver he'd get from her touch. This was the touch he craved, because sometimes touch could be about giving. Tiny snaps of static tingled along his scalp as she pushed her fingertips through his hair. She found her grip just behind his ears and swung her knees onto the mattress over his lap. Heavy breaths clashed between them, a sticky vapor drawing them closer. She pulled his head back, bit into his bottom lip, and her mouth sucked at the cut she'd already given him. He pushed his hands up her thighs and over her hips, latched around her waist, the tips of his index fingers almost touching, thumbs pressing into the ridge of her pelvis. A sharp dig in his back after she'd dropped her arms over his shoulders and dug her nails into his skin. He pulled her against the weak springs in the damp mattress, thought about the difference between them, man and woman, the different types of force. She slid a hand beneath his shirt, her nails grazing against his flesh, tightening muscles beneath his skin, and she pressed her palms into the ripples of his abdomen. When she pushed her thumb against his lip where she'd bitten him, he poked his tongue through to taste it.

NINETEEN

The early morning sounds at the store across the street weren't much different than the sounds he'd heard in the afternoon. The conversations were about the same, as well, and there were really only two or three conversations recycled and handed off from customer to customer as they passed each other at the doors. People had to talk, even if they didn't have anything to talk about. At some point, when people were no longer hunter-gatherers, no longer had to simply survive or fear danger, they stopped listening. They replaced that need to survive with their need to be noticed, with their own noise, as if the absence of something to focus on would deflate their purpose and they'd slip away into the wind like some imperceptible floating particle. They assumed their noise was something other noisemakers wanted to hear. That was human evolution.

Ryan opened his eyes and looked down at the store from the chair he'd slept in for part of the morning. Her breathing pattern had changed earlier in the night, too, and woke him, and he'd watched her move through the room, thinking she was leaving before they had to wake up together.

"Well, this is pretty fucking awkward," she said.

He stood. "I figured you'd want to relish in that—the

awkwardness. I have to go. You're welcome to sleep in."
He shrugged, one shoulder dipping forward slightly, and his
eyebrows twitched.

She pushed herself up from the bed, brought her knees
in, draped her arms over her shins, and looked away from
him as he slung his duffel bag over his shoulder and left.

His jaw hurt, and that's what woke Kurt—pain. From his
jaw, the pain crept around his ear and along the side of his
head to his temple. He lifted his head and the ache rattled
down into his neck, the strain from his head sagging against
his shoulder through the night while he slept in the rocking
chair. He tasted the sour taste on the back of his tongue and
glanced around the wooden floor of the porch to see if he'd
vomited anywhere. A soft breeze blew and rustled the dry
leaves beneath the porch. The boards echoed his footsteps
to the front door, where the shriek of the hinge stabbed into
his ears. He went to the faucet in the kitchen. The sludge in
his stomach shifted when the water hit the basin, and he
scrambled toward the bathroom.

Kurt stumbled from the chair on his porch and entered the
house. He thumbed a mosquito that had landed on his
hand, smearing the bug and the blood it had taken from
him, a slight itch already beginning to rise. The ground was
soft and damp where he sat inside the tree line across the
street from Kurt's house, above the steep banking and the
ditch at the side of the road, behind the narrow foliage of
small growth. Two young cattle in the small pasture trotted
along the back side of the fence. The white tags in their left

ears flapped as they moved. Ryan pressed his back harder against the thick birch he leaned against to relieve an itch gnawing close to his spine.

Vomiting shifted whatever had kinked in his neck, and after he'd splashed water on his face, Kurt felt slightly better. The dizziness faded, and he dried out his gums with mouthwash. The phone rang and he shut the bathroom door and turned on the water in the shower. He let the steam build in the room, until he could feel his eyelids go clammy. The shower helped to push him a bit further toward better function. Then he'd talk on the phone. He'd figure out what to do with Patricia. She'd never not come home. Nobody at the church would let her stay with them without telling him. Malcolm? The sharp, disdainful responses she'd been giving him became more frequent since she started getting better. Discomfort pushed at the back of his eyes as he thought, so he tried to push his thoughts away like a noise he could cover his ears from.

Kurt came from the house, moving slowly and slightly sideways to his truck. He'd changed his clothes, had tucked in his shirt. The cattle stopped to look over at the movement in the driveway, Kurt's truck backing to the small barn then cutting hard through the gravel and out onto the road. He sped down the tar toward town. Ryan waited until the sound of the engine was gone and moved down the embankment and across the street.

He moved along the edge of the barn. The cattle approached him slowly, perhaps hoping he had something to give them.

Their heads bobbed and one of them let out a short grunt as they meandered in his direction. Ryan moved away from them to the corner of the house and around the back to the sliding door that opened into the kitchen. The door was unlocked. He slid it open six inches, sent out a short whistle to check for a dog, and waited. Before he entered, he reached down to peel off the black socks that he'd put over his shoes. He rolled them into a ball and tucked them into his back pocket. Then he stepped inside, onto the clean red-and-white linoleum, the treads of his shoes free of anything he might have tracked in.

The house was gloomy except for the light coming through the picture window. He stood between the kitchen and dining area, the round table to his right, a red vinyl tablecloth over it and white, lacy placemats in front of each of the four chairs. The living area was directly in front of him, two recliners facing the television, one slightly closer than the other, the armrests draped with yellow-and-red crocheted covers. A woodstove sat cold in the corner near an empty wood box. The woodgrain paneling that covered the walls and the textured pattern of the mauve carpet made the place feel like a double-wide trailer.

Trailers reminded him of the tornado targets he'd been through in the flat, rural parts of Alabama and Mississippi, through the Midwest, West Virginia and Pennsylvania, and all the ones he'd seen in New England on the way there. They never changed, and neither did the type of people he'd see in them. The only difference was the landscape and the accent, as if pronunciation were something that lost density as it tumbled downhill from the mountains in New England and slumped flaccid in the Mississippi Delta.

He got a feel for the layout, the doors and windows,

slowed his breathing and moved into the living room, past the hallway that led to the two bedrooms, the bathroom, and the basement door. A tube television in front of the recliners, converter boxes on top of it—the struggle to maintain entertainment with something nearly obsolete. On the wall behind the television, shallow shelves displayed a collection of crystal ornaments. Brass-framed black-and-white eight-by-ten photographs with Skowhegan State Fair blue ribbons attached to their corners. He scanned the shelves, noticed the dust on the television absent from the crystal and the glass in the frames. There were no pictures anywhere else on the walls, nothing of Patricia's past to remind him of his family. Only two of the black-and-whites were Patricia's and neither of those had ribbons. She stood near a river, and the other on a suspension bridge over a waterfall. She was younger in those pictures. The rest were sunsets and meadows and soaring birds of prey, other various wildlife in snow-laden landscapes. None of the photos contained an image of Kurt. The photographer is always present, never seen. Predators are rarely captured by their prey. Ryan moved softly across the carpet, into the bedrooms and found nothing there but made beds and clothing—the decorating style of an old woman.

He went to the bookshelf to the right of the recliners, a china cabinet, actually, that had no doors. All religion. All a bunch of con artists smiling like they'd wiped their ass with tithing. The oldest shakedown in the world, but the thing he hated most about religion was how stupid it made people. TV shows are too violent, so they bring their children to church to talk about a book where a man in the sky killed babies. There's no humanity in religion. And if that were pointed out to them, if they took a minute to read that book, they'd learn that nearly everything that's been used to support one of those minister's arguments is taken out of context. Instead, people accept questions about religion the same way they'd feel if someone took a shit in a baseball hat that represented their favorite team. They don't actually believe in what their religion preaches, just like they don't play for their favorite team. There was nothing else there that he could learn about Kurt, so he moved toward the door to the basement.

The stairs were unfinished wooden planks. He put his hand on the switches to his left and closed the cellar door before turning on the first light that was nothing but a red glow from the right. The second switch illuminated the area below him. He turned off the red light and moved down the planks, both feet on each step, allowing the cool air to chill the thin patch of exposed skin on his wrists. Broom strokes had cut lines through the particles on the cement floor, and he walked over them into the openness of the cellar. The space—a workbench and pegboard above it where wrenches and other tools hung shimmering in the light of the room. Another bench, tripods and camera lenses, exposure trays and camera cases and cables that sagged from the weight of clothespins. The furnace and water heater lonely in a corner, a row of shelving against the back wall behind the stairs with marker-labeled boxes solemn in their wait for the appropriate season to be emptied. Split firewood ran along the wall to the left of the stairs half the width of the cellar, an aroma of piss from red oak. Near the workbench, where an old iron vice was anchored to the wood, there was another water heater tucked into the corner. The copper pipes spiking from the top of it had been cut. Ryan scanned the space again, remembered the clever tricks Benjamin used to store things for clients. Everything down there had a purpose, a reason, a label, even him. Everything except that water heater. The Phillips-head screws on the outside paneling of the nonfunctioning water heater were worn. Ryan pulled a driver from the wall above Kurt's workbench.

The water heater had been gutted, and there was a black milk crate inside. Ryan leaned the panel against the bench and tucked the screwdriver into his back pocket. He set the screws on the plastic top of a coffee can and pulled the plastic bag from the milk crate, a flat, orange hook inside, the sharp point brown up to the curve, *Hale* etched into the wooden handle. He squatted and set the bag down on the cement. The only other contents of the crate were scattered brown envelopes. Like the boxes on the shelves, each was labeled. *Jack Leaving the Tavern. Nicole. Malcolm Hale. Pushes in Embden. Teenagers at Moxie Falls. Sappi Truck at Kennebec. Arthur Carlton. Crews for Moscow, Jackman and Athens.* One of the envelopes was unlabeled. He took them out, worked the metal nibs on the one labeled *Nicole*, and removed the photos inside. Kurt kept the negatives with the photos. Idiot. He scanned through the stack of low-light exposures—Nicole sucking some guy off on the smoking porch of the Tavern. He went to Malcolm's envelope, another low-light series—Malcolm butchering a deer; the hardwood foliage behind him made it obvious the deer had been harvested out of season. He replaced the photos and opened the unlabeled envelope.

The first few photos were nothing but various spreads of hardwood, then Mike Hale on the Carlton woodyard. He continued through the images until he got to the last few in the stack. Then he flipped faster, the images clear and focused, forcing an abrupt change in his breathing. Quickened, like he was rushing uphill toward some reward, but there was not that, only the ruffled cadence of his heartbeat. Malcolm was wrong. Kurt hadn't killed Mike. He looked over at the pulp hook, thought about Simon, what Simon had sent him there for.

"Fuck," he whispered.

He took longer than he should have to decide what he wanted to do, what he should do. The dried blood on the end of the hook came off easily with some paint thinner he'd found under Kurt's workbench. Anything else left on the hook would be gone as well. He replaced it, then tucked all the photos that would expose the truth about Mike's killer into his belt along with the negatives, scanning them to take only the ones necessary. Kurt wouldn't know anything was missing unless he looked through them, and the nibs hadn't been bent more than a couple times. Then he sat back down and went through the rest of the photos to see what else Kurt might know about the people of Ironwood.

Jennifer pinched at the fabric of her uniform, itchy against her skin. She shouldn't have switched cleaners, but the last place busted three of the buttons on her shirt. Webber had brought her a coffee and two Boston creams because she hated them, his non-flirtatious way of getting her to cover for him while he went to the river to fish for an hour. She gave him less shit than normal because she didn't need him looking over her shoulder while she perused the NCIC database.

When she typed in his name, she hesitated for a moment. She debated submitting his information, remembered what he'd done with his mouth, working down her stomach and the teasing bites along the inside of her thigh, her hips. A tingle crept along her knees when she pressed her legs together to subdue the quiver, swallowed behind the flushing skin on her neck while she thought about his tight grip around her throat. Then she remembered the sheets, crawling from them in the night after she was sure Adam was asleep. She'd dug quietly through his duffel bag, where she'd found his red Velcro wallet and lifted it to the window to use the sliver of light from a streetlamp to read his name and information. There was a crease down the center of the picture, so she'd mouthed *Adam Crane* into her memory, tiptoed through the room, back into the bed and wrapped her arm around his stomach to nuzzle against his ribs. Then she thought briefly of the campaign signs in her closet. *Jen Carlton for Sheriff*. The glossy red shimmering behind the few clothes she had hanging in there.

She submitted Adam Crane's information and the screen changed. Three traffic violations, nothing else. She sat back in the chair, glanced over the monitor at the two rookie deputies staring googly-eyed at Henderson, the only other female deputy, who told them about the naked tweaker lunatic she'd taken down all by herself. She omitted the part of the story where she'd drawn her weapon and shot a hole through her pants and the tweaker fell down a flight of stairs. It wasn't until she'd snapped her cuffs on the unconscious man that she'd realized she'd shit herself. Another reason Jennifer wanted to be sheriff, so she could fire that lizard-faced cunt. She scanned the information in front of her. Do better things with your time, she told herself.

She walked around a row of desks, an inconvenient path for her to head out to her truck to begin patrols. "Ask her about how she shit her pants," she told the two rookies on her way by.

TWENTY

Kurt cut into his eggs. Patricia pulled her hand from the man's reach as she approached his booth in the back of The Kodiak. The man followed her slowly, corduroy pants and a polo shirt, a slight smirk on his face. Kurt didn't break his movement with his fork to cut the yoke of his eggs. She sat down and inched closer to the pine board wall in the orange bench seat to give the man room to sit.

"Who's your friend, Patricia?"

The man extended his hand across the table. "I'm Nolan."

Patricia stared at Nolan's hand. Kurt kept his eyes on Patricia.

He took a bite of his food, chewed slowly while he stared at her. "Who is this hippy faggot waving his hand over my breakfast?"

Patricia opened her mouth to speak.

"Kurt, let's keep this civil," Nolan said.

Kurt maintained his stare on Patricia. "The man who's sleeping with my wife wants me to be civil?"

Nolan intertwined his fingers over the edge of the table. "That's certainly a simplistic way to pigeonhole this, Kurt. What you neglect to realize is your failure as a husband."

Kurt snapped his hand over the table aiming his fork over

Nolan's top lip, yoke slinging from the tines, small drops landing against the window and grazing Patricia's chin, which she wiped away immediately with her palm. "One more word out of you, and I'll pin your tongue to the table with this fork." Kurt pressed the tines into Nolan's upper lip just below his nostrils. "In fact, if you don't disappear, I'll be sure to wedge this piece of metal between your fucking eyes."

"Mr. Myers—"

Kurt slammed his fist down on the table and Patricia jumped. The server approaching with a pot of coffee stopped in her tracks. She turned, almost ramming into the man behind her, who quickly avoided contact. Nolan's breathing sputtered.

"Nolan," Patricia said, "I need to speak with Kurt. Please give me a few moments."

Nolan hurried through the side exit.

Kurt went back to his food.

Patricia's hands shook as she clasped them over the table.

"So what is it you want, a divorce?"

She whimpered slightly, pulled a napkin from the holder at the edge of the table. She smeared it against her eyes and then her nose. "The only thing I want is to never spend another moment in your presence. You left me alone when I needed you the most. I had cancer for God's sake, and all you could do was think about Arthur Carlton's woodlot."

"Patricia, I'm going to finish my breakfast and you're going to sit here and watch me. Then you're going to go get into my truck and we're going home to have a nice long chat about this."

"I just told you—"

"You shut your mouth, bitch-fucking-whore."

Patricia stood and Kurt grabbed her wrist across the table. "Let me go."

"Sit your ass down."

"Let me go!" She swung, slapping her hand against his temple.

Silverware chimed toward the front of the restaurant, and the servers and cooks had stopped working. The sound of the slap wrapped itself around Kurt and made his heart race. Beyond Patricia, the server perked her eyebrows. Patricia jerked her wrist from Kurt's grip and charged through the restaurant to the front door. Kurt's jaw quivered, a sneer painted on his face. He swatted the plate of food away from him, and it dumped over the bench where Patricia had sat and onto the floor. He dug into his pocket for a ten-dollar bill and tossed it on the table before taking the side exit to cut off Patricia, where he took a firm grip of her bicep, his fingers digging against the bone on the inside of her arm.

Nolan's voice rose into the clamor of Patricia and Kurt's yelling, pleading for Kurt to let her go. Kurt had opened his truck door and pulled a tire iron from behind the seat. Patricia yanked her arm away and shoved his truck door closed.

The server and the cook made their way onto the deck outside. Kurt jabbed Nolan in the corner of the mouth with the curve of the tire iron.

Nolan latched onto the pain with both hands and stumbled back. He squatted toward the ground. Kurt stood over him and he brought his hands up, held them close to his face and cowered behind them.

Kurt held up the iron in his hand, as if he hadn't realized he'd pulled it from behind his seat. He turned away from Nolan toward the scuffling in the dirt behind him, where Patricia reached beneath the truck for the shoe that had come off. The heat of the day had not arrived, but the sun was high enough over the pines and had been there long enough to dry what moisture had settled on the dirt in the lot. Dust rose as she scrambled to her feet, a sharp rock digging into the tender arch of her bare foot, and she fell to her knees. Kurt's thick-fingered hand squeezed around her elbow and jerked her to her feet.

Patricia yanked her arm free again, hobbled a few feet before another rock gouged her foot. She hopped, but Kurt gripped her elbow again, tighter this time. Rushing footsteps came from behind them. Kurt swung the iron as he turned, thinking he'd connect with Nolan's jaw. His aim would have been true if Nolan had rushed him. The edge of the steel deflected up off the side of the woman's skull. Blood came from the gash and draped down the slope of her hair. Her hand moved up to the wound as she fell. Kurt got a good, clear view of her face and the Somerset County Sherriff's Deputy uniform as Jennifer fell to the ground.

When he turned, Patricia's expression had changed, and he linked it to the impact in his groin. A surge of air rushed out of him, like he had suddenly begun to fall from a tremendous height. His knees hit the ground. Sound left his ears, the watery rush of blood in his head, the panicking drum of his heartbeat pulsed over every other sound. Then the pain wobbled through him. His mouth gulped at air. He wavered. The iron slipped from his hand and he fell forward, a sudden rush of breath coming back to him, rolling heat against the back of his eyeballs. He tasted the charred, smoky flavor of vehicle exhaust that had settled into the dust as he inhaled. Strain yanked along his collar bones as Jennifer jerked his arms behind him and clicked her handcuffs around his wrists.

Jennifer put her knee over Kurt's hands at the small of his back.

Kurt puffed loose dirt as he spoke. "This is a big misunderstanding."

"You thrashing your wife around the parking lot? That's a big misunderstanding?"

Dispatch sizzled through the radio.

"You just starting your shift, Deputy?"

"Kurt, quit talking."

"I've got a lot to talk about, though." Kurt pushed against her knee and whispered, "About a deputy who slept with her sister's husband." His dust-painted lips thinned into a smirk. "How soon am I going to get to the station, Deputy? I want to get out of this whore-filled parking lot."

A sheriff's cruiser whipped into the lot. Deputy Webber. Jennifer stood, staggered a few steps from Kurt, and pointed down at him. She reached for her head and fell to the ground.

TWENTY-ONE

Jennifer tapped at the gash on her head and found the lump, smooth and ovular. Cloud shaped pain rolled over her skull, billowing over the top of the bone. The smell of disinfectant opened her eyes and she shifted on the table. Sticky clumps of hair surrounded the lump. Her fingers felt like tiny hammers as she touched the wound. She went through her memory—Kurt turning toward her, swinging, the cold ring in her ears, the flash of Patricia's movement, the bite of gravel on her knee, then Kurt, yes.

How did he know about Mike?

When she pushed herself from the exam table, her knees buckled, but she caught herself, then drifted to the wall and slid toward the door. The muscles in her legs responded slowly, and it took her a few more minutes of clinging to the wall for them to take the total of her weight. The door handle was cold, and she realized how chilly the room was. Outside the room, where she was a little more stable, the red arrows painted on the walls led her back to the lobby.

"What the hell are you doing, Jen?"

The voice was shrill in her ears. She turned to face Olivia and shuddered. Her mouth went dry. Olivia's stern look jumbled anything she could say. She waited for it. Would

Olivia hit her right there in the lobby? The glossy campaign posters in her closet paraded through her mind in flames.

"Why are you here?" she asked, choking through the words.

"Webber called me. He said that you'd need someone to pick you up—that you took a pretty good hit to the head. What the hell is going on? Kurt hit you? That motherfucker."

Olivia didn't know. Jennifer took a deep breath and said, "I just really want to get out of here."

Olivia gave her a sideways glance then shrugged. "Well, alright. Let's go." She dug into her purse for her keys and led the way out of the hospital.

Jennifer nibbled the skin on the knuckle of her right thumb. She stared out the window, wishing Olivia would drive faster, wondering what Kurt was telling the other deputies, Sheriff Middler. Olivia beside her forced a chill to flash over her face and neck. She thought about the tree that crushed Mike, how it had buried her secret beneath it. Then a squeeze pinched in her stomach.

"Pull over," she whispered.

"What?"

"I'm going to be sick. Pull over."

Olivia checked the rearview and swung the car onto the shoulder. Jennifer was already pulling on the handle before the vehicle stopped, and she leaned out of the car to wretch. More sound escaped than anything else. For a moment, she hoped for an accident, a logging truck too close to the shoulder to end it, but she realized that in her hope, it was only to escape Olivia learning the truth. She pushed against the knotting cramp in her abdomen with her fingers and reached for the handle above the door to pull her torso back into the car.

"You going to make it?"

"Yeah. I think I'm just concussed. I need to lie down."

"You want to go to your place or mine?"

"Take me home. I want to be in my own home."

A logging truck. How fucking cute, she thought. Then it became clear, why Kurt must have been sitting on that information. The lease. He'd been trying to get on her father's land for years. He was going to blackmail her. That must have been his plan before, before he'd assaulted her and got himself arrested. What would he say now?

"Are you alright?" Olivia asked.

"What?"

"You're mumbling shit to yourself. Maybe I should take you back to the hospital."

"No. I don't need to go back to the hospital."

"I'm just saying. You're being weird."

"I got hit in the fucking head. Sorry my behavior's not more normal for you."

"Whoa, Jen. I was just making sure you were alright."

"I'll be alright when I get home. I just need to get home."

Jennifer stared at the white line, trying to find a way to organize things in her mind, to develop a plan, and the miserable frustration of all of it was that she couldn't do anything until she spoke to Kurt. Olivia pulled the car hard into the driveway and slid a little on the gravel. The car rocked and Jennifer felt the edges of her headache. She got out of the car. Olivia walked her to the door, tried to follow her in, but Jennifer turned her away.

Jennifer scrambled inside the house. The phone charger was knotted and tangled on the entryway table. After she plugged in the phone, she hovered over the screen. The lightning bolt logo came on, then the battery logo with a thin red line at the base of it. She pressed the power button and waited for the phone to come to life. The urge to vomit returned, but she choked it down. Around her home, the blankets and clothes were thrown over the back of the couch and the armrests. More clothes hung over the backs of chairs in the kitchen. The sink was full of cereal bowls and coffee cups, dirty plates, the pans stacked and piled on the stove, leaning, ready to fall over in the night and send her lurching from her bed. The trash smelled sour and sweat emanated from the pile of dirty clothes next to the coffee table. And then she saw the couch and remembered pressing her face against the armrest and gripping the seam on the edge while Mike had fucked her from behind—how all of it started. One stupid fucking mistake was about to destroy everything for her. She shook away the thought and looked down at her phone. Nothing.

She stood in the middle of the untidy space, waiting for a knock on the door, her phone to ring, anything that would allow her to move in some direction. The more she stared at her phone, the more the sensation of having her arms pinned to her side settled on her. She tongued her bottom lip, tickling the soft, delicate flesh where she could taste the tang of bile on her teeth. Dizziness again. Cramps began to nestle at the tops of her knees from flexing her quads. Her vision blurred. The phone vibrated. She dropped it and it bounced on the carpet.

She bent quickly to grab it, and when she rose, she clipped the wound on her head against the edge of the side table. Her eyes watered and she screamed obscenities at the object, sweeping the things from its surface onto the floor. A voicemail from Webber told her she needed to call immediately. She hung up, tried to determine what she should do, and she scrolled through her contacts for Webber's cell.

No answer.

She called again.

No answer.

Her cell rang. The station.

"Carlton," Webber said when she answered. "Why the fuck are you calling my cell?"

"What's going on?"

"Where are you? You should get down here."

"Why? What's going on?"

"Middler wants to talk to you about Kurt. Are you at your place? The hospital said you'd left before they released you. I'll send a car."

Her voice trailed off. "Yeah, I'm at my place."

Jennifer moved through the corridor of the station. The electronic buzz from the fluorescent lights made her ears ring until one of the phones rang. That pain bore through each ear and clashed in the center of her skull. Webber rounded the corner at the end of the hall shaking his head. She reached for the wall and dry-heaved.

Webber rushed toward her. "Shit, Jen. Are you okay?"

"Why do I need to be here?"

"I don't know. Sheriff told me to get you down here ASAP. They haven't even booked Kurt, yet."

"What? Why?"

"Fuck if I know."

She righted herself and Webber withdrew his hand from the small of her back. "You look like shit. You sure you're going to be alright?"

Her pain scurried away with the presence of her anger.

"Just take me to wherever I need to be."

Webber led her down the hall to an interview room. The shriek of the heavy door slashed into her ears like crushed glass on a Q-tip. Kurt was at the long folding table, a cup of coffee in front of him and a smile on his face. He continued to talk to Sheriff Middler, who sat across from him, holding his own cup of coffee to his lips—his legs extended, crossed at the ankles. Webber closed the door behind Jennifer. The echo of the door closing settled before Middler spoke.

"Deputy Carlton. How's your head?"

"How's yours, Sheriff? Why hasn't he been booked?"

Middler drew his knees up and adjusted in his seat. He put his cup of coffee down. "That's why I wanted you to come down here. I don't really think that's going to be necessary. I wanted you here as a courtesy."

"Are you fucking serious?" She forgot about Mike, what Kurt knew, remembered back when she'd told Middler that she wanted to run for sheriff. He'd laughed at her. "Wait, what are you saying? We're not charging him?"

"Deputy, I know this is difficult, and in any other situation we'd be behind you one hundred percent. I've known Kurt for twenty years, and he'd never intentionally hurt a law enforcement officer. He's already agreed to pay for the medical expenses."

"For me, his wife, the other man he assaulted, or all three of us?"

Kurt lifted his cup and covered his twitching smile.

Middler scratched the side of his face. "Well, you got mixed up in a family matter. I don't want to ruin this man's reputation over a simple misunderstanding."

"A simple misunderstanding? He hit me in the fucking head with a tire iron."

"Deputy, look. I'm not just doing this for Kurt. I'm doing this for you, too. Think about the paperwork we're going to avoid. Kurt's already made out a blank check for the hospital bill. Go ahead and take the rest of the week off."

Jennifer crossed her arms, tried to go tough, but it was useless, and pointless. Kurt had obviously kept his mouth shut.

"There's something I'd like to say," Kurt mumbled. "Bobby, could I have just a minute alone with Deputy Carlton."

Middler got up slowly from his seat. He sidestepped around Jennifer and shut the door behind him.

"You look a lot different out of uniform. More like a whore." He lifted his coffee.

She drew her fist up and bit her knuckles, an absolute hatred for that word. More than she hated *slut* or *tramp* or *harlot* or any of the other terms that got thrown at her in high school or even after when she'd gone to college in Orono. Names that men used out of spite or jealousy or insecurity or because she wouldn't give her body to them— wouldn't oblige herself to their entitlement.

"Kurt, is this really why I'm in here with you? For you to call me names? This is about the lease, isn't it? You want Mike's yard, and I'm supposed to convince my father to lease it to you or you'll blabber about me and Mike. And who the fuck are you calling a whore, Kurt? Your wife was out taking cock behind your back. What's wrong, you too small to please her? Don't have quite the blood flow that you used to? Maybe she just wanted a real man to fuck her, not some limp-dick faggot who hits women."

Kurt shook his head at her and chuckled. He lifted his coffee again.

"Something funny? Here's something funny: Middler retires in a few months, and that means nobody is going to be here to do you any favors. I'll still be here, though. And I'm going to do everything I can to make sure you end up in jail. At least for a weekend." She stepped to the table and gripped the edge of it—lowered her voice. "Just long enough for some thick-dick convict to slam his cock in your ass. Then you'll realize how much of a bitch you really are."

Kurt's expression had twisted into something painful, like her words had wrapped around his lips in an attempt to twist his face off his skull. "That filthy whore mouth. I'm not talking about you sleeping with Mike. I'm talking about you sinking a pulp hook in the side of his neck."

Jennifer's face went rigid. Her bones felt hollow, like reeds. Her knees almost gave. "M-Mike's death was an accident."

"The tree?" He chuckled. "That was no accident." He twirled his empty cup around in his hand, looking into the bottom. "But you are right about the lease. Now that Malcolm's got himself a helper, it's going to take a little more convincing for your father to cooperate. For now, though, I'm going to go down to Waterville, and get myself a nice steak dinner. You have a good day, Deputy."

Kurt stood and left the room. When the door shut, she sank into the chair he'd been sitting in.

TWENTY-TWO

When she got out of Webber's truck in the parking lot of
The Kodiak, she swayed, her balance similar to that point
between buzzed and drunk, and Webber asked if she was
going to be alright. She wanted a shower. Her inability to
do something, all the ideas that came to her floated in her
guts like buoys being tossed around on choppy water. She
started the truck and moved the dials to blow cold air over
her, and she thought back to that day in the yard with Mike.

*He pinched the upper seam of the reinforced knees on his
brown Carhartts and craned his head toward the handle of
the pulp hook he'd hung around his neck. She waited for
him to say something, that it was alright, that he under-
stood, that he wouldn't tell Olivia. But he didn't say anything. He just stood there tapping his fingers, a glazed-over
look in his blue eyes that was almost as icy as the gust of
wind that surged through the yard.*

*Then he shrugged. "I'm tired of the way this's been eatin'
me up inside. Maybe you should be the one to tell her first.
She'll divorce me, but you're always going to be her sister."*

*When he turned to walk away, she lunged at his shoul-
der, her fingers drifting over the fabric until she caught the*

metal of the pulp hook when he jerked forward. He spun toward her and she fumbled the hook from the ground.

"Goddamnit. I've got work to do, especially before your old man kicks me off his land."

"Don't fucking tell her."

"I've already made my decision."

"Fucking coward."

"Coward? Telling the truth makes me a coward?" He shook his head and reached toward her hand, the pulp hook. "I don't have time for this shit. Fucking whore."

Then she swung the hook.

She came back into the fold and slowed her breathing. There had to be a way out of this, a way to even things out with Kurt, make sure he'd never say anything. He had to have the pulp hook. Maybe she'd find it at his place, or maybe she'd find something on him, something embarrassing enough to keep his mouth shut forever. She backed the truck out of her spot and pulled out onto 201.

Kurt's front door was ajar when she arrived, but there wasn't anyone around. She called out even though she didn't expect an answer, but she wanted to make sure there weren't going to be any more surprises. Her head began to ache again, and she wandered toward the bathroom first to look for something to relieve her headache. She helped herself to the Advil in the medicine cabinet, took a quick look around the bathroom, and noted all the things that were missing, all the things that would belong to a woman. Despite that, there was the sense that one lived there—the towels and bathroom linens were pastel colored and the seashell-designed soaps decorated the windowsill. But there was only one toothbrush, no hair dryer, no makeup, and no feminine products. Patricia must have cleaned her things out earlier. Jennifer threw a few more Advil into her mouth and tossed the bottle over her shoulder. The plastic bounced off the toilet and the pills rained over the tub and linoleum.

She went to the living room and stood at the bookshelf, looking along the spines of the small library. God, God, Spirituality, God, Self Help. Wide-smiling, bleached-toothed Evangelicals telling people how to live and conning their money out of them. A minister instead of a deputy might have been a better career move.

She pulled a book from the shelf and fanned through the pages. Then she dropped it on the floor and walked over to the kitchen. Kurt had been waiting for an opportunity like this. Had it not been for the incident at The Kodiak, he would have approached her eventually. He had to have something. She slid open the drawer to her left and started her search.

Jennifer walked into the Tavern tired and disappointed after her search at Kurt's. The Tavern was quiet. Stacy, the town pill head, was at the video console tapping on flying fish, and Rickety Rob, one of the short-order cooks from The Kodiak, sat at the bar. Rob had hit a moose one night and surviving wasn't necessarily a lucky thing. The wreck had left him permanently hunched and he moved around like a tower of Jenga blocks that would crumble at any moment. He lifted a twisted hand from the bottle of beer he was nursing and punched it through the air in quick little jabs to wave to her. She sat at the corner of the bar between Rob and Stacy and waited for whoever was bartending to return.

"H-h-how's it going, D-D-Deputy?"

"I'm doing alright." She noticed a cut on her wrist as she put her hands on the bar. It must have come from the search at Kurt's. "How are you, Rob?" She scratched at the dried blood and ignored his stuttering answer.

"I h-heard you had a r-rough d-day. Wish you'd a-a-a killed that f-f-fucker."

She almost said, *Me too*, but thought better of it.

Nicole came from the back, the moving dolly wobbling behind her stacked with three cases of beer. The bottles rattled when the wheels hit a divot in the wooden floor. Stacy's sad eyes remained on the game screen. Rob chewed at the air, looking for something else to say, and she watched Nicole's approach in the mirror behind the bar. Two double-barrel shotguns hung above the bar. They'd been hanging there longer than she'd been alive, maybe almost as long as the wall had been standing there. For the first time that day, her thoughts drifted from the worry about Kurt and she envisioned herself walking over the bar and fitting the barrel of one of those shotguns into her mouth, perhaps a curiosity to see if they still worked and if they were loaded. She knew that neither was probably true, and there was nothing left for her to do with the day except end it. Nicole brought the dolly to a stop and moved behind the bar.

"Oh, hey there, Jen. Heard you had quite an exciting day today."

Jennifer could feel herself try to smile. Nothing came to her face but a drab look of annoyance. "Another day in paradise," she said. "Can I get a rye? Double."

"Whoa, definitely one of those days, hunh? You want that chilled?"

"No." That question always bothered her. Who the fuck drinks chilled whiskey?

Nicole whistled. Jennifer scratched the lobe of her left ear, a sudden flash of rage with the shrill sound of Nicole's whistle that made her clench her jaw.

"H-h-h-hey, Nicole. I'll buy the good D-D-D-Deputy a d-d-d-drink if you d-d-d-don't mind," Rob requested.

Jennifer thought about the shotgun over the mirror again, aiming it at the two of them, ending their breathing noises. Nicole had begun talking, and there was a conversation between her and Rob, but the sounds droned through the air in the room, drowned out by the rushing anger that swept through her thoughts. She could feel the taps of a scream on the inside of her lips, something on its last press of politeness before patience completely eroded, but she kept it behind her clenched teeth. Nicole put the tumbler of bourbon down on the bar and Jennifer wrapped her fingers around the glass and slammed it back before Nicole's hand had finished retreating. The noise in the room fell to a tolerable hum.

"Wow. I'd have gotten it over to you sooner if I had known you needed it that bad."

"You're here now." She tapped the side of the glass with her nail. "Be useful."

Nicole poured another double into the glass. "That first one was on Rob," Nicole said, reminding Jennifer of her manners.

"You're a peach, Rob. Thank you for the drink."

Rob twitched and looked down at the dollar bills he'd spread out in front of him, a courtesy he offered the bartenders so it would take less time to count his money. Nicole slipped the bottle back onto the shelf and continued her conversation with him. Jennifer stared at the reflection of the back wall, the line of antique beer cans on the shelf just below the ceiling. Sleep would be the delight of her life at that moment, to have the torments of the day slip away when she drifted into darkness. But she'd have to find a way to fix things. Going to sleep only meant she was closer to tomorrow, and she didn't want it to be tomorrow until she figured out a way to clean up her mess. She thought about the .38 revolver she'd found under the mattress at Kurt's. Somehow, the liquor made things clearer. She just needed to be patient.

And it was that easy. She straightened in her barstool. Tightness in her back lifted from where she'd hunched over the bar. Sleep would come easy when she got home. There, she'd put a set of sheets in the dryer, shower to wash the day from her pores. Then she'd take the sheets from the dryer and remake her bed, climb into it naked, feel the warmth of those sheets against her skin, dream, wake up the next day and go to Bingham for breakfast at Samantha's. She'd stay away from The Kodiak, from Olivia, from Kurt and everyone else—stay low, creep along the edge of her routine and wait for the people in town to forget all that'd happened. Olivia would leave, with a little convincing, cut ties with everything in the town and move on, and then she could take care of Kurt. It could be that easy, as easy as squeezing a trigger.

"Well that's one way to turn a frown upside down," Nicole said to her.

Jennifer caught her own reflection. She was grinning, wide and happy, and her face had taken on more color. She blinked and lifted the glass one last time. "Whiskey." She tipped it back and swallowed. The liquor numbed the pain in her head, both the wound and the headache that had grown with her frantic movement through the day. She got up, quietly, almost ignoring Nicole's stare and Rob's yellow-teeth grin. For the first time, Their voices and sounds had faded out, and hatred for them, why she hated them, rather, became clearer. They were happy with nothing, and nothing was misery. Stacy looked up from her game, nothing but a slight movement of her eyes between blinks.

Tomorrow, she whispered to herself as the Tavern door closed behind her. The rustle of the shade over the window of the door whispered back to her as she walked over the splintering boards and their rising nails to her truck. In the cab of her truck, she caught the smile that was still on her face in the rearview, and drove herself home. She kicked through the scattered items on the floor of her living room, the books and piles of clothes. The television remote spun and found a home beneath the couch. Careful of the wound on her head, she stripped her shirt as she passed the bathroom and ignored the chiming, happy little voice reminding her to brush her teeth. She left the lights on in the kitchen and fell face-first against the mattress after she entered her room. The crumpled sheets were twisted in the comforter, and she rolled her head against the fabric until her head had settled comfortably on the pillow. No need for fresh sheets. A deep breath, and she whispered *tomorrow* one final time, before she fell asleep.

A breeze through her window woke her. It blew over Jennifer's shoulders and down her chest, against the curve of her breasts still harnessed by her bra, like the sweep of a man's fingers. A wavy string of cobwebs hung at the corners of her ceiling. Things needed to be set right, Kurt dealt with, so she could move forward through the sluggish mire that her life had settled into. The earthy smell of soil and wet bark surrounded her, and she realized it must have rained at some point in the night. She rolled back to her stomach and the smell faded. The odor of her own sweat was there in the sheets, and as she pushed herself from the bed, she heard tires rolling over the gravel in her driveway. Outside the room, she grabbed a T-shirt from the armrest of the couch on her way to the door. Olivia. *Fuck.* Jennifer turned and made her way to the kitchen.

She took a glimpse of herself in the bathroom mirror. Her shirt was inside out and backwards. The door rattled as Olivia knocked and the thin metal of the bottom panel clattered when it slammed shut after she entered the living room.

"Jen?"

"Kitchen."

Jennifer leaned against the counter with her hands gripping the edge of the sink. The coffee maker grumbled its initial promise to buff away the tired look in her eyes.

"Why the fuck is Kurt Myers not in jail?"

"Pays to be friends with the sheriff."

"Are you fucking kidding me? Holy fuck, when Dad finds out about this…"

"Let's not talk about this right now."

"How you feeling?" Olivia asked.

"Fucking super."

"Yeah?"

At that moment, she wanted to point to the couch and tell Olivia that she'd fucked Mike there after a night at the bar. Put it out there. Get her out of the house at least. "You're so dense sometimes."

"Fuck you." Olivia scratched the back of her knee.

"What are you doing today?"

"Going to Samantha's for breakfast."

"I had breakfast already with Nicole."

"Wasn't an invite. How's your bestie doing this morning?"

"Bestie? You must have gotten hit harder than I thought. But speaking of besties, I saw your new friend today."

"Who?"

"Adam. He was at the store."

"How is he my new friend?"

"Maybe *friend* is just a nice way of saying, *fuck buddy*."

"What?"

"You really did take a good hit to the head. Malcolm's helper, who you fucking chicken-hawked at dinner. The only guy staying at the Tavern where your truck was early yesterday morning. Did he turn out to be the hard-core criminal on the run you thought he was? Is that what you're into these days?"

As her face flushed from embarrassment, the ache in her skull returned. The noise of the coffee maker. Olivia's voice. That perfect sleep she felt like she'd had when she awoke drifted off somewhere in her memory. She wanted to go back to bed, close her eyes, and find a quiet dream.

"I just woke up. Do I really have to start the day with you giving me shit?"

Olivia threw her hands in the air. "Whoa. Alright. Sorry. Maybe you should go back to bed. I can hang out here for a while and..." She looked back through the kitchen door. "I could help you clean up. Maybe help you look for the carpet. You do have carpet in here, right?"

"Funny. Help yourself to coffee. I'm going to go take a shower."

"Sounds like a good start. Should I fix you a cup when

it's done?"

"No. I might skip the coffee today and go straight to whiskey."

Jennifer's shoulders dropped as she exited the kitchen and turned into the bathroom. She closed the door and sat on the lid of the toilet while she reached into the shower and turned on the hot water. The water warmed, indicating its temperature with the spray that flung itself against her forearm and elbow. She peeled her clothes off and climbed into the tub, letting the water spray over her back, and pulled the curtain closed. The stitching in the gash on her skull tickled her palms. Water soaked through her hair until she had turned completely around again and stood there waiting for some decision to come to her. After yesterday, she didn't want Olivia around. A deep lather slid down her forearms as she stared at the floral pattern on the shower curtain and worked the bar of soap in her hands. Her anger rose, a small buildup of soap formed beneath her fingernails as she dug her fingers into the bar.

TWENTY-THREE

Johnson sat in a wicker chair with his back to Victoria, who lay out on the deck, topless. He'd called that morning, excited, almost frantic. *I've got something big*, he'd said. And Victoria left the cool comfort of the newly fixed air conditioning to be outside in the sun.

"If you don't mind," Johnson said, "I'd be a little more inclined to discuss this if you were a little more..."

"You don't like my tits?" She swatted away a fly that had landed on her nipple. "Do you even like tits, Johnson?"

"Yes. I mean, I have nothing against your breasts except that it seems a little inappropriate to conduct business in this manner."

"I think it's very appropriate. I'm comfortable."

Wendell walked out onto the deck with the glass of ice water for Johnson. He wore a light brown suit, a dark blue shirt under it, unbuttoned down to his chest. Johnson took the glass.

"Wendell," Victoria said. "What do you think about my tits?"

"You have wonderful tits, Mrs. Williams. Thank you for sharing."

"See, Johnson. Wendell thinks I have wonderful tits. And

they're real. Wendell, I don't think Mr. Johnson likes my tits."

"You don't like tits?"

"Yes. I like—it's just…They're wonderful, Mrs. Williams."

"As wonderful as this big news you have for me? Have you found him?"

"I think I have. A man driving the Subaru registered to this Ryan Carpenter fellah was in an accident last week. I went to the jail to interview the man the police arrested after the crash. That fellah's name is Adam Crane."

"And Adam Crane knows Ryan? Does he know where he is?" Victoria pulled her top from the deck beside her and put it on.

Johnson turned to face her. "Not really."

"Not really? That's the big news?"

"I'm not finished. This Adam Crane fellah met this Ryan fellah one night in Dallas. He told me that Ryan gave him some food in exchange for his clothes. Then this Ryan fellah—"

"Could you stop saying *fellah*? It's slightly annoying," Victoria interrupted.

Johnson bit his lip. "Ryan offered the man money for his wallet and ID. So, I guessed that this Ryan fe—that Ryan might be using Adam Crane as an alias. Adam told me that Ryan said something about a bus ticket, so I checked. An Adam Crane did buy a bus ticket from Dallas to Albuquerque."

Victoria looked at Wendell. "Did you hear anything from your cripple? Does he know where Ryan is?"

Wendell shook his head.

"Mrs. Williams, if Ryan's trail stopped in Albuquerque, I wouldn't be here. I called in one of those favors I told you about, my friend with the Marshals. There's a good possibility that Ryan is still using Adam Crane's ID and he might be in Somerset County Maine."

"But you don't know for sure."

"No. I'll have to go to Maine to verify that."

"Mr. Johnson, how do I know that you're not feeding me a bunch of shit to take a vacation to Maine at my expense?"

"I can assure you that that isn't the case Mrs. Williams. Adam Crane was run through an NCIC database from a sheriff's department. Same birthdate. Same ID number. That was yesterday. I have the officer's information. If this Ryan—if Ryan Carpenter is there, I'll find him."

"I want you to get in touch with your friend, the one who handles things. I need this taken care of as soon as possible."

Johnson put his glass down on the small table between him and Victoria then stood to leave. "I'll be in touch Mrs. Williams." He nodded to Wendell and showed himself out.

Victoria wriggled her toes and reached down to wipe away some grit clinging to the side of her foot. "Wendell, dear, is my darling husband in his office?"

"I'll check."

"Thank you."

Wendell turned to walk toward the house.

"One more thing, Wendell."

"Yes?"

"If you ever look at my tits again, I'll cut your fucking eyes out."

TWENTY-FOUR

Two days after he'd found the photos at Kurt's, Ryan sat in
his room at the Tavern with his feet on the windowsill, staring out at the store across the street, thinking about Jennifer
and the pulp hook, what he should tell Malcolm, what that
would do to Olivia. The steady movement of customers
went in and out of the store, and he thought about his birth
name on a piece of granite in the cemetery. There, in a dank
and run-down room above a bar in a town that ran life into
despair, he began to embrace the thought of being completely
isolated, where he wouldn't have to hear the sound of another human voice. Hearing is the last of the senses to go
when a person dies. He would hate to die in that town with
the voices of those people chanting through his thoughts.

He wondered, peering down into the cabs of trucks and
through the back windows of cars to the soft skulls of children in car seats swinging their arms at siblings, what would
have become of him if he'd never had to leave, if his mother
had decided to endure the ruthlessness of his father. How
different would that town have been if there hadn't been
anything they considered legendary to define it? If they
hadn't been afforded the opportunity to embrace tragedy as
a defining characteristic? Did what happen to his family

somehow shape the nature of the people in that town?

And then he thought about Jennifer again, the melding of memories he had of her, the times she'd tucked board games into the closet when he was a child, and how she sunk her teeth into his shoulder the night before. How she was the real reason he was there, and how impossibly definitive despair had finally become. *This is where you are.* None of it mattered. It didn't matter why he was there. What mattered was what he was there to do. Kurt preyed on the weaknesses of the people around him, and from the excited exchanges of conversations about Kurt, and what he'd done to Patricia and Jennifer, Kurt was as good a reason to be there as any. Ryan was there to make someone gone. Simon wanted Kurt gone, so that's what he would do. He'd get the photos of Jennifer to Simon when Kurt was dead. Simon could handle the rest.

Malcolm's truck backed into a space at the store. When he got out, he pulled an envelope from the dashboard and crossed the street to the Tavern. Ryan met him at the door of the room.

"You hear about Kurt?" Malcolm asked.

"Not really a town for secrets, is it?"

"Nope. No, it isn't."

"You should come in. I don't really like standing in doorways."

Malcolm stepped inside.

"This came for you." He held out the envelope.

Ryan took it and tore the flap open. Inside, a birth certificate, ID, social security card, and a passport. His new name.

"So, I went and talked to Arthur Carlton. That's Olivia and Jennifer's father. He's who Mike and I were leasing land from. He's not going to give up Mike's lease to Kurt."

Ryan pushed the papers back into the envelope. "That's not all that surprising, is it? Besides, it's time to deal with what I came here for."

"Really? Now?"

"Yeah."

"When?"

"Within the next couple of days."

Malcolm scratched his stomach. A smile broke his solemn expression as he scanned the room. "This place is a fucking shithole. I've got that trailer on the lot next to mine that you're welcome to. It ain't much, but it's better than this."

"I'll make my way over there tomorrow. It'll be better to move from a place that's so conspicuous."

"Good. Good. Say, let me buy you a beer, hunh?"

"Alright. Let's go have a beer. I'll meet you down there."

When Malcolm left, Ryan went to the corner of the room and moved the dresser. The corner of the carpet came up easily, and he tucked the envelope beneath it. Now, only he'd know where it was. And it would be easy enough to get to. He used a wooden shim that had been jammed into the window to keep it from rattling in the wind and tucked the fraying edge of the carpet back down against the tack strip.

Nicole pulled the two beers from the cooler and carried them over to the bar. She smiled at Malcolm and made it wider as she nudged a beer toward Ryan. Olivia was already at the bar and she moved down the row of stools toward them.

"Hey boys," she said.

Ryan sipped his beer, avoiding the aggressive plea of

Nicole's stare for him to make eye contact.

"Hell, Nicole, you trying to burn a hole through him?" Olivia asked, a little more than a whisper, just enough so the four of them could hear.

Ryan flashed a quick smile. Nicole winked and left to tend to other customers. He kept his gaze just over the edge of the bar after that, so he wouldn't have to acknowledge Nicole again or the clippings on the Tavern's walls.

After a while, the barstools around them began to fill. This was a different crowd—the people who didn't spend their nights in the bar, who lived in that town but hid themselves away from the stain it would leave if they spent too much time out in the open. Those people dressed differently, too. Collared shirts that had been run through a washing machine tucked into jeans. They wore boots that weren't caked with mud or shit, and their hands were clean. The stench of diesel fuel and sweat was absent from them. One man, alone, bobbing his head to the music with a big goofy grin on his face, caught Ryan's eye. The man wore Velcro sandals and socks up to his knees. Like the majority of the other people, he appeared happy. There was a happy side to that town, maybe. When the man made eye contact with Ryan, he lifted his beer, and Ryan noticed the two watches on his wrist. Must be very prompt, Ryan thought. A small circle of people gathered around one of the round tables, propping their guitar cases up against the wall. The Sunday Jam. As the noise level and traffic through the room whirled around him, the more he wanted to slip away. He thanked Malcolm for the beer and drifted through the crowd back up to his room as the music began.

Jennifer pulled into the parking lot, and Ryan watched her with a bit of sorrow as she got out of her truck and crossed the street to the store. Simon might make him deal with her. Simon would expect him to deal with her. Probably, he should just do it, and get it over with, prevent any more fallout with what could happen with Kurt. He went to the bed and rolled into it and put his back against the headboard. The music from the bar vibrated softly through the coils, and he closed his eyes, letting the hum in the metal springs help him drift closer to sleep. At that moment where his consciousness was about to plummet, the knock hit the door. He shook his head to find focus in his vision and climbed from the bed to answer. In the hallway, the sounds of the band had less vibration but there was more noise.

Jennifer lifted a six-pack of beer. "Care to share a couple of drinks with a lady?"

Her hair was pinned over the knot on her head. Ryan took a step back to let her in and shut the door. She twisted the top from a bottle and tipped it up, sucking back a little more than half before offering Ryan one.

He thanked her and moved to his chair, repositioning it so that he could lean against the wall, keep the window on his right and her on his left. "You must be planning for an early night only bringing a six-pack."

"I figured we'd already gotten the foreplay out of the way." She sat on the bed.

"Is that any way to talk to a gentleman?"

She moved the bottle to her lips and drank, keeping her eyes on him. "I don't need anything gentle from you right now."

Every man has a type.

Ryan leaned forward, rested his elbows on his knees, and took a long look at her. He could get away from there. He had his papers. He could slip through Kurt's that night, before he left town. What he needed was on the bed in front of him. That sip of his beer cooled the sides of his tongue as he moved across the room. Jennifer's eyes moved across his chest as he stood over her. He took her bottle and set it on the nightstand as he slipped his other hand over her shoulder and up the back of her neck. With a firm grip of her hair, he ran his knuckles over the corner of her lips, her chin, and down her throat.

TWENTY-FIVE

Malcolm moved down the narrow steps into his cellar. His T-shirt was wet along the spine where he'd sweat in his sleep. The dream faded as he tried to remember it. Maybe he'd find it again in the light of the refrigerator where he went for a beer. Lately, he'd found it difficult to find sleep, but tonight was different. This time wasn't because of the stress that had plagued him for the last couple months. A nervous excitement filled him that he hadn't felt in a long time, since Mike had been born. Then he thought about the stages of Mike's life, all the things he'd wished he'd done for his son—things he should have thought about sooner, like spending more time with him, being a little more present instead of retreating to his camp. He realized that even then, with what he was going to do to Kurt, that it was all more about him than Mike. Kurt had taken away the chance for him be a better father, but it was Kurt who made him realize that. Maybe that's why he wanted to kill Kurt, because Kurt showed him that he hadn't been much of a father. Malcolm looked out on his porch at the silver toolbox, chainsaws, and gas cans stacked against the wall. The tire chains hung from the rafters with the chaps and saw-resistant rubber boots on the floor beneath them. Malcolm finished his beer and left the can on the windowsill that he passed on his way back up to the loft where he finally fell asleep.

Olivia stared at the ceiling from her bed. There was a chill in her room. There had always been a chill, but she'd forgotten about it for a while, until she finally found a desire to sleep in there. She'd turned the face of the alarm clock against the wall to reduce the light that it cast through the space. It sprayed an arc of blue against the wall behind her, the edge of it shining close to the ceiling. She rubbed the ball of her foot against her instep and ankle. Exhaustion. Deep in her body, her legs especially, but her mind kept churning things over and over. She thought about her mother, the days she'd kneel in the garden and turn the soil, murdering the clumps of dirt that had bonded, casting away the stones that had risen, flinging the small weeds behind her where they'd formed a line. The memory became more vivid, and just beyond the slicing sound of the garden spade stabbing into the ground, she heard her mother whispering. That must have been when it started, why they hadn't seen it until it was too late, until she was no longer whispering but screaming into walls in the middle of the night. Eventually, she was cast away like one of those dirty stones, and out of guilt or necessity, Olivia's father had moved them to this wretched town in Maine, a town that twisted and writhed more and more each year, like a root that continues to find a way to burrow through the smallest spaces of rock. Her eyelids finally went heavy, and she wondered, as she drifted off to sleep, if she'd leave that town before she started screaming into the walls.

* * *

The gas station lights were bright over her car. Patricia limped out of the store, the gash on her foot bandaged and cleaned, but the pain was present and it seemed fitting to her as she climbed in. The coffee reminded her of meeting Nolan for the first time, his charm, his continual upbeat demeanor, how it gave her some will to push through those last treatments, helped her develop a new perspective on what she'd do with her life. She wished he hadn't been there that day at The Kodiak, so she could have left Ironwood and gone to him. But she realized during those moments with Kurt that Nolan was just another man who would dismiss her, assume he knew what was best for her, think of her as a possession. It exhausted her, men assuming control of things they thought she wanted. She'd told him that before she left his house, and he hadn't said anything to try to stop her.

Headed south, toward I-95, she would finally get away from Ironwood, out of Maine, south out of New England for the first time, past the Mason-Dixon line, down into the deep South and Louisiana. She'd go all the way to New Orleans, to her brother Simon, as far away from Kurt as possible, far from Maine and Nolan and the haunting memories of her past. Nobody would even care that she was gone. She was finally leaving, and she'd never go back.

Ryan could feel the world sleep around him. It made him vibrant and restless. The night beckoned him, to get out below the stars, taste the damp, smoky flavor of the air. In his mind, he walked through all the different rooms he'd lived in, the walls he'd hunkered behind to watch the world, the places he'd stayed and observed. As much as he didn't belong there in Ironwood, and maybe never belonged there, he *was* there. He was there to bring the town another story, another volume of gossip, and nobody would see how the new was connected to the old, how one story connected to the previous. The darkness in the sky began to fade and cool into lighter shades of blue. He leaned forward slowly until the legs of the chair were on the floor, and he rose from the seat to find a little rest. The stuffing in the mattress muffled the shrieks of the springs from his weight. He tucked his face into his elbow to filter out the air of the room as he breathed.

Kurt shuffled through the despair of his house carrying a bottle of Scotch. Jennifer had been there, looking for things he'd hidden in the water heater. She hadn't found them. He'd already checked to make sure, the pulp hook resting on top where he'd left it. Patricia had taken the .38, though, but that didn't surprise him, not after what had happened.

He stepped around the pile of books, the scattered armrest covers and couch cushions, and wandered into the kitchen where he hunted a small tumbler from the cabinet. Better to drink from a glass, he told himself. He went out to the porch, sat in the rocking chair again, and took a drink without hesitation.

His deep breaths pulled the scent of Scotch from his teeth and into his lungs as he rocked. Specks of sand that had flung from the soles of his boots when he walked onto the porch crushed into the floorboards under the rockers of the chair. He tried to listen for it, the subdued grind as he rocked forward. At the tree line to the west, the spaces between the trees were dark and grim. Fog began to rise from the damp forest floor and the apparition of a body moved through the gray. He took another drink, closed his eyes and saw Mike in his thoughts. Kurt smelled the choky oil and gas stench in the air and got up from the chair and went into the house. He returned with the bottle he'd left on the counter, poured himself another drink, and muttered that the dead should stay dead.

The follicles on the back of her head still tingled on the edge of pain as Jennifer rolled from sleep. The night was quiet save for the sounds of crickets outside. She recounted the events, from that first hard yank that exposed her throat to him, to that last thrust that slammed a faint mist of sweat from her sternum. He'd collapsed next to her, his eyes staring off into the void, somewhere in the corner, and he didn't protest while she fuck-staggered around the room to gather her things, a stupid elation stretched across her face until she'd gotten home and fell into the bed.

She pulled the flat edge of the sheet tight over her chin, forcing her mouth open, letting the air dip into the open space like a toe testing the water of an unfamiliar pool. She exhaled slowly, staring up at the ceiling, debating how badly she wanted a cigarette. The craving drifted down her throat to her chest until she could feel it in her stomach, settling there like a small ball of heat. The sheet ruffled as she yanked it away and rolled toward the nightstand. The pack inside the drawer was empty, and she crumpled it inside her fist and flung it toward the corner of the room. She climbed out of bed, pulled her jeans back over her legs and ass, crammed her feet into a pair of boots that she didn't lace up, and found a hoody in the pile of clothes on her way out to her truck.

A paper clip binding pieces of paper buzzed against the windshield. The sky was clear, and Jennifer ignored the sheer darkness speckled with the light of stars on her way to Skowhegan, to the only store within thirty miles that was open after eight p.m. She'd lost her craving for a cigarette just a short distance from the store but went inside and purchased a pack anyway. The first inhale, the first smoky flume that satisfied what she remembered of her craving, tasted like a food she enjoyed but hadn't had in a long time. After that, the cigarette smoke just tasted like newspaper. Nausea made her speed toward home, hoping she could sleep until noon. She thought about Ryan's hand, the scar and missing finger, how he'd kept it out of sight. Then she thought about Kurt, how little his hands were and those big stupid beaver pelt mittens he wore in the winter. They'd been hanging near the door of his house when she was there. And she realized then that Kurt couldn't have started the chainsaw to cut that tree down that crushed Mike with his mittens on. Her mind began to roll out a plan ahead of her, one that made sense enough in the moment for her to convince herself that Kurt's fingerprints on Mike's chainsaw would mean anything.

Victoria walked quietly into Williams' office. The lights were low and her husband leaned back in his leather chair swirling the cubes of ice in his whiskey.

"Roy?" She crossed the soft, dark area rug to his desk and sat in the leather chair across from him. "Roy, is everything alright?"

"That hardly seems like a question you need to ask." He

lifted the drink then set it back down.

"Roy, Johnson called." She shifted to the edge of her seat. "He found him. He found Ryan."

Williams kept his chin down but moved his eyes to look up at her. "Is this news supposed to excite me?"

"Why wouldn't it?"

"Because the man you found probably killed my son. Did finding him bring my son back to me?"

"No, but we could—"

"We could what? What could we do? You want to bring him back here and keep him prisoner? Make him tell us what he did with Roy? And what if he tells us what we already know, that Roy is dead, that my only son is dead? What then, Victoria? We have him killed? That's what we do?" Williams took a drink that time. "We're—I'm not that kind of person. It was a mistake to let you talk me into this arrangement in the first place, getting Roy relocated. That was the problem. The boy never had to hold himself accountable. His mother spoiled him. You spoiled him. And it got him killed."

"Are you implying that it's my fault if Roy is dead?"

"I'm not *implying* that at all."

"What is it you really want to say, Roy?"

Williams huffed. "You know, that's probably the reason I married you, that confrontational directness of yours. I didn't try to fool myself, though. I never expected you to love me. That's a goddamn miserable show anyhow, people in love. But I didn't expect you to betray me either, especially not with my own son. So, if it's direct you want, then that's what I'll give you. I don't have the means to prove your infidelity, and I wouldn't want to. I wouldn't subject myself to that salacious embarrassment. I've never claimed to be the brightest bulb, but I didn't get myself to this point in life by being oblivious. I'm divorcing you. I've had my lawyer draw up the papers. They'll be in Dallas when you return. You can keep the house there, since it's your favorite, and the condos. As soon as my lawyer gets the signed papers from you, I'll wire ten million into your account. I want nothing to do with this anymore, with you or your hunt for this Ryan Carpenter person or anything else that comes of it." He finished his drink and stood. "I expect that you'll be gone by tomorrow afternoon."

TWENTY-SIX

Malcolm took his time to load the rifle. It's how he'd decided to kill Kurt, how he'd been thinking about killing Kurt since the day he'd found that sloppy notch in the stump on Mike's yard. Then all those days and thoughts, how many times he'd seen himself killing a man, poured into him again all at once. His breath quickened as he pushed his shells into the rifle with the nylon gloves on his hands that Ryan had given him. *Are you sure you want to do this?* Ryan had asked. And when Malcolm told Ryan that he'd been thinking about pushing Kurt's face through the back of his skull for a long time, Ryan had simply said, *Messy*, and waited outside.

Malcolm followed Ryan through the woods, felt the familiarity of the occasional night hunts he'd do, when he had a craving for venison and it was two months away from opening day. Ryan's movement was so slow that a few times Malcolm lost sight of his silhouette in the darkness of the trees and thought he was gone. His eyes weren't what they used to be at night.

Kurt was on his porch, the rocking chair serving as his new post instead of in front of the television in his living room. His chair rocked an inch at a time, the porch light dimmed by the hovering swath of moths and other insects.

Malcolm could have taken the shot there, and Kurt would slump in that rocker until someone finally noticed him. Even then, Malcolm imagined not many would care about his murder. But there wasn't going to be a murder. That's why Ryan was there, to make it look like Kurt had left, shamed by what had happened with his wife. That's what people would think, anyway.

Ryan left Malcolm in a patch of ferns, where his movement to position himself would be concealed, and whatever slight noise he might make minimal. The ferns tickled his ears as the breeze wafted them, and Malcolm waited for that movement of ferns to adjust his feet, lean into the tree behind him and dig his heels into the dirt. He pushed his elbows against his thighs and made sure he could cover Kurt's movement from the porch to the side of the house. Ryan would move through the woods, through Kurt's yard just out of range from the motion-sensor lights, then through the back door up to the front of the house. He'd close and lock the front door so Kurt would have to walk around to the back to get in, where he'd move beneath the sensors and ignite the yard with illumination. He'd squint and look up at those lights as if he were surprised that they were there, hold a hand over his face to block the glare. Then Malcolm would put a .308 round through the base of his skull. *Blood is easier to cover with dirt than clean off a wall*, Ryan had said. Malcolm listened for Ryan's movement but heard nothing. Fatigue spread through him, heavy, like sand trying to push through his veins.

Ryan eased himself down the embankment an inch at a time, listening for the rhythm of tires on the tar, the glow of headlights in the trees. In the ditch, he hovered close to the ground, extending his hand out to palm the tar, feel the day's heat being sucked away from it. He kept his gaze parallel with the road, closed his left eyelid to maintain his low-light vision before he looked down to the bend where the porch light at Kurt's glowed through the foliage.

Across the road, Ryan moved toward the fence post that marked the pasture where Kurt's cattle grazed, and he slipped beneath the barbed wire and crouched at the edge of the yard. In the pasture, lightning bugs flickered their tiny beacons—hundreds of them, maybe thousands, shimmering in the darkness. Those flickers about the amount of time it would take for Malcolm to pull his trigger. Kurt's existence would be torn through a hole and dispersed over the ground along the bullet's path. Ryan followed the fading, iridescent pulse toward the light hovering over Kurt. They were still there, those green flashes, and among them, beyond Kurt's front yard, just inside the tree line from the road, a faint illumination of indigo. The light from a watch. Ryan froze, lowered himself to the ground one knuckle at a time through his hand then inch by inch until he was flat, peering over the fragments of bark and decaying leaves. He worked his fingers over the soil, his hands crawling toward his face to cup as much light from his eyes as possible. It took a while, but he finally saw it, the silhouette between the trees.

He lay there, waiting for it to move, but Kurt moved first, pushing himself from the rocker to his knees. He worked to get to his feet, kicking an empty bottle over the floorboards, and stumbled through the door to his house. Ryan waited for the shot, hoping it wouldn't come, that Malcolm would be patient enough to stick to the plan. Kurt's door closed, and Ryan seeped out a breath of relief against the moist dirt touching his lips. The silhouette moved carelessly out to the tar and walked down to a cut-in between the trees on the other side of the street. There was the sound of an engine. The truck pulled out onto the road, drove quietly past Kurt's, then threw the headlights down the tar. Jennifer's truck.

Back at the camp, Ryan stood against the wall just inside the door watching Malcolm slowly pull each round from his gun. He thought to tell him then, the truth about Kurt and Jennifer, and a sudden guilt swept over him. He'd nearly let Malcolm murder a man who, despite how much Malcolm hated him, wasn't responsible for his son's death. Malcolm would still be angry that Kurt used his son's death in an attempt to gain something for himself, but Ryan didn't see Malcolm as the type of person who wanted to kill because he was upset. He didn't see Malcolm as the type of person to kill, even if he believed that Kurt did kill his son. Malcolm put the bullets on the table, lining the primer ends with the edge.

"I put him in my crosshairs. Almost took the shot."

"I'm glad you didn't. That would have been a bigger mess than we were ready to handle."

"The truck that passed by, that looked a lot like Jennifer's."

"It was Jennifer's."

"What the hell was she doing?"

"Same thing we were."

Malcolm set the rifle against the wall. "What the hell is she thinking?"

"She's angry. Kurt got some special treatment, and she wants justice. She'll cool down. We'll get another chance."

Malcolm scratched his chin. "It wasn't the same."

"What's that?"

"I've put a lot of things in my crosshairs, a lot more than

I've ever killed." He massaged his palm with his thumb. "You know, the two tours I did in 'Nam, I only killed one man. Black boy, maybe only a couple years younger than me, but it was his first tour and a tour aged a man different over there. I was on my second. He was bad off, had pongee sticks all through him, from his ankles to his asshole. I don't know how they got him out of that pit, but they did, and they called me up there and there was nothing I could do for that boy. I told someone to get the chaplain, I think. I was waiting for someone, I remember. During that time that I was waiting, that boy held my hand and begged me for morphine. I knew what he was asking me, and at first I couldn't see myself doing it, but I looked down and saw the mess that pit had made of him and I wondered what his mother might think of me if I saved him, got him sent home so she could hold her boy again. And then I thought about how I would feel if I were that boy, and I had to go home to my mother all maimed to shit. Having her wipe my ass, hold my cock while I pissed, listen to me scream in the night like a goddamn baby." Malcom's face shuddered, and his tears came. "I overdosed that boy on morphine before I could think twice about it, and he was gone almost as quick as a bullet to the head would have taken him. I've never felt guilty about that. But tonight, when I saw the back of Kurt's head in my scope, I thought about what it would mean to take a life like that, to murder someone. I probably shouldn't feel that way, with what Kurt did, but I do, and I don't think—I can't kill that man. I don't want to. I'm not a murderer. I think that maybe, tonight went exactly the way it should have." He wiped his tears from his face. "I'm sorry that you're here, that you came all this way for nothing. I'll understand if you're angry about that."

"It's a good feeling to know that you're human. Don't be sorry about that. You should get some sleep. Kurt will get what's coming to him. You don't need to be the one to do it. In the meantime, I'm here, and I'm here because Simon wants me to be here until what's done is done. It's best if I continue my role as your helper for the time being."

TWENTY-SEVEN

Victoria sat in the sunroom of her Dallas home with Johnson, looking through the stack of photos that he'd provided. *The Ironwood Tavern.* Must be a gem, she thought. She flipped each photo gingerly, by its corner, and moved them face down on the coffee table. Ryan appeared weary, tired, more so than he had when she'd first met him. It was hard to imagine the man in the photographs as quippy as she remembered, but it was definitely Ryan. When she finished with the stack, she neatened them back into a pile and set them on her knees.

"I'd like to keep these for now."

"You paid for them," Johnson said, his hands still, finally.

"What's with the two watches?"

He lifted his arm. "Just in case one breaks. Old habit from the military."

"And this friend of yours who can handle the rest of the job. How do I go about acquiring his services?"

"I've already contacted him, briefed him on some things. He's available for hire."

"And when do I get to meet him."

"You don't."

"No?"

"No. You don't meet him. You don't get his name. All you get is a number. You wire the funds to that account and the job gets done. Funds in full, by the way."

"And what happens if the job's not done? The reason I'm in this mess in the first place is because a job wasn't done."

"These are the risks, Mrs. Williams. I can assure you that my contact is quite reliable."

Johnson pulled a slip of paper from his pocket and handed it to Victoria. "My contact has the details. He'll begin as soon as the funds are transferred. But you only have twenty-four hours to make your decision."

"This isn't good enough. I'll need proof. Can your associate provide that?"

"That's standard."

She looked down at the numbers, then back at Johnson. "Are you serious?"

"About what?"

"The fee?"

"Yes. Again, that's standard."

"It's ridiculous."

"Oh?"

"Yes. I've paid *you* much more than this."

"Groundwork is expensive."

Victoria reached to the table and picked up her glass of wine that she hadn't touched since Johnson arrived. "Apparently so."

"Is there anything else, Mrs. Williams? Any special instructions on handling your issue?"

She took a drink. "Yes, actually." She set the glass down and leaned back on the couch. "After your guy finds out where Melissa and her son are, I want Ryan Carpenter's face taken off his fucking skull."

Johnson stood to leave.

"Johnson."

"Yes?"

"How soon will this be done?"

"I can't guarantee a date, but the job will get done. You'll be notified upon completion."

Johnson left. Before he'd driven down the driveway to the gate, Victoria wired the money.

TWENTY-EIGHT

It took six days to finish the fields, two of them interrupted by rain—an angled deluge that left the low parts of the fields where they'd already hayed a shallow marsh. The gray roads glistened black and the worms crawled out of the ground and over the tar. Some of them were smashed by tires. Ryan embraced the solitude of the fields while he was working. The bales of hay that he moved from the field to the trailer and then to the lofts in the barn had worn against his forearms, scraped the skin down to the points of capillaries—enough for him to feel his skin burn, but barely ever enough for his blood to seep through. Ryan had kept an eye on Kurt, and Jennifer, unable to do what he needed to do before he could leave.

They'd taken a day off before they headed into the woods, down to Mike's yard. The camper smelled of mothballs and stale grain, old rags that had collected dust for a decade. It was quiet except for the owl that he heard almost every night, the nights there weren't coyotes yipping in the distance. Some nights, he thought he missed the drone of voices from the Tavern, but the absence of human sound helped him to sleep, like he was alone somewhere far away from people and Ironwood and all the noise in his mind that reminded him of who he was.

Droplets of water clung to the side of Malcolm's Dodge. The front quarter-panels shined in the sunlight. When Ryan opened the passenger door, he saw the muddy sand clinging to the edges of Malcolm's boots.

"How about a coffee?" Malcolm asked.

Ryan pushed the chainsaw chaps to the middle of the seat and climbed in. *I don't wear 'em,* Malcolm had said. *Chaps are for cowboys and faggots.*

At the store, Malcolm walked with a sway in his shoulders. The same after they left and walked back to the truck. Coffee streamed down the sides of the Styrofoam cup he carried, the bounce in his shoulders spewing coffee from the small oval hole in the lid. The left corner of his lip hung slightly more open than usual, a shifted smile on his face. He drove hunched over the wheel, holding the coffee cup on the dashboard. There was a chill in the air that would be gone within an hour or so, but the gap in the passenger window forced a shiver through Ryan.

Malcolm slowed the truck at the crest of a hill and steered between two giant maples. The road to the yard sloped down through the field on the east side of Arthur Carlton's house. The sun had finally surfaced above the tree line on the far ridge and made the dew-wet field a sheet of silver. When they passed into the tree line at the bottom, the brightness weakened beneath the pine branches. There was a shack to the right, fraying blue tarps stapled and tied to the wood holding it together. It looked flimsy, but Malcolm said it held heat, and that it was a goddamn relief during the cold, bitter days that the wind swept down through the field and spun through the yard. Malcolm pulled the truck next to the skidder, a yellow-brown steel monster with cables sprouting from its back end.

He led Ryan across the skidder trail to the wood splitter and pulled the tarp that had blanketed the hydraulic machine. Under the steel I-beam frame of the splitter, two chainsaws lay side by side, like lovers or rabid creatures that had died together. Malcolm strutted over to the cabin and pulled a rusty toolbox from just inside the door. The weight of the tools inside made the handle creak.

"Grab those saws," Malcolm told him.

Malcolm let the tailgate down and rapped the dented metal hard. Ryan put the saws down on the tailgate and Malcolm rifled his thick fingers through the grease-blackened tools in the box. He pulled out a round file and grabbed one of the saws, maneuvered it against the edge of the tailgate, and hunkered over it. The sound was smooth, almost soothing, as he pushed the round file against the teeth of the chain. Ryan measured the angle, counting the strokes, the teeth. He expected Malcolm to speak to him, to explain what he was doing like he had when they'd done the haying, but Malcolm remained silent as he worked. When he had pulled the chain around completely and sharpened that side of the chain's teeth, Malcolm turned the saw around and tucked it under his opposite shoulder. He repeated the ceremony with the file on the other side of the chain.

For the first hour, Ryan did nothing but watch Malcolm prep the saws and check the chains of his skidder. He'd been down the day before to turn the skidder's engine over, admitting it had been longer than it should have been since he'd done that. It took a while for the machine to start, but it did, waking slow and clumsy before chugging to life. After Malcolm had let the skidder idle in the corner of the yard for a while, he took it down the trail, leaving Ryan there to wait. Ryan thought about following, to see where the road headed, to see the giant machine yank logs off the ground. The ragged tail of cables and chains clinked together, and why Malcolm called the skidder *Marley*, finally made sense. He judged how far Malcolm had taken the skidder by the changes in the engine's volume. The cables made a different noise and before long, the skidder was approaching again but had replaced the chain melody with the harsh sound of snapping branches. Malcolm dragged the logs close to the splitter. He moved a lever in the cage and the thick ends of the logs he'd dragged dropped to the ground, vibrating through the roots and the dirt under Ryan's feet. Malcolm hopped down, pulled his chainsaw from the cage, and had it whaling into the air by the time he passed the enormous back tire.

Malcolm walked a meter-length stick, an international rule, down the trunks of the logs, cutting a line where he'd stopped measuring out the board feet, a spray of bark flinging through the air. He repeated this for all the logs then cut off the tops and left those for Ryan to cut into stove-length pieces of firewood to split while he went back into the woods.

The saw sliced through the logs, hungry to sink through the wood. Ryan expected it to grind and tear, but it didn't. The thing that it would tear through, though, was flesh. He finished cutting through the twitch that Malcolm had dragged up then started the splitter. The solitude of the work, the smell of hot oil and wood, the motor's exhaust mixed into the new flavor of the air, gave Ryan a sense of reassurance. There was something else he could do, work that he could find redemption in—something he could seek out when he moved on from Ironwood. He lay the first log in the path of the wedge on the splitter, another chunk of steel that would crush bone and mangle flesh should it get in the machine's way.

The next twitch was all white pine. Malcolm climbed from the skidder with the rule and his saw and walked down the length of the trees, the way he'd done with the hardwood. The chainsaw cut through the soft wood faster than the oak and maple that Ryan was splitting into firewood. There were two piles growing taller behind him, heaps of what would eventually be reduced to ash. One way or another, the trees returned to the ground, like everything else. Would it be better to grow old and rot or to be felled and burned? He thought back to the house he grew up in, the smell of the woods his father had carried.

At noon, Ryan had worked the split wood into three separate heaps, large mounds of nearly a cord each. He'd worked quickly, finding a rhythm with splitting, stopping the wedge at the point where a log would fit just inside the gap. Malcolm had collected a truckload of pulp for the paper mills in Skowhegan. Ryan kept working, his head down, until Malcolm shuffled over to him. He stopped the motor on the splitter and when the noise left the air, Ryan could still feel the hum of the machine's vibration in his forearms and elbows. It tingled, like he'd been gripping a wheel too tightly for too many miles over uneven gravel.

"Time for lunch," Malcolm said. Then he pointed over Ryan's right shoulder to the pile of wood. "Not bad for your first day. And you still have all your fingers and to—" Malcolm stopped speaking. He looked down at Ryan's left hand. "Shit."

Ryan curled his four-fingered hand into a fist, bunching the empty finger of the glove against his thigh. "I'll be extra careful to keep the ones I started with anyway."

The truck ride out through the field put the sun directly over them, shining on the cracked dashboard. The wet smell of dew was gone, and the air was drying, carrying more the scent of granite. Ryan balled his hands into fists, working out the kink that had settled in the meaty part of his palm below his thumb—a pain that had become present when he stopped slumping logs onto the splitter. Malcolm reached down under one of the blankets over the seat of his truck and pulled a blue racquetball from the tangle of the blankets. He tossed it over to Ryan.

"It'll help with the stiffness. You might have to give them a soak in Epsom's later tonight. Try using the pulp hook if it gets to be too much."

Ryan worked the ball, first in his left hand, but it forced too much pain in the pinky knuckle, so he switched it to his right. Sheep scattered through the field on the right side of the road as they passed, and the air was damp again with the smell of shit. It faded after they'd gone down the stretch of tar past the fields they'd hayed. The metal roof of the barn glinted in the sunlight, reminded Ryan of the grass that morning on their way to the yard. A shimmer caught Ryan's eye and he looked in the side mirror. A truck sped toward them. Kurt.

Malcolm adjusted in his seat, pulled his ball cap off and tucked it onto the dash in front of the wheel. A band of matted wet hair haloed his head. Malcolm ran his fingers through the black mess.

Kurt parked across the street at the Tavern. He lumbered from the cab of his truck and slammed the door. Then he stomped up the steps to the bar.

They sat in the truck facing the bare white wall of the store and unwrapped the sandwiches they'd bought. Malcolm complaining about how little meat they'd put on his pastrami sandwich, the wilted lettuce dangling from the edges. Dust and clutter on the dashboard did little to keep Malcolm from laying the top layer of bread there. A thin line of mayo streaked the windshield. He opened the truck door and swept the lettuce onto the ground and muttered obscenities.

"You want half of mine?" Ryan asked.

"Nope." It came out sounding more like *Note*.

"Something on your mind?" Ryan asked.

Malcolm sighed. "I really hate that motherfucker. Maybe I should have just manned up and done what had to be done that night."

"You were smart not to do something that night. You're smart to leave it alone. Hindsight, regret, those are just distractions from what you really feel. This isn't yours anymore. You could have done something, yes, but you didn't. You chose to make your own decision. Kurt makes you angry, but you didn't allow him to make you hate yourself. You've won. When Kurt's dead, he's not going to feel any pain or remorse or guilt. He'll just be dead. And if you're the one who makes him that way, you're the one who's going to feel all of those shitty things. Fuck that guy. He hates you now. Make him hate you more by being happy. That's real revenge."

When they got back to the yard, Ryan noticed the splitting maul propped against the door of the shack. He got out of the truck and walked toward it, grasping the fiber-resin, break-proof handle. The end had been gnawed, what looked like teeth marks from a dog. The texture of small sharp edges came through his glove, the weight at the other end of the maul. Unlike an axe, the weight of the tool was what split logs, smashing its way through the grain, where the wood could be split the easiest.

"Might be a little faster splitting at first, but it'll wear you out," Malcolm said.

Ryan looked at him, the sad defeated look Malcolm had in the Tavern that first day. And then there was the pinch of something else, not in his throat, but in his stomach. He wondered if the only real happiness Malcolm had ever experienced was that morning, when the world was something he had a little control over, before Kurt's presence became a reminder of all that he'd lost—an inadvertent taunting.

"Just be careful," Malcolm said. "Catching the end of that in the shin ain't gonna tickle." He lumbered toward the skidder.

The machine started behind Ryan, the rumbling something almost rhythmic. He measured the weight of the tool in each hand, alternating the heavy end between each grip and discovered that it was comfortable either way, but more with the end of the handle in his right hand. Strange how much power the weakest finger of the hand holds. Ryan looked over the wood. Life is waiting to be split—the fragments flailing out into the air as stove-length pieces of fuel. Some pieces split harder than others, like those days of waiting for something to happen, but even those eventually split apart. And they'll be fed to flame, crumble to coals, and turn to ash. He chose the most crooked piece he could find, hoping to find a part of himself to take out of it.

There was a hovering weightlessness just before he swung the maul, that perfect moment from where he'd drawn it up, and just before he brought it down, that natural pause in breathing. Then the fibrous twitch of thin muscle rolled down the back of his hands and up his forearms to his shoulders and then widened over his back and the motion of the head of the maul was so quick that the split-second bend in the handle wasn't visible. The shock of that sudden stop at impact sent a jolt down the handle and into Ryan's fingers and forearms where it died out somewhere near his elbow.

Ryan had smashed through the toughest of the logs by the time Malcolm returned on the skidder. Chains rattled and the twitch dropped to the ground.

TWENTY-NINE

Jennifer pulled a loose string from the third button of her uniform. She squinted at the sun, even behind the Ray Ban aviators. When the string came loose she held it in front of her face and twisted it through the sun's glare that toppled over the roof of the Tavern porch across the street and flailed itself from the hood of the patrol truck and through the windshield. For days she'd been watching Kurt. The Tavern had become a daily venture for him. That morning, she'd lain in bed after she'd been awake for hours thinking about him, how a few moments of bad judgement crept between the threads of her tight little life, which had been stretched to a point that everything would slip through. She realized when she'd put on her uniform that morning that control was something taken, not offered.

Kurt walked out of the Tavern and charged across the street to her window. He breathed heavily. The stink of Scotch hurled through the cab and she turned her face from him and the string and the sun. The American flag on the front porch of the Tavern snapped in the wind. An Audi with Quebec plates blasted by her. She fetched a breath of untainted air and looked back at Kurt.

"Back on the sauce again? Quite a head start for the day, too."

"Why the hell is Malcolm cutting on the land?"

"Wasn't my decision to make."

"I told you what would happen. I warned you goddammit."

She clenched her teeth and glared at him as he marched away and got into his truck. His brake lights pulsed as he backed out onto 201 and headed toward home. The wind flattened and the snapping flag on the porch of the Tavern went soft and lay still in the air.

After a right turn onto Indian Hill, she saw the dark color of Kurt's truck a half mile up the road. He rounded the bend to the long stretch of empty road. She reached over to the console and flicked on the flashing lights. The engine lagged for a moment after she'd pressed the gas pedal to the floor. Then the truck lurched forward, screaming and flashing down the quiet street.

She'd rolled her grip from pinky to index finger on the steering wheel as she sped toward him. The truck eased onto the shoulder. She pulled in behind it and climbed from the cab. The tar was clean and black. New. A paving crew had spent three weeks in May redoing that stretch of road. The heat made the tar feel soft under her feet. She touched the tender bump on her head from Kurt's tire iron then unsnapped the button on the holster of her service weapon—habit.

Kurt's voice lolled to her as he spoke into his mirror, watching her approach. "What the hell are you doing?"

She stepped to the window. "Kurt, you've been drinking today. I need you to step out of the vehicle." She took a step back so Kurt had to crane his neck to look back at her.

He shook his head. "Are you—"

Jennifer drew her service pistol and shot him in the side

of his face. His last words were heft into the air from a tired, dry breath. The bullet blew through his cheek. Blood poured down his neck and spilled over his chest like hot sap. His eyes looped in circles and he choked, blood dribbling over his jaw. She looked in both directions for approaching vehicles then stepped to the window, raised her pistol, and fired again. Kurt flailed over the seat, gone almost instantly, leaving a dark splash of blood on the passenger window to replace the scene where his expression had gone dumb and wide-eyed. The passenger window shifted then tiny squares of glass rained down on the sand and tar and the seat and floorboards. She checked the road again, where she stood, the two brass shell casings at her feet. Then, she pulled out the .38 that she'd taken from Kurt's house from the inside of her shirt.

The back of Kurt's skull was a bloody mess behind his ear. The shot had rolled him from his seat onto the floor. She opened the door and reached over to his wrist, pressed his fingertips onto the handle and cylinder and barrel of the gun. Stepping back, she checked the road again, then reached in to grab the weapon. It clattered on the tar near the door where she dropped it, and she reached in again to push her fingers against his neck where she knew there wouldn't be a pulse. A soft, whimsical smile emerged on her face as she keyed her radio and called it in.

She took flares from a box behind the seat in the patrol truck, sparked them one at a time, then tossed three into the road ahead of Kurt's truck. More behind hers. The trees shaded the tar and the scene was just a strip of bizarre action from above, where the birds sat silent in the branches looking down through the leaves. A crow squawked up the road, calling for another that was off somewhere in the woods.

Three flew over her when she looked up into the edge of the sun that was cresting over the shade of the trees on the east side of the road. The caws echoed, like the sound came from an empty wooden barrel, and she waited for the faint sounds of the sirens that she heard in the distance. A car slowed as it approached from the opposite direction Kurt had been traveling. It stopped at the edge of the flares and she held her palm out as it approached. Bill Kerrigan climbed from the small black sedan, his music blasting into the air like a wind trying to turn over the leaves.

"What the hell happened?"

"Bill, I'm going to have to ask you to go back to your vehicle and remain there."

He looked past her, almost as if he didn't hear, and stepped toward the flares.

"Bill, I need you to back away."

Bill lifted his arms, peered over the thick glasses toward Kurt's truck. "That Kurt's truck? He in there? The hell's going on?"

"I need you to step away and get back into your vehicle."

Bill spotted the gun on the road. "You kill that sonofabitch? Did you?"

"Please back away, Bill."

Bill's shoulders shook and vibrated down into his hips. His smile went a little wider and he nodded several times. "Ding dong," he said. "I'm off to see the wizard." He turned and took two long strides back to his vehicle. He reversed, turned in the road, and sped away. She didn't care to stop him.

* * *

The adrenaline started to settle as she gave her initial statement. The sun had crested and drove its heat straight down on her. She wanted a cigarette. The craving made her entertain the fantasy of stepping off into the woods, as if she could simply sneak off to the side to have a smoke. What would the scene look like from there, behind the leaves? Everything shuffled and the moving parts around her seemed faster, drowning out the murmur of words. Sweat tickled the softer flesh on the inside of her arm, her ribs just below the edge of her bra. She wanted to take that off, unclasp it, roll the shoulder straps down, and pull it through the sleeve of her uniform. What would they all say? Nobody spoke to her. There were no more questions, wouldn't be until later, from people in suits.

The Tavern moaned with a steady throb of patrons. Nicole's brow sweat as she tried to keep up with the movement, the traffic to and from the bar, the constant noise of loud voices and yelling. The laughter. People had begun pouring in just after she'd taken over the afternoon shift. It wasn't evident why so many people had abandoned their routines to venture out in pursuit of celebration until Bill Kerrigan told her what had happened. He was at the bar, eagerly drumming his fingers against the change and keys in his pockets. He'd told her immediately, and the news fell on her with a panic—what Kurt had drunkenly whispered to her the night before: *I know something about Mike that nobody else knows.* And when she'd pressed him, sliding another drink over the bar even though it was past last call, he vaguely responded: *Jennifer will make a good sheriff if Olivia doesn't find another husband who strays.* She'd dismissed it as nothing more than drunken garble, but the news of Kurt made her fetch some connection in his rambling. Olivia had mentioned Mike's affair right after the funeral, and Olivia had made it obvious she thought it was her who'd slept with Mike. The crowd demanded her attention, so she let the thought of Jennifer and Mike slip away.

Even if they'd been asked, none would admit that it was celebration, but the full parking lot, the gathering of patrons that filled the bar, made it nothing short of that. They were celebrating a man's execution, and even if they'd known that, they wouldn't have cared. They were happy that Kurt Myers was dead. Some of them, those whose small mistakes had suffered the brunt of Kurt's maliciousness, were relieved.

Bill was directly responsible for spreading the word. He'd carried it to the store, then the Superette and the post office. Bill stood in the corner of the bar, his gossip-induced pride fading. People had stopped asking him for the story. And Bill was no longer part of it despite how much he'd projected himself into the narrative. He thought back, while he stood in that corner, alone, of the life he'd taken, the years he'd spent in prison trying to remember that night in the whiskey-dim darkness of his memory. But all he'd ever found was the last taste of whiskey he'd ever drank and the pale morning that he found his victim in the driveway with an axe lodged in his chest—fragments of his body over the ground like the contents of a trash bag that had been torn open overnight and shaken out on the lawn.

Olivia's car was parked at Malcolm's and she jumped out as he crested the hill. Ryan saw the frantic look on her face as Malcolm eased the truck onto the gravel next to hers.

Her mouth moved the words, as Malcolm walked toward her, and even though Ryan couldn't hear them, he knew what they were, what Jennifer had done.

Malcolm looked over at him as he climbed out of the truck. "Kurt Myers is dead." Malcolm said, a frown that seemed truly genuine. "Jennifer killed him."

A sweep of relief flushed through Ryan, as if his body sucked coolness from the ground and pushed it through the air above him, off his shoulders. Malcolm stepped past Olivia to take the worn path in the grass to the porch at the back of his home. Olivia followed. Tree branches waved their deciduous flags in response to the mild tremor of the breeze.

He was finally free to leave.

THIRTY

The next day, the town hummed with a different vibration. People moved slower, eyes squinting against the sun's reflection on the windows of the store as they walked in for their morning coffee. Twisted Tea and Allen's Coffee Brandy hangovers pillaged the normal balance the town would have held in the morning. Blisters whined from the palms of Ryan's hands, almost a yelp from the raw meat tint where the skin had torn away on his palms just below his thumbs.

While Malcolm was in the store, Ryan walked through the parking lot down to the post office. He stood at the blue bin outside the lobby door with the envelope he'd addressed to Simon, *Omaha* written where he would have put Simon's name. In his mind he saw Simon opening the envelope, seeing what Jennifer had done and maybe having a faint, shameful realization that his guidelines sometimes failed. For a moment, he thought about tearing the envelope in half, putting a flame to the photos right there. *This is where you are.* The envelope swished away when he let go of the corner. The clumsy donging of the lid vibrated through the blue box and he walked back up to Malcolm's truck.

In the yard, Ryan sat against the pile of white pine and Malcolm hunkered down through the woods on the skidder for a twitch of hardwood. He closed his eyes. The rumble of the skidder engine and the dangling chains faded. Scraping. A faint, smooth sound of steel on stone, and Ryan tried to associate the sound with the skidder, but it came from behind him, at a much slower rate than the drag of chain over rocks. He opened his eyes, saw the slow hover of wasps at the corner of the shack. A flicker of movement caught his attention then a sharp, slicing sting slammed through his left forearm. He turned his head toward the gnawing pain, a knife buried there between the bones and into the soft flesh of the pine. A burst of pressure slammed into his chest. His sudden exhale erupted through his mouth and nose, blowing snot and spit onto his outstretched legs. The man stepped back, posting himself a few feet away.

"Sitting down on the job?" The man asked. "Tsk. Tsk. Tsk."

There was a cool expression on his wide face, stoic. The man from the bar who'd tipped his beer at him. A black beanie pulled snug over his head to his ears. His cotton shirt hung tight over his chest and shoulders. Baggy cargo pants. Sneakers. Ryan reached for the knife, snapping pains in his chest daisy-chained down his sternum. The knife was stuck, solid, and he couldn't pull it out. The man moved toward Ryan and extended his leg, mashing the right side of Ryan's face with the bottom of his sneaker, turning Ryan's face away from his free hand. He gripped Ryan's wrist. A thin burn flew over Ryan's right knuckles, flared through his fingers. The man backed away, wiping blood from another blade against the thigh of his pants.

Ryan stared at him, shock and surprise wearing off. His eyes full of tears, pain spinning through his arm. He knew exactly why that man was there, who'd sent him. What he didn't know was *how*. But that didn't matter. It only mattered that he'd gotten so close, and it would end there. With each breath, Ryan tasted and smelled more and more of what the wind carried—cedar, the decaying leaves on the ground, wet soil, the waxy scent of pine pitch. Death. Ryan swallowed, pushed the pain out of his mind, slowed his breathing. The rumble of the skidder continued to move farther away. Calm. He accepted the notion of death, how it had arrived.

"I didn't think you would be so easy to get the upper hand over."

"Pun intended?" Ryan coughed.

"Hunh? Oh, yes. You are a clever one." The man looked down at his watches. "I've always enjoyed a challenge, and your clever little move with Adam Crane would have gone almost seamless had you not given the man your car keys."

That was how.

"For fuck's sake, dialogue? Just kill me already."

"I can't *just* kill you. I have special instructions."

"Were general instructions too complicated for you?" he asked.

"Victoria Williams wants your face."

"My face? For what? To sit on?"

The man pushed his knife into a horizontal sheath along the belt hitched to his waist. "I didn't ask."

He walked over to the tarped shack and picked up one of the chainsaws, hefting it from the ground, and returned to Ryan. He set the saw at Ryan's feet and looked down on him, at the quivering hand he'd just sliced open.

Ryan jutted his chin toward the saw. "This looks like quite an adventure."

"I think it will be quite painful. I could make it quick. All

I need to know is where the girl and her son are. And what happened to Roy."

"You know, your voice reminds me of a slow, wet shit. I bet you make all the ladies tremor with lust when you whisper in their ears."

The man twisted his lips into a disgusted frown.

"Oh. I see." Ryan smiled. "Impotent? That explains the knives." He nudged the saw with the toe of his boot. "Overcompensating, aren't you?"

"I wonder why people place such emphasis on sexual prowess, especially to insult people. Even worse, to insult the person who's about to kill them."

"Probably because insulting people is fun, and sex is just another way to insult them. Your mother probably liked sex a lot, until you and that big fucking head of yours came out of her." Ryan spit on the ground. "That's it." He pointed at the man with his free arm, his hand dangling and bloody. "That's exactly what your voice sounds like. Childbirth."

The man reached down to pick up the saw and gripped the pull cord.

"You should have a nickname." Ryan scratched an itch on the right side of his face with his shoulder. "How about Fuckhead? Get it?"

The man yanked on the cord. The saw sputtered.

Ryan shook his head, stared at the saw. "It's probably the choke."

Another yank and the saw sputtered again.

Ryan pointed his toe. "You need a hand?"

The saw ripped to life, chain spinning.

"There you go, Fuckhead."

The first few clouds of exhaust smoke were thick and gray and blew into Ryan's face. He swallowed. That was the last sound he'd hear. The grinding and tearing of that spinning chain against his flesh. The man stepped over Ryan's legs, straddling his knees, and held the bar close to the side of Ryan's face. Closer and closer. Ryan felt the motion of the chain in the air against his ear. Vibration, the metal clicks riding through the guide, and there was nothing he could do but watch those teeth whir by, the exhaust smoke spilling out in eager breaths of viciousness. The chain nicked his ear and the man stepped back, held the tip of the bar at the center of Ryan's face, fragments of wood and oil whipping against his cheeks, into his eyes.

This is where you are.

He lowered the bar a little at a time, to Ryan's chin, his throat, collar bones, sternum, solar plexus, navel, belt line, and then let the end of the saw hover just over Ryan's crotch. Ryan's insides tightened. He waited for the pain, the ripping snap of the fabric of his pants before the tearing of that bar through his flesh. He wondered how quickly his body would go into shock, how much of that pain he would have to feel. The engine wound down.

A smile spread over the man's face, a smooth streak of bliss. "Nothing to say now? Maybe the location of the girl and her son? Roy?"

"I think you have the wrong guy."

"Oh, no. I have the right guy. You're not as tough as you think you are. You'll talk."

"You know something, my mother tried to kill me. When that happens, everyone else who tries to do it is pretty much a joke. But you're no joke, Fuckhead. You're not even laughable. The only fucking punch line around here is that saw. So, fuck you."

The man revved the saw and stepped to Ryan's side,

where his arm was pinned to the log. Ryan closed his eyes, thought back to a weekend of camping, that Fourth of July romance and nine-dollar bottles of wine. That was the last face he wanted to see. He put her there, Laura Quinn, that moment she sat across the fire from him and shifted, and he realized that she was crawling around the heat to him, flashes of flame in her eyes, and she mounted him and put her mouth against his, the taste of wine—that first taste of love that he'd never get out of his mouth. He whispered her name, the last thing she'd said—*I'll think of you fondly, and I'll think of you often, but that's all it can ever be.* The sound of those words was easy to purge into the throaty hum of the saw.

A moist, wooden thump drifted through the air. The rushing sound of the saw rose, kept rising, moving away from him, and then he felt the tumble in the ground. Ryan opened his eyes, saw Malcolm there, heaving in breaths, the saw bucking over the ground to the man's left. The man was on his back, a stiff-armed reach for the sky, fingers clawed around an invisible ball, an axe buried in the bridge of his nose. Malcolm stepped toward the saw and pinned the engine to the ground with the heel of his boot, then grabbed the handle and lifted it to turn it off. Ryan's breath rushing into him made his ears pop. He turned his head to his right and puked.

Malcolm dropped the saw and knelt by Ryan; the man's arms still quivering in the air over Malcolm's shoulder. Ryan gagged a few more times, wiped the stickiness from his lips with the back of his wrist, and turned to Malcolm.

"You alright?" Malcolm asked.

Ryan looked over at the knife pinning his arm to the tree. "I'm pretty fucking excellent."

"Wh-who is that guy?" Malcolm pointed at the man whose arms were just beginning to drop.

Ryan spit the residue of vomit from his tongue. "Him? That's Fuckhead."

THIRTY-ONE

Malcolm swept the clutter off the table. The bullets he'd set at the edge from the night at Kurt's and scraps of paper, knife-sharpened pencils, and a handful of change spewed over the floor. The first aid kit popped open when Malcolm slammed it onto the table before he went to the cabinet below the kitchen sink, where he pulled out bottles of peroxide and rubbing alcohol. He brought them to the table and sat down. Ryan stood in the doorway, his left arm pulsing, swollen with blood pooling beneath the skin around the knife, his fingers bloody. The gash on his knuckles was pursed and open. Malcolm thrust himself from the table and up the stairs to his loft. He returned with a bottle of whiskey, pulled the cork out with his teeth, and spit it onto the floor with the rest of the things he'd cast there.

"Getting a little dramatic, don't you think?"

Malcolm tilted his head. "You forget there's a goddamn knife through your arm?"

Ryan lifted his arm, pain hurling from the wound to his brain. "Yeah, that." He sat at the table, in the chair Malcolm nudged out with his foot.

Malcolm took Ryan's fingertips in his hands to inspect the knife through his arm. The rough texture of Malcom's skin distracted Ryan from the pain. Malcolm pushed the bottle across the table. "Drink."

Ryan tipped the bottle up.

Malcolm stood and yanked his belt loose. It snapped through the loops and he draped it over Ryan's wrist, then lashed it to the arm of the chair. "Drink," he said again.

Ryan took another shot.

Malcolm took the bottle of rubbing alcohol, flicked the top open. He gritted his teeth, looking down on Ryan. Ryan tipped the bottle again. Malcolm moved his arm toward the knife.

"No."

Malcolm paused.

"Not yet." Ryan hammered down a long pull. "Fuck it. Go ahead."

Malcolm took Ryan's wrist and squirted the point of the blade first, then the wounds on both sides of Ryan's forearm. He checked the tightness of the belt. Ryan tensed against it, growled behind his clenched teeth and his legs marched in place. Malcolm drew his hand to his shoulder and backhanded Ryan across the cheek, simultaneously yanking the knife from his arm. Blood spurted from the wounds, rained over Malcolm's chest and shoulder, Ryan's lap, then dribbled down to a slow leak. Ryan's head dropped, and he let out a throaty moan.

"Did I tell you how much I hate being touched?" Ryan asked. "Intimacy's not really my thing."

"D'you think this was a date?"

Malcolm wiped away the blood from the wound with the towel and shook his head. "This might be worse than the last time I worked on you."

"No shit? Maybe you should stop saving my life." Ryan

tipped the bottle.

"You ready for the fun part?"

"You're a smooth talker, Malcolm. How can I resist?" Ryan lifted the bottle again.

"Nope." Malcolm grabbed it. "That's enough." He set the bottle down with the rubbing alcohol. "Ready?"

Ryan winked. "I hope you use protection. Be gentle. It's my first time."

Malcolm doused Ryan's knuckles with the alcohol, held Ryan's shoulder against the back of the chair as he screamed through his teeth and jerked his arm. Ryan's eyes went moist and he dropped his head back, the burning like that knife cutting deeper, rapid strokes through his flesh. Malcolm put the bottle back in Ryan's hand, and he gripped the neck and squinted his eyes and pushed his forehead against the mouth of the bottle. Malcolm put the alcohol down and dabbed the wound with a towel.

"Not as bad as I thought," Malcolm said.

"I might have lied about it being my first time." He took a drink, his speech beginning to slur. "You know, I should make it a tradition to take a shot every time someone tries to kill me."

"This happen to you a lot?"

"No. It's a fairly recent achievement, like being born again."

"Hunh?"

"Yeah, born again. You know, having an absolute supreme intolerable hatred for yourself that forces you to become religious so you can justify a sanctimonious judgement on everyone else to make yourself feel better."

"Not sure I'm following you right now."

"Yeah, I don't know where I was going with that.

Speaking of which, where the fuck did you come from back there?"

"I saw a car down on the tote road. Then I heard the saw. There was nothing you needed to be cutting. I got a bad feeling, I guess."

"A bad feeling...I've had one or two of those before." Ryan handed the bottle up to Malcolm. "You might want to take this. I'm having one of those bad feelings."

Ryan draped bags of frozen corn that Malcolm had given him over the bandage on his forearm and knuckles at the shabby table in the camper. He leaned forward and pressed his head against the wall. When those first few drops of rain hit the thin rectangular windows of the camper, he thought of his mother. As a boy, he'd lean into his palms at the screen in his bedroom on the days it rained too hard to play outside. The rain was more fun to play in, but his mother wouldn't allow it.

Malcolm had done a good job bandaging his arm, his hand. His grip wasn't entirely gone in his left hand, but it wasn't enough for him to spend hours on the road. And he hadn't even thought of that, where he would go, what direction he'd drive, but Victoria would find out that another attempt had failed. What would she send there next? Who would she send? How long would she keep sending them?

Maybe they were already there.

It rained into the night, and a ring emanated along his bones from the pain. It throbbed at his fingertips, almost became a numbing quiet before rising to a pitch that brought a tinfoil-chewing bore through his teeth. He left the table after the rain slowed and lay on the bed, staring at the ceiling, arms out and hanging slightly off the mattress. That, he discovered, offered some relief and he welcomed the itchy tingling. The drumming of the rain on the fiberglass roof began to fade as he found sleep.

THIRTY-TWO

Kurt's blood that had dripped onto the ground had dried in a dark, formless patch against the tar. The rain had taken it and made it the ground's, passed on to a path Jennifer couldn't see, carried along the ditches where dead leaves and branches from the forest tangled at the edges of the roads, then it seeped through the tiny rivulets of earth where it would tumble over the small rocks in the streams flowing into the Kennebec. And the river would carry it to the ocean.

Jennifer leaned against her truck with her arms folded, sipping her coffee, staring at the space that held the scene from the day before. The consequences of killing hadn't inspired much thought until then, until she'd plotted it out and it was a matter of methodical motion and not reaction. The natural flow of it surprised her, the time between action and final result. The excitement that had inflected the tones of everyone's voice gave her a sense of justification. She thought about it enough to be conscious of her own reaction to it. Control had never felt so close to her. She denied her own urge to go to the Tavern, to become a part of the swelling tumor there. It would have been the first time anyone at the Tavern would have been happy to see her walk in, and that gnawed on her thoughts for a while, because it might be the last time anyone was happy to see her. She questioned her hastiness with Kurt, but her chances, as she assessed, were better then.

The first sound of tires on the road above the bend nudged her from her thoughts. She climbed into the cab of the truck and drove to Bingham to meet Olivia. It was then that she felt something. She remembered the last time anything like that had crawled through her—the pain of never seeing someone you cared for again. She finally felt safe. All of her worries about how Olivia would react were gone, because Olivia would never know.

Olivia was in the back corner of Samantha's Diner holding the menu over her mouth as if she were whispering secrets to herself. Above the counter was a row of animal trophies, a twelve-pound brown trout with a layer of gray dust over the dark ridge of its back. Mounted deer heads that looked like any movement at all would shake off the fur. The walls held old, orange-tinged photos of the town's once established forest industry and the last log run in the country where a seventeen-year-old made history as the last man to die on a run. His first and last. The two patrons at the counter, old men in green Dickies pants and black suspenders over their large round torsos covered in plaid shirts, stopped their quiet conversation to look at her. The server, the only other worker aside from the cook, held a pot of coffee at her waist behind the counter and watched Jennifer move through the restaurant and sit across from Olivia, where a cup of coffee was waiting for her.

Olivia moved the menu to the side of her face to shield her mouth from the two old men and the server. "So, wonderful weather we're having."

Jennifer tried to shun the smirk coming to her face. "Been here long?"

"Long enough to hear your praise several times over. Oh, and don't be surprised if the general public wants to elect you sheriff."

She couldn't stop her smile then.

"Holy fuck," Olivia whispered. One of the old men coughed as he and his friend peered at Jennifer. Olivia glanced at them. She leaned forward. "You can't be alright with this."

"With what?"

"The fact that you killed someone." She drew back slightly then leaned forward again, still whispering, "Yesterday."

"That's what happens when you pull a gun on a cop."

"I can't believe that he tried to—" Her hands shook as she reached for her glass of water. "If that motherfucker had been in jail like he should have been, this wouldn't have happened."

"It's for the better."

"Shit. How can you be so, I don't know, weird about this?"

"Kurt was a piece of shit. Nobody else cares. Why do you?"

"Well, not nobody."

"What the hell does that mean?"

"I don't know." She bit her lip. "I said I wouldn't say anything."

"Spit it out, already."

"Nicole. She called this morning. Well, last night and again this morning. Kurt was babbling about Mike at the bar the other night. She said it was important, that she had to tell me something." She took another drink of water. "I think she's going to admit to sleeping with Mike."

Jennifer let out a deep breath. "What else did she say about Kurt?"

"Nothing."

"You sure?"

"Yes."

"Positive?"

"Yes. God."

"Then why do you think she has an admission about Mike?"

"Because she said it's her last night at the bar. She's leaving town. She said she was coming by later tonight."

"Later?"

"After her shift. I told her I'd come to the bar, but she said she had to talk to me alone. I think I'm going to go down to the bar anyway."

"No."

"What? Why?"

"Look. If you really want her to come clean, you can't put pressure on her. Let her do it on her terms."

"Yeah, but—"

"Listen to me. She's not going to say anything at the bar. All you're going to do is make her nervous and she'll clam up. Make her feel like it's okay, like you don't even care. Make her feel like her confession will make you better friends."

"But what if she leaves town?"

"If she leaves town without telling you, you'll have your answer. The truth."

Olivia bit her lip and reached for the menu. "Let's just order."

The server came to the table with a big, nervous smile on her face. She held the coffee pot out. "More coffee, Deputy?"

Jennifer looked down and stared at her full cup of coffee. Her thoughts jolted to a childhood memory. When her and Olivia were little, their father let them take turns sitting on his lap as he drove the tractor around the border of the fields of his new land right after they'd moved to Ironwood. Olivia had refused to wait and chased them down into the field and she fell as she reached for the step of the tractor. Their father, a cigarette dangling from his mouth, slammed the shifter into reverse and dropped the bucket, jarring her into the steering wheel. His cigarette fell from his mouth and toppled over her shoulder down the inside of her shirt, burning her stomach. He'd stopped the machine millimeters before the back tire crushed Olivia. Jennifer remembered the strength of his hands as he hefted her from his lap and held her over the ground before he dropped her, where she collapsed on the ground batting at the burning cigarette. He climbed from the tractor and jerked Olivia to her feet, her eyes red and moist. Her whining cry echoed through the field and he slapped her across the face. She stopped crying immediately, looking up at him in shock. Jennifer saw, too, the grainy wear of his face, the tears leaking from him like something had sliced him open. Olivia told her once that was the most pain she'd ever felt, seeing him cry. Jennifer shook her head at the server. An even bigger, more profound betrayal took root in her mind.

Jennifer slipped into a pair of sweatpants after she returned from Samantha's. Comfort, finally. Yesterday had been a long day, and the night was going to be longer. Fibers of muscle along her neck and in her chest vibrated with electric pulse. Her fingers quivered as she opened a bottle of wine hoping it would dull the tremors of her thoughts. It wasn't quite time for something more potent. Webber had called shortly after she'd gotten home, and she invited him to come by. She was curious to know what was going on at the department. When he arrived, he stood in the doorway with his thumbs tucked into his service belt. His forearm was bandaged, a small square taped off just below his elbow.

"New tattoo?" she asked.

He slipped his sunglasses off and pushed the temple inside his shirt at the top button. Then he pushed his thumb back into his belt. "Yeah. I couldn't keep cancelling the appointment. I would have gone in yesterday, but something else came up."

"I hope I didn't ruin your day."

"When do you have to see the shrink?"

"I don't know. Middler said next week some time. I don't remember. How is our fearless leader, anyway?"

Webber sputtered his lips. "Well, he's doing his best to get this ordeal over with. Press is all over him. They haven't found out about the incident at The Kodiak yet, though."

"Wouldn't that be a charming story."

"Are you alright, Jen? You seem a little indifferent."

"I'm fine. Administrative leave. I've wanted to take a vacation for years."

"They found a bunch of weird shit at Kurt's. Pictures."

Her heartbeat went erratic, like the clamor of dishes falling from a counter. "Pictures? Why were you at Kurt's?"

"Middler wanted to be sure he hadn't killed Patricia. Nobody can get in touch with her. They found some other stuff, too, I don't know what exactly, but it looks like Kurt was maybe blackmailing some people. They're questioning folks."

"What do you mean, blackmailing?"

Webber pointed at the ottoman near the couch, the only spot to sit where there wasn't a pile of clothes or other fabrics. "Mind if I sit?"

She shrugged, focusing on compressing her breaths, keeping her chest from heaving.

"Now, I don't know a whole lot, but some of the pics are sexual in nature. Those are the only things anyone is really talking about. But there are a couple from Mike's yard, possibly around the time that he died."

Her teeth went icy; she could feel it seep into her jaw. "And?"

"Well, don't you think it's strange that Kurt had those pictures?"

"Kurt did a lot of strange things."

Webber shrugged. "I guess. Not much there anyway. Nothing exciting. Not like the others."

"Did you see the pictures? All of the pics on Mike?"

"Yeah. Just him and a bunch of snow and trees."

"Kurt didn't have anything on you, did he?" She feigned a laugh.

He squinted at her. "No. I saw a few of Nicole that weren't very flattering."

Jennifer took a sip of her wine. Her body started to calm. "Not surprising."

"Yeah, well, Nicole likes to have fun. Anyway, they might ask folks a few questions about them, but I don't think it's going to be a big deal. Not much they can do about Kurt now. You took care of that."

She tipped her wine glass toward him and took a sip.

"You know who they're going to ask questions to?"

"Nicole, maybe. It's not like she broke any laws or anything."

She shook her head. "Man, I'm going to feel sorry for her if anything comes up about her and Mike."

"Her and Mike?"

She shrugged. "Yeah. Liv thinks Mike was fucking her. Nicole told her she had a big confession to make, and Olivia seems to think that it's about Mike. Mike admitted to having an affair before he died."

Webber mulled it over. "I'll pass along the information."

"Look, Web. Don't say anything right away. Things have been tough on Liv."

"Well, I'd better be going. I really just wanted to check up on you on my way home. I'll keep you posted."

"Thanks, buddy."

Webber pulled his sunglasses from his shirt. "You know anything about this new guy in town working for Malcolm?"

Jennifer took a sip of her wine, almost choked on it. "Not really, why?"

"Kurt took a lot of pictures of him. More than anyone else, actually. And I saw a couple of the same photos on Middler's desk. I thought maybe your sister might have said something about him."

"I don't know anything except that he's working for Malcolm and his name is Adam Crane."

THIRTY-THREE

Jennifer reversed her truck into a space near the back of the Tavern parking lot. She marked the edge of darkness, where the beams of her headlights faded into the ground just short of where Jack stacked firewood for the bar, an effort to conceal the patches of rot in the clapboards and an inconvenience for the bartenders tasked with lugging in the firewood during their shifts in the winter months. Nicole's vehicle was parked at the rear entrance of the building to the right of the woodpile. Two other vehicles were parked in front of the bar, and she sank in her seat and waited for them to leave, which wasn't long. The Tavern closed early at the beginning of the week. Jennifer killed the lights and slipped over the center console to the passenger seat to wait.

When the last patron had left the bar and driven out onto 201, exhaust rumbling up the road, Jennifer slid from the cab of the truck and moved quietly over the gravel to Nicole's car. She knelt at the front passenger side tire and let the air out of it—a noticeable hunch in the vehicle like some crippled animal sinking to the ground. At the edge of the building, she slunk through the dark to the fire escape and made her way to the second-floor hallway, the way she'd done her first night with Ryan.

The barroom smelled like bleach—the odor fading quickly against the decades of liquid saturating into the floorboards. Nicole was ringing out the mop as Jennifer moved into the doorway.

Nicole grabbed an Allen wrench from the register, hurried over to the front entrance, and turned the small bolt to release the push-bar. The latch took, and she pulled the shade over the window. She turned to move toward the side door that led to the bathrooms and the stairs to the rooms above. She gasped at the sight of Jennifer there looking up at the moose head.

"Jen? What are you doing?"

"That's such a wretched way to be remembered, don't you think?" She looked from the mount. "I've had a pretty rough week, and I thought maybe I could get a drink. It's early to be closing, no?"

Nicole shrugged. "Not much business tonight."

Jennifer jutted her chin toward the mop and bucket. "You still have a few things to do. I won't be in the way." She moved toward Nicole and stood next to her. "You don't mind if I sit at the bar, do you?"

Nicole's hands shook. "Well, let me lock this door before anyone else decides to come in."

"You nervous, Nicole?"

Nicole smirked. "Nervous? What would I have to be nervous about?"

"I don't know. Seems like maybe you're scared or something."

"Scared? What's there to be scared of?" She pointed toward the side door. "Just let me lock this up."

Jennifer kicked her heels over the floorboards on her way to the bar. Nicole shut and bolted the door and turned toward Jennifer.

"What can I get you?" Nicole asked as she passed and moved behind the bar.

"I'll take a shot of rye." Jennifer drummed her fingers over the bar.

Nicole pulled two freshly washed rocks glasses from the right side of the wash basins.

"So are you sipping or shooting?" Nicole asked.

Jennifer squinted, a tingle in the back of her mouth in anticipation of the drink. "That supposed to be funny?"

Nicole dug her fingers below her collar and scratched at the base of her throat, looking away from Jennifer. "No. I'm not trying to be funny."

Jennifer flashed Nicole a wide grin. "Kidding. Let's see how we feel after this one."

Nicole made the pour. She lifted the glass in her shaky fingers and took her drink down in one shot.

Jennifer lifted hers and sipped it. "I guess you're shooting."

Nicole took a deep breath and pushed from the bar to retrieve the bottle.

Jennifer took another sip. "Good stuff. Thank you." She drummed her fingers on the bar, waiting for Nicole to make eye contact.

"So what's got you so riled up to talk to my sister?"

Nicole snapped her head. "What?"

"Liv told me Kurt said some things to you and you needed to talk to her about them." Jennifer lifted her drink. "I was curious as to what that was all about."

"That? It's nothing, really. I just, you know, wanted to tell her what Kurt said."

"What was it that Kurt said?"

"He just said that he knew some things about Mike."

"Like what?"

"I don't know."

"If you don't know, then what is it you're going to tell Liv?"

"Honestly, Jen, that's something I'll talk about with Olivia. I should probably call her to let her know I'm running a little behind."

"You know what she thinks you're going to tell her, don't you? That you were fucking Mike."

"What?"

Nicole stared hard at Jennifer. Then she began to cry.

"Do you think crying is going to work on Liv?"

Nicole smeared her palms against her face, trailing the tears onto her fingertips. "No. I don't think so."

"So it's true?"

Nicole pushed another batch down her cheeks. She flinched when Jennifer reached out to touch her hand, a light graze over the edge of her thumb.

"I think the best thing would be for you to just clear out. Head out of town. I'll talk to Liv for you. Tell her that it's not true."

"You'd do that for me?"

"Of course."

Jennifer reached out to her again, this time a more firm pat on Nicole's wrist.

Nicole pulled her hands back and wiped her tears away, her expression almost immediately back to normal. "That's so sweet of you, Jen."

"Well, it's—"

"Considering I'm not the piece of shit who fucked my best friend's husband." She grasped the bar. "You are."

Jennifer slipped her hand to her pocket, thumbed the clip

on her spring-assist knife. "So that's what Kurt told you."

Nicole reached over and grabbed Jennifer's shot glass and put it down on the sink. "Not in so many words. But now I know for sure. How could you do that to Liv? Your sister? And people think I'm a slut. Good luck running for sheriff." She pulled her purse from the bar and dug her hand into it. "You're not going to come in here and try to intimidate me. I don't care who you are."

"Let's not get carried away, Nicole. I'm sure there's something we can do to fix this."

"You're right. You can get the fuck out of here."

Jennifer smirked, leaned her head back toward the ceiling. She thought of Ryan, almost wished he was in the room above her, and then a better idea crept into her thoughts. "You're making a mistake, Nicole. A big one. Olivia's the one that's going to get hurt the most out of this."

"Leave, or I'm calling the sheriff. I'm sure he'd be interested in what I know, too. That's why you killed, Kurt, isn't it? Because he knew."

Jennifer held her hands out and pushed herself from the barstool. She moved toward the gap in the bar. Nicole drew a snubnose revolver from her purse, extended her arm, and trained the barrel on Jennifer's chest. Jennifer stopped and without a sound, turned and left.

Moments later, Nicole burst through the door and stopped at the front fender of her car, looking down at the flat tire. "Fucking bitch," she muttered.

Headlights broke into the darkness from across the street and spilled halfway through the parking lot. Nicole dug into her purse, her head down. As she turned to walk back into the Tavern, Jennifer emerged from the darkness and stuck the blade of her knife into the side of Nicole's neck. She moved to wrap her hand over Nicole's mouth and get behind her, holding the blade in place to minimize the blood flow. The neck was a vulnerable spot. She remembered that from Mike. Nicole's eyes were wide. The vibration of her pulse through the knife stopped and Jennifer slumped Nicole down to the ground near the woodpile. She slowly loosened her grip on the knife. Blood ran along the edge of her index finger and thumb onto the cuff of her shirt. She frowned and reached into her pocket for her keys.

The rain beat down on her porch steps, the deluge furious for a few moments, like a naturally linked phenomenon that made the effort for her to wash Kurt's blood stain from the road, and the ground where she'd killed Nicole. Jennifer saw the torrent through the occasional swipe of the wiper blades. The green, haunting glow of the console display pushed against her wet T-shirt, the streaks of mud and dirt there from the efforts she'd made to dump Nicole's body. The radio was on, but barely audible. The DJ spoke about tips for life, health, an appropriate diet for losing weight. She wasn't focused on it, but the man's voice and the content made her wonder about people, how they woke up in the morning and pushed through the day with the delusion of ambition, the terminal cycle of week-to-week, day-to-day hourly pay for the goal of financial progress. Where was the recognition in that? What part of that made someone a human being? How could people be so complacent with just being—with no desire for the world to recognize them or their efforts? Maybe that was their purpose after all, to recognize the people who had the drive to stand above. Where was the happiness and joy that people so often craved, those brief moments of satisfaction with a bank deposit, a final car payment, a fresh coat of paint on the living room walls, the orgasm when they'd finally fucked the person they'd been pining over for so long? Those were all just moments lost in the hollow glory of redundant or meaningless accomplishments. There were no battles won. She thought for a while about Mike and Kurt and Nicole. They were all the same. Simply barriers and obstacles—annoyances in the path that she was taking. She had somewhere to be, something that was redeeming, something that would give her the control to vindicate the absurdity of it all, living among those people.

Olivia snapped awake on the couch. A current habit of sleeping in late brought more frustration into her day. It wouldn't be long before her team leader at New Balance finally wrote her up. Her watch beeped from the coffee table. She moved from the couch, sweeping her tongue over her teeth in an attempt to clear away the residue of wine. The bathroom was cool and the sounds of rain pattered against the windows. She stripped her clothes, turned the shower on, and draped a generous portion of toothpaste over her toothbrush before pushing the curtain aside to step in.

She squatted into her jeans, gripping at the belt loops and lessening the tension in them from their cycle in the dryer. The warmth of the T-shirt she pulled over her torso soothed the ache beginning to whirl behind her eyes. The rattle of the ibuprofen bottle that she pulled from the junk drawer in the kitchen made a feeling of resentment for Nicole rise, as if her presence the night before would have somehow relinquished that day's hangover. Olivia sighed at the silliness of the thought and went to the refrigerator for something cold. She eyed the foamy remnants in the orange juice container, told it to *fuck off*, pulled it from the fridge, and rushed out to make her way to work. A short moment of relief presented itself when she saw Nicole's vehicle still parked at the bar. Then anger came that Nicole had ignored her, but she was angrier with Jennifer sticking her nose in again and probably scaring Nicole off into a drunken frenzy instead of her finally admitting what she'd done.

She scrambled across the parking lot when she got to work, the rain drenching her by the time she got inside. Her team leader was waiting for her at the time clock with her write-up in hand, documenting her late arrival.

THIRTY-FOUR

A sheriff's cruiser was parked in front of the Tavern when Olivia drove by on her way home. The rain had stopped, leaving long pools of muddy water at the edges of the roads. The clouds had rolled away, nothing but iridescent blue and the blaze of the sun. Nicole's car was still in the lot at the Tavern. She pulled in and parked. The bar door was open and Jack's voice echoed inside the empty room as she walked across the front porch. Webber held a notepad out and a few scrawled lines on the sheet. He tapped his pen against the pad, looking down at her as she stepped into the doorway.

"Olivia, shit. Do you know where Nicole is?" Jack asked.

He was sitting in a stool at the corner of the bar.

"No. She was supposed to come by last night when she got done, but I don't think she showed."

"You don't think she showed?" Webber asked.

"No. I fell asleep. She may have come by, but she didn't wake me up if she did." She thought about Nicole's text message but decided she didn't want to mention it.

"Does she come to your house after work often?" Webber asked.

"Sometimes. I don't know what you'd consider often."

Jack cleared his throat, shook his head, and slapped the bar. "She probably took the money and split. I knew she was fucking stealing from me."

Olivia took a step inside the door. "She's never stolen a goddamn thing from you, Jack, and it doesn't matter how often you accuse her of doing it or how much you want to blame someone else for this shithole's lack of popularity. It's not true. Besides, her car is still in the parking lot. Where'd she split to?" She wondered why she was defending Nicole. Habit, maybe, or more that she hated Jack.

Jack scoffed. "Whatever. The bank bag is missing. You see her, you tell her she's fired."

"Fuck you, Jack. You tell her. In fact, have you even called her?"

Webber raised his eyebrows at Jack.

Jack raised his palms. "What, am I a fucking babysitter now? No. My money is missing. I called the sheriff."

"You're such an asshole." Olivia spun and strode back to her car.

Olivia saw Webber peeking out at her. *What the fuck are you looking at, Webber?* As she backed out, she realized that she wanted to find Nicole to hear that bitch tell her she'd fucked Mike, tell her that shacking up with some guy was more important than finally coming clean. She peeled the rings from her fingers as she pulled onto 201.

Nicole's front door was locked, both the knob and the deadbolt. The back door was usually unlocked, for some reason, as if Nicole believed any intruder wouldn't think to check the back door. After Olivia had kicked through the thick grass that was still damp from the rain and the dew that morning, she noticed how quickly her heart was beating. The drone of her hangover had diluted an emotional perspective, but it became more conspicuous then. Olivia was afraid of what she'd find in Nicole's, hoping that she would be passed out with some guy she'd drug out of the bar and perhaps had hidden the bank bag somewhere else.

A clear trash bag full of empty beer cans and plastic soda bottles was tied off and next to the sink cabinets. A pile of dirt and fragments of leaves lay in a pile in the corner, the broom leaned against the trim and hovering over the gathered pile. Olivia moved toward the living room. The house smelled like the damp air around bath towels in the dryer that hadn't finished drying. The echo of *Nicole* rolled through the house when she called out. Cautious as she moved through the kitchen, she noticed her posture at the threshold. Stalking. The living room had been tidied, but Nicole wasn't a sloppy person, Olivia reminded herself. She must have shacked up at someone else's house. Plots from all the crime dramas Olivia had seen on television made her imagine herself looking for clues about Nicole and Mike somewhere in the house. When she spotted the roll of cash in the corner of the bookshelf tucked tightly above one of the books, she began to move faster. Her heart thudded. Her fists clenched. She called out again and rounded the corner to the hallway leading to Nicole's bedroom, already imagining dragging Nicole onto the floor by her hair.

The bed was made. The vacuum had been left in the middle of the floor in front of the closet, still plugged into the wall. The blinds were drawn, a packed suitcase next to the door. She moved over to the dresser where Nicole kept her keys and purse. Nothing. And nothing implicating in the top drawer of Nicole's dresser where she kept her souvenirs—things she liked to keep from her trysts—Bic lighters, Zippos, dip cans, belt buckles, pocketknives. Once, Nicole had pulled a guy's rearview mirror off. More rummaging through the tin of Nicole's trophies. Nothing of Mike's. Down to the next drawer, she found only clothing and two of Nicole's dildos. The last two drawers were just clothing—sweatpants and tank tops. She turned to the closet and movement at the corner of her eye startled her. Jennifer.

"What the fuck are you doing?" Jennifer asked.

"I went by the bar. Nicole was supposed to come over last night, but she didn't. I came here to check on her."

"Why didn't you call me?"

"Why would I call you? Seems like you already invited yourself into more of this than you were welcome."

"What's that supposed to mean?"

"Nicole texted me last night that you came by the bar. She said she was on her way to my house and she never showed. What the fuck did you say to her?"

"It's really not what I said to her, but what she told me that you should be interested in."

"That *is* what I'm interested in, but I want her to fucking tell me. I knew I should have gone to the bar last night." She ground her knuckles against her temples. "I fucking knew this shit was going to happen." She squinted, trying to keep herself from crying. "It's fucking true, isn't it?"

When she relaxed her fists, her hands waved and they started trembling.

"I'm sorry," Jennifer said.

THIRTY-FIVE

Malcolm toed the boots off his heels, feeling the layer of skin that had blistered cling to his sock. The sound of tires and a car engine rolled down the road past his house, and he leaned forward in his chair. The mess that had been on his floor when he left to get rid of the dead man's body had been picked up and stacked on his table. Ryan. The rumble of chains was still in his head from dragging the body down to the muddy section of road near the brook. He'd put the body there, drove it into the ground by backing over it a few times with the skidder to push it deep into the mud. Then he'd plowed earth from the sides of the road onto it. When he finished that, he dragged the car down the old skidder trail to the bog and watched it sink into the mud, the sludge crawling up over the sides of the car and through the open windows. Nobody would ever find it.

In his loft, he stripped his shirt, grabbed a dry T-shirt from the top of the dresser, and put it to his nose to check for any odor, unsure if he'd worn it already. Then he pulled it over his head and stepped into a pair of moccasins. On his way out the door, he grabbed the whiskey bottle from the table and passed through his yard to the camper in the next lot. Ryan sat in the folding chair outside the camper facing the woods, looking up into the trees. His arms rested over his stomach.

"Got one last small request for you if you don't mind."

Sunlight spilled into the bottle of liquor, a light, soothing brown like the dead pine needles on the forest floor. Ryan lifted his hands. "Don't know if I can do much for you. I'm in a bit of pain."

Malcolm chuckled. "Well, a drink or two might help dull some of that. Is it getting any better?"

"My range of motion is a little better, but mostly because I'm not pinned to a tree."

"You're welcome to stay here as long as you want."

"Yeah, well, I don't really think I can handle any more surprise visits."

Malcolm walked behind Ryan and grabbed one of the collapsible nylon chairs leaned against the camper. He pushed it open and shook the dead leaves and needles from it, then plopped it next to Ryan and sat down, sighing and feeling the tightness in his back. "Hell. I might not get out of this seat tonight." He pulled the cork from the bottle and offered the first drink to Ryan.

Malcolm slipped his feet from the moccasins before he lifted the bottle. He took a pull, rolling the damp pine needles against the bottom of his feet. He lifted his toes to push his heels into the bare earth, a slight relief against the burn from the torn skin. He took a breath and spoke. "I'm sorry, Ryan. I'm sorry Simon sent you here. I know I told you that already, but I don't feel like I can say it enough."

"If Simon hadn't sent me here, you wouldn't have been around to save my life. I don't think you need to apologize."

"Yeah. I suppose." He sighed and took another pull. "You mind if I ask you something?"

"Go ahead."

"This might be a bit shitty for me to ask, but what was going through your mind when that motherfucker was holding a chainsaw to your face?"

"Other than the fact that I was about to die a horribly painful death?"

"Yeah. Besides that." Malcolm took a pull and handed the bottle to Ryan.

"I was thinking about a girl I met once."

"Oh. Must've loved that one."

Ryan took a drink. "Maybe. Probably not."

"Hard tellin' not knowin', ain't it? Think it could have been love?"

He took a drink and handed the bottle back to Malcolm. "I usually see the worst in people first. Not much of a life if you want to spend it with someone. Certainly no love."

They sat silently, passing the bottle back and forth, two men staring into the trees, as lost in their thoughts as something dropped from a pocket out there in the forest ahead of them. Malcolm thought of his failures, the people he'd lost, and the whiskey haze that had begun to paste itself around his vision. He remembered back to Mike's funeral and the frost on his windshield as he drove away thinking about Olivia, before he realized that Mike's death wasn't just a dumb mistake, when he only had feelings of sorrow for Olivia and how much she was hurting. The worst was knowing that despite how much she felt betrayed, Mike had loved her more than anything or anyone. He knew that about his son. The sun sank down below the tree line. Malcolm thought about the next day, it already becoming lucid in his mind. He'd get up and go down to the yard in the morning, trample over the ground that his son had worked, where he'd died.

THIRTY-SIX

Jennifer was finally able to take a full breath of relief just before Webber pulled up in front of her house. She'd spent much of the afternoon at Olivia's, silent, watching her clean appliances and reorganize the canned goods in the cabinets. Laundry, vacuuming, window cleaning—Olivia had done all of that while she repositioned herself in various corners of the rooms out of the way of her sister's housekeeping rampage until she couldn't stand there anymore with nothing to say. Even when she told Olivia she was leaving, Olivia had simply thrown a hand up into the air to wave goodbye as she tossed silverware into the drawer.

Jennifer went to the freezer and pulled out a bottle of tequila as Webber trotted up to the front door.

"It's open," she called out to him before he could knock.

His approach had been quick, but he moved slowly into the house and stood against the wall just inside her door.

"Drink?" She held the bottle up.

He shook his head.

"I guess we're at the point of just dropping by now."

"Actually, Jen, I'm here officially."

"Oh?" She took a drink.

"Yeah. Have you spoken to your sister today?"

"I have."

"So you're aware that Nicole closed the bar last night and there's money missing."

She took a drink and nodded.

"I was just at Olivia's. She said that you saw Nicole last night. Well, she said that Nicole texted her that you were at the bar."

"So you already know I spoke to my sister today. Why the question?"

"I guess I'm just making sure you understand this is important. I'm trying to track down the money, but with what you told me about Nicole and Mike, I have to look at things in a different way. Your sister's involved. I need to make sure I'm getting straight answers."

"No. Your first priority is tracking down the money. Then, in another, what..." Jennifer looked down at her watch. "Thirty-six hours or so, if someone files a missing person report on Nicole, you change the scope of the investigation."

"I'm kind of hoping that doesn't become the case."

"Because if it does, Olivia is the first person you'll begin to question."

Webber bit his lip. "This isn't easy for me."

"No? Seems like the difficulty in this is you jumping the gun. It's only been a few hours. Nicole, you know as well as I do, probably found some hick from Athens to thrash her around for the night. I'm sure she'll wander back home soon, and in the meantime, Jack will probably find the money that Nicole supposedly made off with."

"I'm not jumping the gun. This doesn't seem right, any of it. I'm here out of respect for you, a professional courtesy. I have to file this report. If Nicole doesn't turn up in two days, then it's a different report and I have to do my job, which means the first person they look at is Olivia, or, well, you. I'm trying to get the information I need to prevent that."

Jennifer crossed her arms for a moment, then relaxed and lifted the bottle. She took a sip. "When you come inside your wife, does she say your name or the guy she wishes was fucking her?"

"Wow, Jen. You see the shrink yet?"

"Fuck you, Web."

"Fuck you, Carlton. What the fuck is your problem?"

"My problem? I told you about Nicole and Mike yesterday, and Nicole does some sketchy shit. Stealing isn't totally out of the realm of her capability, and you're hammering down on this like it's a fucking murder investigation. What the fuck? Why are you so focused in that one direction? Seems to me that you want this to be more than it is."

Webber blinked and brought his hands up to push his palms against his eyelids. "I'm sorry." He dropped his hands to his sides. "I really think something's not right here. I called every other bartender. Granted, Jack makes accusations about the bartenders stealing all the time. I'm sure that this is just an oversight on his part, as much as that guy drinks, but all I'm really trying to do is prevent the fallout if this goes beyond a simple theft. That's why I'm here."

"Look, I'm stressed. This shit doesn't help. You here asking questions. I was at the bar last night. I went down to talk to Nicole about Olivia. I wasn't there long, and I shouldn't have gone, but it's my kid sister. Believe me, when Nicole admitted that she'd been fucking Mike, I wanted to drag that cunt over the bar by her hair. I told her she owed it to Olivia to tell the truth and then I left."

Webber brought his hand up to pull his notebook from his shirt, but relaxed and moved his hand back down to his side. "Do you think you might have scared Nicole? I mean, you did just kill someone."

"Yeah, well, maybe. I'd think that, but when I left some guy walked into the bar."

"Who?"

"I don't know. I was already in my truck and pulling out. I wasn't paying attention. I just saw his silhouette as he entered. I figured it was Nicole's fuck buddy for the night, and I got a little more upset and came home. I was going to go to Liv's, but I didn't want to deal with her disappointment when Nicole didn't show, which is what I figured would happen when I saw the guy go into the bar."

"Details? What did he look like?" Webber made the reach for his notepad. "You mind if I write this down?"

"Go ahead. But I don't have anything for you. I know the job. If there was something I could tell you, I would. Now, I'd really like to be alone, so if you don't leave, I'm going to call your wife and tell her you're going down on me."

Webber jotted his notes. "You really do need therapy."

"I need to get fucked." She winked at him. "You need to go home to your wife."

Ryan was caught just on the edge of sleep, the furry brush of whiskey beginning to form on his teeth, when the tapping on the camper door brought him back to consciousness. He opened his eyes and pain surged through his forearm and knuckles, fading slightly as he adjusted to the darkness. He waited, listened. The knock came again and he pushed himself from the cushions and approached the door. His heart was already whirring in his chest. Already here, he thought.

He'd only put off his death. It wasn't easy to move in the camper silently, but he got to the window and peeked through the slit in the curtains.

Jennifer stood before the metal steps outside in the faint light from Malcolm's porch. She took a step back while Ryan struggled to turn the knob and pull the inner camper door open. Her white T-shirt stood out in the darkness. Ryan tapped at the wall and a pale light shed through the room. He staggered back to the cushions and sat.

"What did you do to yourself?" She asked as she stepped into the space.

"Nothing productive."

"Such a smartass. Really, what happened?"

"I fell against something sharp out on the yard."

"You should be more careful." She went after an itch on her ribs, digging into it. The movement forced her breasts to shake. "You're moving up in the world," she said after taking a look around the camper. She took a step forward and sat next to him, palming her knees. "It's been a rough couple of days for me. I was hoping you'd be up for ride and a few beers. It would be nice to spend some time with someone who doesn't need or want something from me." She bore a stare into his eyes that made him blink.

In that moment, he wanted to give her the knowledge that he'd acquired. He would have, but another urge formed inside him unlike how he'd been taught to live and duck into the darkness and shadow whenever possible, be obscure, vanish. He had another truth he wanted to give her. He wondered what it would sound like coming out of his mouth, his real name—Everett Waugh. "Yeah, let's take a ride."

His heart beat desperate thumps as he tried to decide how he could tell her that they'd shared part of their childhood together, that the scar on the back of her hand was from a wound she'd gotten when she'd freed his feet from a tangle of barbed wire, that they both had secrets. He swallowed, rubbed the tingling in his right hand, and followed her from the camper.

She'd parked on the road at the base of the hill. When he asked her why, she told him she didn't want to wake Malcolm if he was sleeping. Ryan got in the truck, thinking back to that night at Kurt's when he'd seen her in the woods. She pulled away from the road before he'd settled in the seat, which helped his effort to shut the door.

They rolled through the single blinking-light intersection in the center of town and continued north on 201 toward Jackman. She clutched the speed of the truck to the posted speed limits and Ryan thought of all the times he'd driven across the country—through the mountains and the deserts, the monotony of the Midwest that made him wish the Great Lakes were even greater and spilled through that awful region of mid-sized cities protruding from corn fields, windmills towering through the distance. The scattering of porch and flood lights faded and the road was just a dark path toward where they were going. He didn't ask and the silence as they drove allowed him to focus on how little the pain in his arm was fading. They crossed over the edge of tar onto gravel.

The truck rocked as she veered around divots. Ryan brought other thoughts into the fold, the time he'd lived as though he'd never return to that place, those people, the memory that Jack O'Brien decorated his bar walls with. The hum of his experiences in the days that he'd spent in unfamiliar places were like echoes in the empty rooms of a house he'd once lived in, like he'd dreamed everything up to that moment.

She slowed at a small turn off and cut the wheel to make a sharp right. Arnold Portage. He caught a glimpse of the sign as she turned the truck and then turned again on a narrow road that led them to the edge of the lake, a campsite even few locals knew about where the river that fed through the *Ice Box* dumped into the lake over a cluster of broken limbs and storm felled trees that had tumbled over rocks and wedged between the growth of fir trees at the mouth of the river.

Jennifer pointed toward the oak that grew at the edge of the lake. "There's a rope swing in case you want to show off."

"I'm not feeling all that acrobatic tonight."

She shrugged. "Well, I guess we can just sit on the tailgate and listen for the loons."

Jennifer climbed from the truck. Ryan got out and moved toward the bed where she had lowered the tailgate and yanked a cooler toward her. She pulled out two cans of beer and handed one to him.

"It's a shame you're leaving, you know. We could have had a lot of fun together."

Ryan held the can between his knees and cracked it open. "We have had a lot of fun together. How'd you know I was leaving?"

"Maybe I should have said *more* fun." She opened her beer and held it out to him. "Here's to one last night."

Ryan tapped her can. He let the unanswered question go. Malcolm had probably said something to Olivia. The loons howled in the distance and he took in the echo over the sound of the stream and the beer he poured into his mouth. The beer wasn't very cold, and it tasted sour after drinking whiskey with Malcolm.

"Ever been on a lake and not seen any lights?" she asked.

He checked the lake, oblivious to that reality when they'd first gotten there. He should have noticed that. It was true. There was nothing on the lake. He could see a denser shade of dark on the opposite shoreline where the trees lined the edge of the water. The loons howled again, spooky and haunting from some edge of the lake he couldn't determine.

"It's a good spot," he muttered. He finished his beer and she opened the cooler as he pulled the can from his lips.

"You thirsty?" She winked and took another beer from the thin layer of ice cubes.

"Yeah." He thumbed off the mist over the sealed opening of the can and pulled the tab. A sharp metal click. "I have something I should probably tell you—about why I really came here."

She reached out to the edge of his beltline, her fingers sweeping to his wrist. "I want to show you something first."

He left his arm there, dangling against the soft, kneading wilt of her fingers until she closed them into a grip. Her grip, the same gentle touch that she'd placed on him to guide him and his brother to the house at dusk when it was time for them to initiate their nightly routine before bed when they were young. She led him toward the sound of the stream, and he followed through the bracken hue of the night.

She stopped when their footing reached the soft, sinking edge of land where the mouth of the stream fed into the lake. He heard the click beside him and her flashlight parted the darkness with a beacon.

"I'm—" he held his breath for a moment, looking at the ground. The edge of the light spread over him as she backed a few steps behind him. "I'm not..."

The illumination of her light splashed against the length

of an old pine caught in the chaos of other trees at the mouth of the stream. And he saw her, Nicole, her face the blue tint of the edge of a flame. Her chin drooped against her chest and her hair and legs wafted with the current. A chill spiraled up the center of his back, and he took a breath.

The sounds around him were vibrant—the gurgle of the stream and the sleepy lapping of the water at the edge of the lake. The distinct, subtle click of the safety on her pistol. The loons in the distance shed out another shrill call and he could tell that they were on the north end of the lake. If he turned, there'd be the barrel of a gun and another woman at the other end of it. If he darted right, he could dive into the water, possibly quick enough to swim along the bottom of the lake and out of range. He could do that in one breath. He could get away like he had before. Maybe she'd clip him. Maybe she'd get more than a finger. He caught the shimmer of light on the water, and the faces of all those people he'd moved from one state of living to another rose to the surface. He closed his eyes, the words he'd so often used glided along his tongue. *This is where you are, and you can never go home.* He turned toward Jennifer, digging his toes into the soft earth for traction, flexing the muscles in his legs.

She aimed at his chest, her lips parting to speak. "The world is a very cruel place, sweetheart."

"Everett Waugh."

His voice startled her and her hand twitched. The gunshot echoed across the lake.

A muffled whimper.

The bullet pierced the smooth spread of his skin, tore through and ripped at muscle fibers and blood vessels. It shoved him back and he lost the sensation of balance, compelled to drift, his heart hiccup-thumping and shoving blood through the bullet hole. He dropped back, crashed over the rocks at the edge, and splashed into the water. Cold slipped in through his fingers, wiping away the pain like dust from stainless steel. The current jolted his body and nudged him farther into the lake.

THIRTY-SEVEN

November

A few days of heavy wind and rain purged the orange and red from the branches of the trees and made the landscape up and down the valley gray and dark. Fog rose like smoke from the river to the tree branches and the murmur of rumors had finally settled. The river, too, was calm, lower, everything sinking once again toward the ground. After those rains, fall remained dry, and the temperatures slowly crept their way down, like something that wanted to be underground.

Malcolm sat in the empty lot where the camper had been, before the state investigators hauled it away as evidence. They'd released it, and told him he could pick it up, but he told them to add it to their next auction. He kept a chair next to him, in case Olivia came by, but she'd left town a few weeks before they elected Jennifer sheriff. Only the dead leaves found rest in the seat. Olivia wouldn't say it, and he'd assumed from her silence that she blamed him for what happened to her sister, and Nicole. What she thought happened anyway. His skidder was parked in front of his house. He'd posted the FOR SALE sign on it that morning, but that was all the advertising for it that he'd done. It could have been sold, but the previous year, the only other man cutting in Ironwood had bought a brand-new skidder. He thought of Olivia, missed her coming over, the sound of those plastic tires on the cooler she dragged around with her—the banging of the cans inside, sloshing around with the melting ice. She'd given him something else to focus on even though she was a steady reminder of Mike. He pulled a pack of Lucky Strikes from his shirt pocket and flicked the bottom to push a cigarette from the torn opening in the corner of the pack. He lit it and blew a stream of smoke from his nostrils. Behind him, a vehicle slowed and pulled into his driveway. Jennifer walked to the edge of the lawn and waved, then put her hands on her hips to wait for him. He took another couple drags from his cigarette and stood, pushing against his thighs, to meet her at the back door of the camp.

"I thought you quit," she said when he met her at the door.

He shrugged and led her in the house. At the refrigerator, he reached in for a beer, cracking it open as he turned, leaning on the open refrigerator door. He noticed her uniform. "Did you get a new uniform, or did they just change your name tag and badge?"

"I got the whole ensemble." She brushed some flakes of cigarette ash from her sleeve. "I'd love one of those beers, if you've got another."

Malcolm smirked and reached into the fridge. "All I got is cans. That alright with you?"

"Fine with me."

He handed her a beer and she tore at the tab.

Malcolm pointed over her shoulder at the boxes on top of the freezer chest in the corner. "That's all that I could find of Mike's. I hope it's everything."

"I'm sure Liv will appreciate that."

"How's she doing? She settling alright down in Portland?"

"She's making it. She seems happy. I'm headed down there this weekend."

"You know, I have a little whiskey left. You care to take a nip with me? My congratulations for your success."

Jennifer pouted her lip and folded her shoulders slightly. "Sure. Why not."

"I'll go grab it." He shot her a grin and moved up the stairs to retrieve the bottle.

Upstairs, Malcolm stood at the edge of his bed looking at the bottle, the .357 beside it on the nightstand. He wasn't sure which he wanted to walk down the stairs with. He could do it, move down the steps and tuck each piece of lead into her the way he'd cramped them into the brass that made the bullets he'd loaded the gun with. But then everything would remain crooked. A pulp hook rested on the dresser. He'd put it there on his final day down on Arthur's lot when he cut his last piece of timber. It was cold in his hand. He grabbed the bottle. Warmth. On his way down, he hung the hook on his neck.

Jennifer's eyes squinted at the orange steel dangling on Malcolm's shoulder when he entered the room. He stepped past the fridge and grabbed a clean glass for her. There was another glass in the sink that he took out and set on the counter with the bottle. There wasn't a towel so Malcolm used the corner of his flannel shirt to wipe out the glass he'd taken from the sink. He poured two drinks and turned to offer Jennifer hers. She took the glass, staring at his chest.

Malcolm tapped her glass after she took it and they each eyed each other as they sipped the whiskey. Dark brown lapels and pocket flaps accented her tan uniform, the same pattern when he wore one. "Kinda wish Olivia was here for this," he said. "I remember the first time Mike brought her by the house. I'd never seen a boy so proud. And he wasn't proud in the way that he was gettin' some from the pretty girl. He was proud that she actually liked him. We stood right here in this room and sipped this exact brand of whiskey. I was proud to be a father that day, that I'd raised a boy who would find a girl like Olivia." Malcolm sipped his whiskey again. "That girl gave Mike some purpose. She was the only thing he ever loved more than fishing or cutting wood. I still can't believe he'd tarnish that." He finished off the drink and reached for the bottle to pour another. "I'm surprised you never picked up on that, given how protective you are of your sister."

She chased her sip of whiskey with beer. "Wasn't really my place to stick my nose in her marriage."

"I suppose you've got a point there." He finished his beer and reached into the fridge for another. "You need one?" He asked and placed his empty can on the counter.

Jennifer shook her head. "You know, Malcolm, I've had a pretty busy week." She tipped up the glass to finish her drink, then guzzled down the beer. "I suppose I should get these things out of the way."

"You know, there is something I've been meaning to ask you about." Malcolm took a drink. "Now, I went up to the yard after we got Mike out of there. I remember the tree that fell on him, and I remember the notch I saw at the base of that tree. Same kind I told him not to use. And that was the first thing I ever taught him about felling timber. Cutting too close to the hinge gives the tree a chance to spin. Seen that happen."

She tightened her grip on the can, and relaxed when it crinkled. "I'm not sure I know where you're going with this."

"Just thinking out loud, really." He scratched a cold tickle on his neck from the edge of the pulp hook. "I saw a tree fall on a man once. Broke him right in half. Sounded almost like a piece of wood snapping. Maybe it was wood, but I don't think so. Bone sounds different when it snaps. I guess I should be thankful Mike was on the ground when that tree fell on him."

She set the beer and the glass down on the freezer chest and stacked the lightest box on top of the other. She gripped the corners and lifted. "I should probably be going. Thanks for putting this together for Liv. I know she'll appreciate it."

"That's real kind of you, bringing her Mike's things. Mike always said she was the tough one, the kind of person to do what was right no matter who she upset. I can't help but feel like I lost a daughter as well as my son."

"I'm sure she'll come around. She just needs some time."

"Funny thing about time, isn't it? As much as it passes there are still some things that hover in your mind like they happened yesterday. I remember back when I was a deputy, you and your sister were still in grade school when those boys got shot up by their mother. You were friends with them, weren't you? Yeah. As I recall you used to babysit for the Waughs. I threw up after I found Mrs. Waugh on the lawn." He took a sip of his whiskey. "Fuck, I found a piece of her skull twenty yards from where she'd put that shotgun in her mouth. Twelve gauge makes a hell of a mess out of a person's head." He lifted the glass to look at its emptiness. "Almost as much as guilt does." He set the glass on the counter. "Oh, well. I guess now we have another legend for

Jack O'Brien's barroom wall."

"Maybe you should take it easy on the whiskey tonight. Seems like you're sinking a little deep here." She adjusted her shoulders to the weight of the boxes.

Her small hands clutched the boxes far away from her weapon. He reached toward his shoulder, the handle of the pulp hook. "I'm real sorry I brought Adam here. Well, whatever his real name was. Paper said Adam was an alias. Anyway, I'm sorry that he crossed paths with you. I don't think that's something I can ever forgive myself for."

Jennifer's eyes widened and she took half a step back from Malcolm as he pulled the pulp hook from his neck.

"I never found Mike's after his death, but I bought this at the same time I bought his. I'm sure Olivia would want it." He turned the hook in the air, focusing on the point. "Really is a great tool, especially when your hands are beat to hell or your knuckles are split open and can barely grip the wood anymore. Maybe knives are easier to hold. That's what Adam, or whoever, came at you with, right?" He held the hook close to her face before he placed it in the box. "I'm glad you're going to be the one to give this to her." Her face paled, and after she backed through the door of the camp and made her way off the porch toward her truck, Malcolm grabbed the bottle and poured what was left of it into his glass.

THIRTY-EIGHT

The ceiling fan pushed a gentle lilt of air against Victoria's satin sheets. She lay in the center of the bed, her body rustling from sleep. At that point in the morning, the air had settled into a comfortable temperature and it was quiet, well past the time that the birds would chirp and sing with their awakening. Victoria rolled to her stomach, spread her arms over the California king, and extended her limbs to stretch the muscles through her back. She relaxed, then pushed her pelvis into the mattress, tightening her ass, curving the covers, her bare skin against the sheets.

"Oh, morning," she mumbled into her plush, down pillows.

It was ten forty-three a.m.

She pulled her arms in to push her torso from the bed, the weight of her tits swaying beneath her chest, and she craned her head to work out the lethargy in her neck. Her back cracked. She rolled over and pushed her hands down her stomach, feeling the warmth of her body. The soft flesh inside her hips and her inner thighs was faintly sticky from the brief sweat she'd given off in the night. She rolled her thumb over her pubic region, teased her clit for a moment, debating whether to masturbate or not. She opted for not and pushed herself up in the bed.

In the shower, she waited for the sound of Wendell's trombone, a practice that she allowed for the hour she was engaged in her morning rituals so long as he had the twenty-ounce mocha latte on the counter in the kitchen by eleven a.m. The sound of Wendell's horn warbled through the house while the hot water sprayed over her. She wondered what day of the week it was while she scrubbed the exfoliating lavender soap over her skin.

In front of the mirror, she dragged a fresh towel over her hair—a new cut, just below her ears. *Very Peter Pan*, Nelson, her stylist, had told her. And that reminded her of Ryan. She took her robe from the hook on the door, warm from a fresh cycle in the dryer, which Wendell also did before his practice, and ventured to the kitchen for her latte. She passed the empty room where Wendell played his horn and swooped her drink from the counter on her way to the trophy room. Ritual had become easier after Roy left. Before that, the only ritual was avoiding him. She sipped her latte on the way there. It was perfect.

In Roy's former trophy room, she kept a suede sofa and a small martini bar. There was a Persian rug over the hardwood floor, but she'd grown tired of it and was shopping for a new one. Over the mantle of the gas fireplace, she'd hung the newspaper clipping in a frame. *Deputy Escapes Clutches of Killer*. At first, she'd been surprised that Johnson's contact was a woman, a cop no less. And even more so of how it had been orchestrated so quickly. She was happy that a woman had put him down. Men, and their constant accusation of women's emotional weakness gave her a deeper appreciation for the job done. She often wondered what it would be like to meet Jennifer Carlton, the small-town local hero.

She took a sip of her latte and as she lowered the cup, caught a shimmer of movement in the glass of the clipping. A ringing pain shot through her head between her ears, and the last thing she saw before everything went dark was her blood sprayed over the clipping and the bullet hole near the center.

THIRTY-NINE

Snow came earlier that year, before the leaves had finished their descent to the ground. The cold followed, more relentless than the year before, and the people of Ironwood were already fretful of heating bills and their supply of firewood. The lakes had been long frozen, and state investigators refused to keep sending divers in to find the body. Jennifer thought back to that night, wished she'd gone into the water after him, kept him from slipping into the current. His body had sunk somewhere in the lake, and she'd dream about his sinking corpse settling into the mud.

She'd been waking with those thoughts often, snapping her eyes open to the feeling that someone else was breathing in her house, right beside her, as if they were blowing a stream of air against her lips. The ashtray spilled when she shed the blankets, and the cigarette butts fell to the floor. The ashtray rocked like a spinning quarter that wouldn't settle. At the edge of her bed, she saw that there was just enough light outside to illuminate the fluttering through the part in her drapes. It was snowing. She stood and shucked the drapes to the sides.

The tree line was still except for the flitting wave of snow falling through bare branches of the hardwoods. She rotated her head in a semi-circle to soften the hard kinks in her neck, bent over to touch the floor and stretch the taught ridge of her hamstrings. She relaxed as she stood, glancing over the new bibs she'd bought for riding the sled. Fresh powder. It'd be a good day to ride. She rolled the edges of her feet over the cold wooden floors as she walked into the kitchen to the coffee maker that was already gurgling a brew of caffeine for her morning.

In the kitchen, she saw the glow on the horizon through the window, a golden pulse in the drab skyline, not the power plant across the river, and it was the wrong direction for sunrise. It was closer, too, near the center of town and the post office. She pulled the coffee pot from the machine and dumped the black liquid into the mug she'd drawn from the dishwasher. She wondered what it was, and turned to walk around the island to grab her phone. Her body shuddered when she saw the man in the corner. The mug slipped from her hand, cracked and broke in half against the floor, splashing coffee over the insteps of her feet and ankles. He was small, thin, a smooth and fluid wispiness. A slithering gaze. She was suddenly aware that all she was wearing were her sweatpants.

"Good morning, Sheriff."

Her body trembled as she took a step back, heart stuttering as she waved her fingers for the drawer near the sink and pulled it open. Screwdrivers and Altoids tins rattled inside. She rolled her fingers through the objects, looked down to see that the pistol she kept there was gone. Instead, she latched onto a flathead screwdriver. The man standing in the corner took a step toward her, the suit he wore was almost like wet fabric the way it fit over him—skin. He drew his hand up and pointed a taser at her.

An electric jolt struck through her body, blurring her vision. The room sprawled out into a thin, uneven plain. She had no sensation of falling, only realized that her physical response was gone when she heard the cluttered thumping of her body hitting the floor, the cold linoleum against her skin. In the darkened vision of her awareness, pressure of another body straddled hers, gripping her hair and mashing a wad of fabric over her mouth and nose and darkness tucked her consciousness away.

When she came to, Jennifer tried to shake the haze from her vision and realized her inability to move. Her forearms were clammy against the grimy fabric on the armrests of the chair she was restrained in. The room was dark, but she could make out the silhouette of the man in front of her, similar build and posture of the last man she'd seen. She squinted, reopened her eyes and let them come into focus. He was older, white hair slicked over his scalp, horn-rimmed glasses in front of his eyes. His tongue clicked against his teeth, the little popping sound irritating her. She struggled against the cord that bound her limbs. Her fingertips burned and she fanned her fingers out, each tip wrapped with gauze and medical tape except the pinky of her left hand. Immediately, she thought of Adam, whatever his name had been.

"Welcome to Tulsa, Ms. Carlton. Take as much time as you need to focus. You have been out for a few days." Simon pointed at her hands. "We used that time to sear off your prints, something significantly more painful when you are awake."

She used her tongue to pile away the dryness in her mouth. Tried to remember what the man had just told her.

"I'm a sheriff. Do you realize that?"

"Yes, Ms. Carlton. That is exactly why you are here."

She clenched her fists, wincing through the pain in her fingers. "Who the fuck are you?"

He crossed his legs and clasped his hands in front of him. "I help people navigate their way to new adventures."

Simon slid his hand along the edge of the table he leaned against before thumbing a corner of the picture frame from its surface to grab. He gripped the frame with both hands, looking down on it, then stepped toward her to place it on her lap.

"I took that off the wall of your local drinking establishment."

She recognized the clipping, the frame, the holes at the top and bottom where Jack had screwed them to the wall around the archway of the Tavern. *Deputy Escapes Clutches of Killer.*

Simon clapped his hands together in weak applause. "Very impressive."

He pulled another frame and set that on top of the one on her lap. She glared at him, tingles dancing in her toes and fingers. *Needles*, Olivia used to call them. Simon extended his palm toward the frame for her attention.

Four Dead in Massacre on Indian Hill. Another that she recognized, and she thought about the time she'd spent with that family.

"That, too, I removed from the wall, and subsequently had that place burned to the ground."

"What the hell is this about?" she mumbled. "Jack?"

"No, Ms. Carlton. It is entirely about you, unfortunately. You see, both of these headlines are incorrect."

"How so?"

"Well, the latter, for example, states that there were four dead when, in fact, there were only three. And the first, well, I think you know exactly how that headline is incorrect."

She moved her head slowly from side to side, her face beginning to shift into an expression of panic she didn't want to reveal. Her eyes misted, her throat beginning to ache.

Simon stepped forward again and put a smaller photo on top of the frames. He spoke with a more subdued tone, quieter. "And this we took from your home, from a cardboard box on the top right-hand shelf of your closet."

The photo showed Lucas Waugh sitting on the grass, shirtless, his cut-off shorts dirty with streaks of mud he'd wiped from his fingers. Behind him, his brother Everett, his chin down and giving the camera a devilish smirk. And she stood behind him, her hands on each side of his upper arms, her shitty haircut. She remembered that day. Part of the fields had just been mowed and she could smell the fresh-cut hay as well as she had back then. Her father had just bought Olivia a camera that she'd wanted for her birthday—always his favorite, ever since that day on the tractor. And that was the first picture she'd taken with it. A drop of water hit the glass on the top frame. A tear, she realized. Everett had been her favorite, that sly little smile, the way he'd shrug and tear off into a sprint when she'd begin to scold him for some mischievous behavior. She remembered after the fire, and the whole town swelled with the volume of people talking about what had happened. She'd remembered thinking, believing actually, that if she became a deputy, she'd keep things like that from happening again. She remembered how it hurt so much, losing those boys, riding by that pile of charred wood with Olivia on her way to school. She'd never wanted to have another person in her life that could hurt her by being taken away.

Another tear streamed over her face. "Why? I don't understand."

"I am aware of that." He offered a sympathetic expression.

She screamed at him, "What the fuck does this have to do with me?" And her yell trailed away. "What is this?" She lowered her head, squinted so she wouldn't have to look at that picture any longer.

Simon pinched the edges of his suit coat and ran his fingers down to his belt. "I need you to look at me."

"Fuck you."

A grip on her hair jerked her head back and she pushed her eyes to the left and right, trying to find someone there, but she couldn't.

Simon tilted his head and held a palm toward the person behind her. "Gentle, Annabelle," he said.

The grip left her hair. Simon pushed his hands into his pockets.

"Ms. Carlton. You shot Everett Waugh."

She huffed. "Everett? What the fuck are you talking about? What the fuck is this?"

"The man you shot and tried to frame for Nicole Walsh's murder was Everett Waugh."

She caught movement at the corner of her eye at the door. The man from her kitchen. She looked back at Simon. His disappointed look—a kind face smeared with a slight sneer. He pinched the ends of his fingers.

Annabelle's voice whispered against Jennifer's ear, "Adam Crane *was* Everett Waugh."

She turned to catch sight of Annabelle's face, but it slipped away as she tried to move. The information rushed through her mind; she remembered the boy, his meek demeanor, his devilish, hysterical laugh, the way he shrugged, how much he craved physical attention. Then Adam, in his room, that's what she'd noticed. The shrug. And then she remembered what she'd thought she'd heard at the lake that night, the words he'd said, muffled by the gunshot.

She took a breath, deep through the raspy popping in her lungs. "That's not possible. You're lying. You're a god-damn liar."

"Twenty-five years ago, a woman shot her husband and son then herself. She tried to kill Everett, too, but that evasive little imp managed to slip away. As far as you and anyone else in that carrion basin called Ironwood was concerned, he was killed as well. Malcolm Hale found him hiding in a rock pile, and we managed to get him away from that sewage depot. I sent him back there because Malcolm Hale was convinced that Kurt Myers killed his son." Simon took a deep breath. "Picture getting a little clearer, Ms. Carlton?"

"Everett?"

"Yes. The man you shot at Wyman Lake was Everett Waugh, which is how I know that you were the one who murdered that girl."

She thought back to her sister, in Nicole's house the day after she'd killed her, how she couldn't let Olivia get tangled into that. Vomit rose in her throat, but she choked it down and shook her head. She'd never expected to feel it, the look she remembered from Mike and Nicole and Kurt—that sudden surprise, the overwhelming realization of the truth of death, that they were about to be gone. And then she remembered Adam, how he'd turned and given her that little shrug, tucked his chin into his shoulder just before she'd shot him. The quiver started in her face, shook her body.

She opened her mouth to scream and Annabelle slipped a tightly rolled facecloth into her mouth. Her complexion was dark, but her green eyes, her face seemed to offer some understanding of her torment in that moment.

Annabelle slid a pair of pruning snips around Jennifer's smallest finger. "This will help with the pain," she whispered.

Her finger rested in the open pair of snips. Tension. Simon nodded.

The cloth tasted like soap. There was a sharp pull at the bottom of her hand, pressure, a quick snap, and then a release. The finger fell to the plastic beneath her and rolled against the instep of her bare foot. Her tears seeped in the corners of her mouth, as she pushed the cloth from her lips with her tongue. There was less pain than she expected and somehow, it calmed the clamor in her mind. Drops of blood began to fall against the plastic. Tap—tap—tap—tap—tap.

"If you're going to kill me," she said looking directly at Simon, "please don't shoot me in the face."

Annabelle's voice in her ear again. "The last thing you're ever going to want anyone to see is your face."

"It is very important for you to understand that you are going to die." Simon pulled the purse from behind him and held it up. "But I am not going to kill you." He shook the purse. "You will die a Ms. Wendy Miller. Everything you need for your new life is right in here. New name, ID, a small amount of money in a bank account to get you started. The point of this is that you take us seriously, and that you understand why you are here, in this room right now. I am not the kind of man who enjoys doing devious things to innocent people. Think about your sister. The memory of you as a hero is what she has, not the woman who killed her husband and her best friend."

Jennifer's hands trembled, scattering blood over her toes. "Don't do this. Please, just kill me now. Please." She inhaled through her mouth, drawing in her tears and the saliva webbing her lips. She licked what lingered away, tilted her head. "Please."

"You are already dead. An accident with your snowmobile on Wyman Lake. Out of the nine people who have died in that lake over the past twenty years, only six have been found. Your funeral was this morning."

"Fuck you. Kill me you son of a bitch. Kill me now, goddammit."

"That is not your choice. As I said. You will die a very natural death. Should you decide to die another way, then Olivia will learn the truth and the state of Maine will have to learn that its first female sheriff was not a hero, but a murderer." Simon pulled one last photograph from the table and put it on her lap. Her killing Mike with the pulp hook. "That is hardly the legacy you want to leave behind."

Simon moved toward the door. Patrick pushed himself from the wall, stretching a latex glove over his hand. He moved to Jennifer, bent over, and picked up her finger. The glove made a convenient wrapping as he peeled it from his hand around the severed digit and pushed it into his pocket.

Simon turned at the door to face Jennifer. "My associate will stay with you to see that you are taken care of."

The men left, and Jennifer could see that it was evening outside. Blood continued to drop from her wound, the only sound or movement, and she slipped into the realization of what she'd done, Adam flinging back into the cold water of the lake, the praise, the landslide election win.

Annabelle put the point of the snips under Jennifer's chin and lifted her head. "The man you killed saved my life. He was the only man who could keep me from becoming a monster."

There was a click, and then the rushing air of a propane torch. Jennifer swallowed.

Annabelle leaned over Jennifer's shoulder, blew a soft breath against her lips. "This is where you are, and you can never go home."

Outside, in the car, Patrick adjusted the rearview mirror. "A natural death?"

Simon smoothed the seatbelt against his chest. "Yes. In the world of killers, Annabelle is as natural a death as any."

FORTY

The yipping was mostly contained in a room down the hallway. Occasionally, there was a deeper bark from the other room just behind the counter. Beside the clock on the wall behind receptionist was a calendar, pictures of cloudy skies and verses of Psalms captioning the photos. Mary-Grace, the receptionist, looked up at the man who'd just walked in. A thin, beat-up corduroy jacket was tight on his shoulders. He wore a dirty trucker hat, the fabric frayed at the edge of the brim. Mary-Grace adjusted her shoulders at his approach, touched the cross around her neck, and leaned back in her chair.

"Can I help you, sir?" She asked, her pitchy drawl skipping around the room. She pushed a pen behind her ear.

"Ah, yes, ma'am. I believe you may have my dog here? X?"

Mary-Grace gave him an accusatory look. "Oh, X? She's been here for quite some time. Well, in and out. In fact, she just came back from her temporary home. She was just a little too hyper for their family."

"I know it's been a while, and I actually thought she was gone for good until I saw your ad in the paper."

"What paper was that?"

The man smiled. "I'm not exactly sure of the actual

name, but it was one of those free, local coffee shop papers. I saw it this morning."

"So you say that X is yours? Do you have a copy of her registration receipt or an ID?"

"I have an ID." The man reached to pull a chained billfold from his back pocket and pushed his ID across the counter.

The girl took it and studied it for a second. "This has seen better days. Did you know your ID is expired?"

"No. I didn't know that. Will that be a problem?"

"I don't think so." She pulled a form from a folder on her desk. "You'll have to fill this out, though. There's a space at the bottom where you can detail the reasons that X wasn't claimed before now. Then it'll have to be approved by Miss Sothesby. She'll be in tomorrow. You don't mind if I make a copy of this do you?"

"It's a free country."

The man began filling in the form. Mary-Grace made a copy of his ID at the copy machine behind her. When she finished, she slid his ID on the counter and sat back down in her chair, eyeing him with a subdued expression of disdain.

"You see," the man said. "I was in a car accident. That's how I lost X in the first place. It's taken me some time to get things squared away. Things have actually been pretty rough on me, but I kept my faith in the Lord. And this morning, while I was counting out my last bit of change for a coffee, that's when I saw the advertisement for X." The man's lip quivered, and a tear struck his eye. "I knew it had to be her. You know, when I finished counting out my change, it was exactly the amount for a coffee. That's awful coincidental, don't you think? I know the Lord works in mysterious ways, and I have enough faith in the Lord to pay attention to those things. I think, if the good Lord didn't want me there at that moment to give me an opportunity to reunite with my precious X, I guess he wouldn't have made it so obvious that I should have been there to see that advertisement."

Mary-Grace covered her mouth. Her eyes went moist and she drew her hand away. "Well, I'm so sorry to hear that. I'm glad you're okay."

"Me too. I'm very blessed." He pushed the form across the counter to her. "You see, ma'am, I'm about to head out to California to do some charity work with my parish, and well, I was hoping I could reunite with X sooner than later."

Mary-Grace looked over the paperwork quickly, mulling over her decision. She stood. "You know what, I'm betting Miss Sothesby would be mighty disappointed in me to keep you from reuniting with X, so I won't delay your reunion any longer." She spun away from the counter to the steel door. "Come on back."

He moved around the counter and followed Mary-Grace through. She walked quickly to the back, her arms swinging, to the second to last kennel. She flipped the latch up and opened the gate. The man knelt a few feet from the opening. X's body shook as she came out of the cage, her tail wagging in quick, wide swings. She licked his face. "Oh, yes, ma'am." He hooked the leash he'd brought to her neck and held the sides of her head. He whispered in her ear, "In the end, the good guy always gets the girl." He stood and followed Mary-Grace back out to the counter, X trailing behind him on the leash.

Mary-Grace smiled at him as he passed her at the door. "So happy that you two are finally back together."

"Thank you, so much, ma'am," he said and led X to the exit.

"Adam. Mr. Crane, you forgot your license."

He turned to her. "It's expired. I won't be needing it."

"Well, alright." A bewildered look struck her face. "So, what does X stand for, anyway?"

The man paused, brought his left hand up to scratch an itch just below his eye, the pinky missing. "Exodus."

JOE RICKER is a former bartender for Southern literary legends Barry Hannah and Larry Brown. He has also worked as a cab driver, innkeeper, acquisitions specialist, professor, and in the Maine timber industry. He currently lives in Reno, Nevada, and spends much of his free time walking uphill.

JoeRicker.com

BOOKS

On the following pages are a few
more great titles from the
Down & Out Books publishing family.

For a complete list of books and to
sign up for our newsletter,
go to DownAndOutBooks.com.

Driving Reign
The De La Cruz Case Files
TG Wolff

Down & Out Books
April 2020
978-1-64396-087-6

The woman in the stingy hospital bed wasn't dead. The question for Detective Jesus De La Cruz: did the comatose patient narrowly survive suicide or murder?

Faithful friends paint a picture of a guileless young woman, a victim of both crime and society. Others describe a cold woman with a proclivity for icing interested men with a single look.

Beneath the rhetoric, Cruz unearths a twisted knot of reality and perception. A sex scandal, a jilted lover, a callous director, a rainmaker, and a quid pro quo have Cruz questioning if there is such a thing as an innocent man.

Coldwater
Tom Pitts

Down & Out Books
May 2020
978-1-64396-081-4

A young couple move from San Francisco to the Sacramento sub-urbs to restart their lives. When the vacant house across the street is taken over by who they think are squatters, they're pulled into a battle neither of them bargained for. The gang of unruly drug addicts who've infested their block have a dark and secret history that reaches beyond their neighborhood and all the way to the most powerful and wealthy men in California.

L.A. fixer Calper Dennings is sent by a private party to quell the trouble before it affects his employer. But before he can finish the job, he too is pulled into the violent dark world of a man with endless resources to destroy anyone around him.

Stay Ugly
Daniel Vlasaty

All Due Respect, an imprint of
Down & Out Books
February 2020
978-1-64396-096-8

Eric is an ex-con, bareknuckle boxer better known around his Chicago neighborhood as "Ugly." He wants to shed his past, build a life with his family, but his past won't be so easily left behind.

His junkie brother Joe has stolen $100K from a powerful drug dealer—and Ugly's on the hook unless he hands Joe over.

Which is gonna be hard considering he has no idea where Joe is.

Chasing China White
Allan Leverone

Shotgun Honey, an imprint of
Down & Out Books
September 2019
978-1-64396-029-6

When heroin junkie Derek Weaver runs up an insurmountable debt with his dealer, he's forced to commit a home invasion to wipe the slate clean.

Things go sideways and Derek soon finds himself a multiple murderer in the middle of a hostage situation.

With seemingly no way out, he may discover the key to redemption lies in facing down long-ignored demons.

Made in the USA
Columbia, SC
03 May 2020

95731794R00186